CW01332585

PETER CUSHING'S MONSTER MOVIES

PETER CUSHING is an internationally famous film actor whose portrayal of the great roles of terror such as Baron Frankenstein – The Monster Maker – and Dr Van Helsing – Dracula's courageous adversary – have been hailed as the most distinguished of their kind. PETER HAINING is a full-time writer whose books include *Elvis in Private*, *The Great English Earthquake*, *The English Highwayman*, *Charles Dickens' Christmas Ghost Stories*, *The Supernatural Coast* and most recently *Masters of the Macabre*. Previously a journalist and a publisher, he brings to his work the resources of an extensive personal library of books and periodicals. He is married with three children and lives in Suffolk.

PETER CUSHING'S MONSTER MOVIES

Edited by
Peter Haining

ROBERT HALE · LONDON

*Copyright © Peter Cushing and Peter Haining 1977
First published in Great Britain 1977
This paperback edition 1994*

ISBN 0-7090-5455-6

Robert Hale Limited
Clerkenwell House
Clerkenwell Green
London EC1R 0HT

The right of Peter Cushing and Peter Haining to
be identified as authors of this work has been
asserted by them in accordance with the Copyright,
Designs and Patents Act 1988.

2 4 6 8 10 9 7 5 3 1

Printed in Great Britain by
St Edmundsbury Press Limited, Bury St Edmunds, Suffolk
Bound by WBC Bookbinders

CONTENTS

List of Illustrations	vii
How I Became A Monster Hunter *Peter Cushing*	1
The Masked Ball *Alexandre Dumas*	14
The Mortal Immortal *Mary Shelley*	23
Dracula's Guest *Bram Stoker*	36
In The Footsteps Of The Abominable Snowman *Josef Nesvadba*	48
The Ring Of Thoth *Sir Arthur Conan Doyle*	79
The Gorgon *Gertrude Bacon*	96
The Man Who Collected Poe *Robert Bloch*	107
The Ghoul of Golders Green *Michael Arlen*	122
There Shall Be No Darkness *James Blish*	155

Acknowledgements

The Editor and publishers are grateful to the following authors, agents and publishers for permission to include copyright material in this collection. Messrs Victor Gollancz Ltd for *In The Footsteps of the Abominable Snowman* by Josef Nesvadba; Baskerville Investments Ltd, Jonathan Cape Ltd and John Murray Publishers Ltd for *The Ring of Thoth* by Sir Arthur Conan Doyle; The Scott Meredith Literary Agency for *The Man Who Collected Poe* by Robert Bloch; The Estate of Michael Arlen for *The Ghoul of Golders Green* by Michael Arlen; and Laurence Pollinger Ltd for *There Shall Be No Darkness* by James Blish.

ILLUSTRATIONS

1. My début as Baron Victor Frankenstein in my first horror film, *The Curse of Frankenstein* (1957)
2. Feeding my creation in *The Curse of Frankenstein* (1957)
3. Christopher Lee as the undead count to my Dr Van Helsing in *The Satanic Rites of Dracula* (1973)
4. Valerie Gaunt playing a vampire is stopped by a crucifix in *Horror of Dracula* (1958)
5. On the set of *The Abominable Snowman* (1957) with Forrest Tucker
6. Christopher Lee with a stranglehold on me in *The Mummy* (1959)
7. My appearance as Dr Namaroff, a brain surgeon, in the grisly story of *The Gorgon* (1964)
8. With Jack Palance in *Torture Garden* (1967) in which I played the obsessive collector of Edgar Allan Poe memorabilia
9. With the lovely Susan Denberg in *Frankenstein Created Woman* (1967)
10. Another of my ghoulish operations in *Frankenstein Must Be Destroyed* (1969) with Simon Ward and George Pravda
11. My part as a bedevilled collector in *The Skull* (1966) based on the book, *The Skull of the Marquis de Sade*
12. *Tales From the Crypt* (1979), the film in which my character, Grimsdyke, is turned into a walking corpse

FOR HELEN who is always with me

HOW I BECAME A MONSTER HUNTER

I actually began my career as a film actor by quite literally stepping in where angels feared to tread, and I suppose that considering many of the parts I have since played that was perhaps a most appropriate beginning. For back in the 1930s I deliberately took myself to the very centre of the film industry, Hollywood, and asked for a part – and, much to my surprise and that of everyone else, I got one!

But I am getting a little ahead of myself, for I have been asked in this introduction to write a brief autobiography of my life and to do so I must go right back to the very beginning.

I was born on 26 May 1913 in the small Surrey village of Kenley and my father was a quantity surveyor, a profession he encouraged me to follow when I left school. However, I was already a great film fan – the cowboy star Tom Mix was my idol – and I had my heart set on acting. One of my grandfathers had been an actor, apparently, also an aunt and an uncle, so there was something of a family tradition, though one not followed by my parents.

I decided to be a dutiful son, though, and for four years I was a surveyor's assistant at the Coulsdon and Purley Urban District Council. I was not a very good one, I am afraid, for I was already involved in local amateur theatricals and always asking for time off to rehearse. Even when I was in the office I remember that I spent a great deal of time in the loft supposedly filing maps and things and instead rehearsing my lines to an audience of mice and spiders!

At this time I was also reading the *Stage* and answering the advertisements offering jobs. I kept trying for so long with my own name and getting nowhere that I thought a change might help. As I was in the throes of my first love I thought Peter Ling – from darling – might be a good name and immediately got busy with my pen. But it was not long before I changed it back again because one theatre manager replied quite bluntly, 'I don't think there's much scope for Chinese actors in the repertory business these days.'

But finally my persistence paid off when I got a reply from Bill Fraser who was running a company in Worthing. I had been writing to him for months when at last he asked me to come and see him. I was overjoyed and, quitting my job at the Council, jumped on a train to Worthing.

When Bill saw me he said, 'Who are you?' and I said 'Peter Cushing'. So he said, 'Oh, I'm so glad you've turned up. It was just to ask you please not to keep writing to me because I've got so much else to do without answering all these letters.' Well, I just burst into tears on the spot. But he took compassion on me when he heard how hard I'd been trying to get into the theatre, and he put me in a play that very same night. It was J.B. Priestley's *Cornelius* and I played a creditor – it was my very first professional appearance. I was just 21 years old.

For the next four years I played in repertory all over the country and it was a marvellous experience, apart from being a great training ground. You're literally involved with three plays at one time: you're playing one, rehearsing the next and learning the lines of the third. It demanded great concentration not to come out with the wrong part when you got on stage.

In time, however, I got tired of this and realized that if I wanted to further my career I would have to go elsewhere. I recalled those Tom Mix epics that had so delighted my childhood and decided the answer lay in Hollywood. I only had a few pounds to my name at the time, so with some trepidation I went home to my father and asked him to lend me the fare to America. Despite the fact the very idea must have seemed lunatic to him, he handed over the money. I had enough for a one way ticket: it never occurred to me then how I might get back if all failed.

Once in America it was very much a case of a fool stepping in where every angel would fear to tread – but through ignorance I did frightfully well. Of course I knew no one in Hollywood, but by pure coincidence I went to Edward Small's studios. At the gate I was immediately confronted by a policeman bristling with guns. I told him boldly that I was going into the pictures and he looked at me absolutely dumbfounded.

Subsequently I learned that it was apparently my very Englishness and obvious innocence that opened all the doors to me. The policeman, and the others in the studio, were so amazed that they thought, 'This man's an idiot or he's very honest,' and they let me in to see the casting director.

My extraordinary good fortune did not end there, for it so happened that there was a vacancy in the picture *The Man in the Iron Mask*. The star, Louis Hayward, was playing twins in the film, a good brother and an evil brother, and the director was looking for someone to play opposite him for the split screen process so that he had someone to 'speak' to. They wanted someone who could 'act' in inverted commas rather than just a continuity girl reading the lines. Luckily I convinced them I was their man – though all my experience had been on the stage – and so I went into films. Because of the nature of the part I played, I was literally snipped off in the cutting room and Louis Hayward ended up talking to himself!

I did have the opportunity to see the rushes and I nearly fainted when I saw myself for the first time. I was dreadful! My voice sounded awful and I was as round as a dumpling. However, as the weeks passed I got better and I even ended up with a one-line part. I was the Captain of the Guard and had to gallop on to the set and cry, 'The King wants to see you!' I am afraid the story that I actually played the man in the iron mask in some of the scenes is not true, Louis Hayward played them all himself!

I did have the chance to dress in period costume, though, which was a great delight. The film was set in the period of Louis XIV and they wore lovely big hats with feathers and spurs. So when I went to get costumed I remembered the marvellous sound Tom Mix's spurs made, and got myself a huge pair. Then I leapt on this horse – having never been on a horse before, my mother's bicycle serving as Tom Mix's horse in my youthful adventures – and the animal took off and pulled down all the scenery! I also had sashes around me, both of which fell down and pinioned my arms, and the stirrups locked, and in the end the film crew had to lasso me and bring the horse to a standstill. What a come down for a would-be cowboy star! In any event I was de-spurred on the spot and told that I would cost the production several hours delay, not to mention several thousand dollars.

Nevertheless it was a marvellous experience because it gave me a chance to study the great Hollywood stars at first hand – and earned me $75 a week which was an absolute fortune because I had nothing. By a curious coincidence, too, the director of *The Man in the Iron Mask* was James Whale who had made the famous Frankenstein pictures for Universal in the early 1930s. I had no idea at the time how this story would later feature so largely in my own career, but I do recall that Whale was an incredibly patient and tolerant man with a beginner like me.

The fact that I had worked in this picture, and that I had an English accent, undoubtedly helped get me a much bigger role in the Laurel and Hardy film *A Chump at Oxford* made in 1940, and then later the second male lead in *Vigil in the Night* with Brian Aherne and Carole Lombard. The war was then in full spate and there was an enormous shortage of young actors. The film was based on a story by A.J. Cronin about hospitals, and the producer wanted someone who could assume a North Country accent that the Americans could understand and would be acceptable in England as well. So I was able to immerse myself in this important part.

When the picture was over, I felt homesick for the first time and I was also worried about what was happening in England. Even though I had very little money I knew I must return and offer my services. It was not that I wanted to fight, it was just I knew I must go home.

As all the boats were being commandeered for the war effort, I thought that the only way I could get home would be at the expense of the British Government so I must head for Canada. I decided to go by way of New York earning what money I could on the way.

When I reached New York, the first thing I saw was a notice outside a hospital saying, 'Give Blood for Britain'. As this was the only thing I had to give I went straight in, gave a pint, and walked out. And then fell flat on my face so they had to pull me back in and give me two pints to revive me!

Such was my first contribution to the war effort – brought about, I suppose, by my general poor state of health, through not eating much during my impoverished Hollywood days.

The first job I had in New York was as a car park attendant – but that only lasted two hours! You see there I was trying to carefully manoeuvre these huge Cadillacs into the parking spaces, when the man in charge told me they had to be bumped in as quickly as possible or else the company lost money. He got into the driver's seat, drove forward into the car in front, reversed into the one behind, and completed the job in thirty seconds flat! I protested that that was no way to treat a car – so he said if I couldn't do it he would have to fire me. So he did and I was left with wages of one dollar for my principles!

I lasted a bit longer as a cinema usher at a theatre where they seemed to be constantly playing James Cagney. I remember they gave me a uniform that didn't fit and had no fly buttons on the trousers. When I complained about this the manager said that no one would notice in the dark and I should hold the torch in front of myself – which looked far worse! Anyway it proved a most lucrative job, because the ushers got tips for showing people to their seats, and by moving people around to accommodate their particular wishes I could earn quite large gratuities. I always used to make sure that lovers got seated together, which wasn't always popular with other patrons trying to watch the film. So you see I have experience of the cinema from both sides of the screen!

A bit later on I was able to move out of the city and get myself a job with a small theatre company playing a summer camp at Warrensberg near the Canadian border. The pay was quite good and not only was I able to build up my strength a bit but also improve my finances.

There was one more incident that happened to me before I got a ship home. It seems amusing now but it was quite frightening at the time. After I had left the summer camp and actually crossed the border into Canada, I was once again short of money and went to a small film studio which was doing some incidental work on the Eric Porter film, *The 49th Parallel*. Although they had no work for an actor, the art department was looking for someone to make some war insignia.

Now ever since I had been a schoolboy I had enjoyed painting and making cardboard models (something which I still do occasionally today when I am at home) and I offered to make what they wanted – lots of miniature Japanese and Nazi flags to be pinned on a huge map. They had no space for me to work in the art department and gave me the materials I needed and told me to do it where I was staying.

In fact I was in the local YMCA hostel where I was also doubling as the night porter to earn a little extra money. My room was so tiny that I could hardly turn round, there was only just enough room for the bed, but I set up my equipment and began making the insignia. During the time when I was downstairs serving as the porter, a maid would go into my room to tidy up, and because she had heard me talking about making things like a grand piano (in miniature, of course) thought I was a bit mad. And when I announced one morning that I had actually lost this piano in my room she was convinced of it.

Well, when I returned to the hostel later that day I found two huge Mounted Policemen waiting for me. They immediately grabbed me by the shoulders and said they were taking me to the police station where I was to be charged for being a spy!

I immediately asked why and they said they had received a report – obviously from the maid – that I was acting strangely and claimed to have lost a grand piano. And when they had investigated my room they had found the collection of swastikas I had been busy making. These seemed to confirm their suspicions about my nefarious activities and they hurried me off to the station. Fortunately, I recovered my senses enough when we got there to have them call the film studio and get the producer to explain just why I was making the little flags! And as if that wasn't enough, when I was released and walked out of the police station, I was so thrilled to be free that I didn't look where I was going and tripped on a sheet of ice, cracked my head badly, and had to spend two days in hospital to recover!

My sea journey home to England was not without incidents, either. It was in Halifax that I finally managed to find a ship on which I could get a berth. It was an old banana boat which was equipped for the tropics and we were to cross the Atlantic in mid-winter. I have never been so cold in my life!

I remember that I was very lucky to get a place on this boat at all, for when I approached the captain he said he had a full complement and he could only take me on if any member of the crew failed to turn up. At midnight, after waiting for hours in the cold, I was finally told I could come on board as one man had not turned up. So I got a passage home to England by courtesy of a deserter.

Once we were at sea the captain asked me what my occupation was and when I told him an actor he shook his head with dismay. The only thing he could think of for me to do was to serve as a lookout and so I had to climb up to the crow's nest. Although I was terrified, I managed to clamber up there, but then things got worse.

What with the rain and spray the crow's nest soon began to fill up like a water butt, and as it got colder the water began to freeze. I became really frightened then, for I was stuck firm, and began calling for help. I kept waving and shouting until they realized something really was wrong, and finally they sent someone up in a breeches buoy to rescue me. I nearly froze to death that day.

Realizing I was really of very little practical use on a ship, the captain put me in charge of the ship's cat and that at least I managed to do without any more problems.

Although we did not encounter any German ships on the crossing, life in a convoy can be full of tension because you are never sure if a submarine will suddenly appear or you might run into a mine. My ship happened to be among a group of huge oil-tankers so one couldn't help feeling like a sitting duck. Nevertheless, as I later learned, the commander of the convoy had taken a daring gamble by steering us along the normal peacetime route betewen Halifax and England in the hope that the Germans would think that no one would be stupid enough to use such an obvious course.

As it was the ploy worked, and after ten days Liverpool finally hove into sight and we all heaved a great sigh of relief. Our relief was all the greater when we heard that the famous German ship, the *Tirpitz*, had actually been in our vicinity during the crossing!

I was January 1942 when I stepped on to English soil again, and I hadn't the faintest idea what I was going to do. In fact there was only one course open to someone in my profession – join the entertainment group for the forces, ENSA, or 'Every Night Something Awful' as we called it.

This proved one of the most significant moves of my life, for I was put into the company touring with Noel Coward's *Private Lives*, and the leading lady was Helen Beck, the beloved Helen whom I was to marry shortly afterwards. It was she who was to light my life and encourage me to reach for greater things as an actor.

For almost two years we toured together with the play but our happiness was marred by Helen's failing health, and we both had to leave the group and move to London. Immediately Helen devoted herself to managing my career, a task she did so selflessly and successfully right up to the time of her death.

For a time I was able to get parts in several major plays, including Dame Edith Evans' successful production of *The Rivals*, but after the war, things got much tougher and for a time Helen and I had a struggle to make ends meet. However, a stroke of good fortune kept the wolf from the door at this time thanks to my artistic leanings.

One Christmas, not having enough money to buy Helen a present, I decided to hand-paint a piece of silk as a scarf for her. And it just so happened that a textile manufacturer saw this when we were out one night, and learning it was my handiwork gave me a nine-month contract to design more scarves. The money was an absolute godsend.

However, I was still trying to get acting jobs all this time and went to see Laurence Olivier who was auditioning for the young male lead in *Born Yesterday*. When I got to see him, the first thing he asked was whether I could speak American as the character was an American. I had to be honest and say no, because I think there is nothing more phoney than an English actor trying to speak American.

He looked at me and said, 'That's awfully honest of you. You've saved us a lot of time – we shall be in touch again.' I thought that was very kind of him, but believed it was really just a polite brush off. I was soon proved wrong.

No long afterwards I was playing a Frenchman in a play at the Kew Theatre and apparently favourably impressed one of Laurence Olivier's assistants who was in the audience. He went back to Olivier and told him, 'There's an incredible Frenchman in this play who I seem to recognize. Come and have a look at him.'

So Olivier's party came down to a matinée and the great actor took one look at me and said, 'Well, that's the chap who said he couldn't speak American. But he can certainly speak French!'

Anyway he was impressed by my work and asked if I would like to appear in the film of *Hamlet* he was making. I jumped at the chance and asked him what parts were available. There was only Osric – so that's who I played. (Although we never met at the time, this was also the first film in which Christopher Lee and I appeared together.)

Olivier was seemingly pleased with my portrayal of the courtier, for he offered me the same part in the Old Vic Australian tour which he led with his wife, Vivian Leigh. When I returned to England, however, I was struck down with illness and had to leave the company.

Once again Helen came to my rescue and sensing the developing importance of television wrote to dozens of producers about me. In December 1951 I made my first TV appearance in J.B. Priestley's play *Eden's End* – once again that Yorkshire maestro had featured at the start of a new development of my career. Thereafter I had three solid years of what was laughingly called 'live' television (there were no recordings) and this undoubtedly established me in the profession.

It was immensely hard work and each play I did amounted to four weeks work – three weeks of rehearsal, then the live performance – and the salary was a meagre 36 guineas for the entire month. So I literally went out of one production and into the next, though there was the advantage of appearing in plays that were a foregone success and had already been made famous on the stage by great actors like Olivier and John Gielgud. Virtually every part was different, from straight acting to comedy, and naturally people became intrigued by me. That was also the time when there was only one channel so one had a really captive audience.

During this time I was lucky enough to win the Best Actor Award three times, and appear in two quite outstanding television productions, *The Creature* (later filmed as *The Abominable Snowman* in 1957) and the controversial version of George Orwell's *1984*. I played Winston Smith and to me it is the only true *horror* film I've ever done, for the sort of horror pictures I normally appear in are pure fantasy and impossible to a degree. But *1984* is not only possible – it's practically happening. You only have to look around you, and nearly everything Orwell predicted has come true – and unless we are very careful it will *all* come true!

1984 was not a film, of course, but live television, and put out as a serial week by week. We did it live on Sundays and then repeated it live on Thursday. It is a grim story of a totalitarian society and there were lots of protests about it being unsuitable, I remember, particularly after the scene where I was threatened by hordes of rats. Although this caused outrage at the time, and people actually tried to stop the Thursday repeat, the real story about the rats is quite amusing, I think.

Because the BBC were anxious to make the production as realistic as possible they got hold of the last remaining rat catcher in London to provide them with some genuine sewer rats. Now I never actually saw the rats during the scene, for they were in another studio and I just had to react as if they were attacking me. You see the technicians were getting these bedraggled, pathetic-looking creatures to seemingly scratch my face by rearing up to catch food dangled above them – and then the pictures were mixed.

In any event, after a few days we all got rather fond of these rats, and what with the warmth of the lights and the regular meals, they got very docile and sweet and so when they were supposed to rear up for the morsals of food they just curled up and went to sleep! It was a terrible thing from the point of view of the play, and the producer had to ring up a pet shop and quickly get a couple of tame white rats which were then painted black and starved for a couple of days to take the place of the real thing!

In my opinion Winston Smith is one of the greatest heroes in the world of fiction, for he stood alone against everything. He knew the odds and he was certainly frightened, but he stood by his principles. And although he was defeated he stands as an example to us all.

One good thing that came out of all the controversy was that it helped to get me better known still. However, I wanted desperately to get into films in England, but there seemed to be a general resistance among the film people to anyone working in television because they were keeping audiences out of the cinemas. The one exception to that rule were Hammer Films, and in particular the managing director, James Carreras. It was he who was to give me my biggest chance and changed the course of my acting career.

Hammer had done quite a number of successful films from television series, and as James Carreras liked my work they had several times asked my agent if I would do a film for them. In fact I was just too busy to take them up until early in 1957 when I read in one of the trade papers that they were to make *The Curse of Frankenstein*. Straight away I knew this was a part I wanted to play because I had seen the original James Whale version with Colin Clive and Boris Karloff and enjoyed it immensely. Nevertheless I still wanted to be sure that I was getting into the right thing and asked to see Hammer's latest film. It was called, *X the Unknown* with Brian Donleavy and I thought it was splendid. So, on the strength of this, I said that if they were interested I'd love to play Baron Frankenstein – and that is how it all started.

The Curse of Frankenstein was in fact only one of five pictures Hammer were making that year, and they obviously had no idea of the spectacular success it was to enjoy. Nor did anyone anticipate the enormous snowball effect which has carried on to this day.

Although the picture only cost £65,000 which is nothing in film-making terms, it looked as if it had cost £2 million, the quality was so good. It also struck the right chord with audiences, just the way tales of terror have been doing for years. I believe that both films and stories of this kind will always be popular, at some periods more so than others.

Of course, since I made that first Frankenstein film, there have been great advances in medicine, and people like Dr Barnard have almost caught up with what I was doing on the screen. At first Hammer thought it would be the end of the series, but instead people are even more intrigued to see how Dr Barnard does transplants as opposed to Cushing as Frankenstein. Needless to say I have taken special instruction from a surgeon on how to handle surgical instruments correctly for my parts, because I think it is important for an audience to believe you can actually do what you are attempting.

In some ways I see Frankenstein as rather like Dr Robert Knox, the anatomist, not as a villain, but as someone trying to make people understand that this envelope that we live in for three score years and ten is not important. It is the spirit and the soul which matter. The religious and medical authorities of the time would not hear of the body as something likely to be confined to the waste-paper basket when it was finished with and so they opposed Knox. He, then, had to close his one good eye to the way Burke and Hare supplied him with cadavers so that he could show how the human body ticks for the good of all mankind. For his pains he was hounded out of Edinburgh, just as Frankenstein is always being hounded out by villagers.

As a consequence of this, I have always based my playing of Frankenstein on Robert Knox, though with variations based on the demands of the script and differing degrees of ruthlessness because no one will leave him alone to work.

It was in *The Curse of Frankenstein* that I first played opposite Christopher Lee and we have subsequently appeared twenty-five times together, becoming very good friends. We were also teamed up immediately after this picture in the remake of the Dracula story, in which Christopher played the vampire count and I was his adversary, Dr Van Helsing.

To me, Van Helsing is the essence of good, pitted against the essence of evil, and I think the Dracula films have the same appeal as the old morality plays with the struggle of good over evil and good always triumphing in the end.

The problem that has subsequently emerged with both the Frankenstein and Dracula stories has been finding some kind of new variation. Because like the Western, where the audience expects the gunfight in the saloon or main street, in these films you must have a man who creates a living creature which goes berserk and a man who lives on human blood. The writers have tried many ideas, including bringing the central characters into the modern era, but they are wearing a bit thin. Still they do come up with good ideas from time to time, and the public interest is as strong as ever.

I was again with Christopher in *The Mummy* (1959), the third Hammer film which I think finally established all of us – Hammer, Christopher and myself – as leaders in our field. Since then I have made a whole string of terror pictures, and if this is what the producers and audience wish me to do, I shall be happy to go on making them for as long as they want.

Despite the grimness of many of the stories, I always enjoy my work on the set and there are occasional moments of light relief. I remember one particular incident with Christopher Lee when we were working on *The Gorgon* which I think is typical of many more. I was actually playing a bit of a baddie in the film, Dr Namaroff, and I had developed for myself a nervous cough to use as a mannerism when I was in a difficult situation. After one shot I was sitting with Christopher and he asked me what the cough was for, so I explained. He grinned at me for a moment and then replied, 'Right, then I shall now call you Baron Nastycough!'

In view of the fact that, apart from my reminiscences, this is an anthology of short stories, it gives me an opportunity to mention that one of the anthology films I appeared in for that other British horror film company, Amicus, *Dr Terror's House of Horrors* (1964) actually gratified a long standing ambition. I had always loved trains, and in that picture my entire section took place in a railway carriage as I played the link man, Dr Schreck, who dealt out the tarot cards of fate to his fellow travellers.

In another of this type of film *Torture Garden* (1967) I played opposite Jack Palance in the sequence *The Man Who Collected Poe*. I was the title character, Lancelot Canning, and Jack was the man who came to see my extraordinary collection — which included Poe himself in a back room. We were involved in a fight and after one scene, Jack, who is one of the strongest men I have ever met, asked if he had hurt me. I said no, and he replied that he certainly thought he had by my expressions! I was quite pleased at the compliment because I could only add, 'Oh, I was just acting!'

Perhaps, though, the favourite of all my anthology parts was as the old man Arthur Grimsdyke in *Tales from the Crypt* (1971). I was actually first offered another part in the film, but when I turned it down the Amicus people asked if any other role in the script appealed to me. Now I was attracted to the part of this little old man Grimsdyke, but originally it was a non-speaking part – all the commentary was done as a voice over.

I said that in the normal way an audience would not accept a solitary man talking to himself, but here was a special case, and if they would give him some dialogue I would take the part. You see my dear wife had died not long before this and I used to talk to her when I was alone and to her photograph. So I knew I could make the part convincing because it was something I did myself. And that was how the part evolved and it became instinctive to me. It was a real delight when the picture got such a wonderful press and people actually wrote to me saying how sympathetic they found the part. I even won an award for it in France, which was doubly satisfying for something that was created out of nothing.

So there we are, those are the main details of my life, which has been so overshadowed by the death of Helen who did so much to bring me out of obscurity in the profession that I love so much. I like to keep working for her sake for I know she is watching me and I eagerly await the day when I shall be reunited with her.

Let me say that I am very happy to be what people call a 'horror actor' for I know that these kind of films give entertainment to a great world-wide audience. It is difficult to explain exactly their appeal besides the fact that a lot of people tell me in their letters it is the triumph of good prevailing over evil. They are also, I think, an escape valve in a world surrounded by the menace of catastrophe – a vicarious form of outlet amidst pressures which tend to squeeze us into tight corners.

The same is true, of course, of horror or terror stories, and, with my good friend Peter Haining, I have enjoyed selecting a number of tales which are linked with my career either through the author who wrote them or their subject matter. Whether playing Frankenstein, Dr Van Helsing, Sherlock Holmes or any other part based on a classic character in literature, I always go to great trouble to read the original books and stories and I believe this can be seen in my acting. All the stories here I think you will find reflect my screen life as a hunter of monsters – which, I hasten to add, is a very different me to the one in private life!

Finally, I hope that the stories and photographs in this book will give you just some of the enjoyment and pleasure that, over the years, acting in the films associated with them has given me.

THE MASKED BALL

Alexandre Dumas

Although the stories in this book are mostly about monsters of one sort or another, it seems most appropriate to begin the collection with a tale by Alexandre Dumas who wrote The Man in the Iron Mask — *the very first film in which I appeared. As all lovers of great literature will know, Dumas is an exuberant and colourful writer, and in the story here — which also deals with a masked figure — he mixes drama and jealousy with sinister effect.*

I said that I was in to no one; one of my friends forced admission. My servant announced Mr Anthony R. Behind Joseph's livery I saw the corner of a black frock-coat; it is probable that the wearer of the frock-coat, from his side, saw a flap of my dressing-gown; impossible to conceal myself.

'Very well! Let him enter,' I said out loud. 'Let him go to the devil,' I said to myself.

While working it is only the woman you love who can disturb you with impunity, for she is always at bottom interested in what you are doing.

I went up to him, therefore, with the half-bored face of an author interrupted in one of those moments of sorest self-mistrust, while I found him so pale and haggard that the first words I addressed to him were these:

'What is the matter? What has happened to you?'

'Oh! Let me take breath,' said he. 'I'm going to tell you all about it, besides, it's a dream perhaps, or perhaps I am mad.'

He threw himself into an armchair, and let his head drop between his hands.

I looked at him in astonishment; his hair was dripping with rain; his shoes, his knees, and the bottom of his trousers were covered with mud. I went to the window; I saw at the door his servant and his cabriolet; I could make nothing out of it all.

He saw my surprise.

'I have been to the cemetery of Père-Lachaise,' said he.

'At ten o'clock in the morning?'

'I was there at seven – a cursed masked ball!'

I could not imagine what a masked ball and Père-Lachaise had to do with one another. I resigned myself, and turning my back to the mantelpiece began to roll a cigarette for him between my fingers with the phlegm and the patience of a Spaniard.

While he was coming to the point I hinted to Anthony that I, for my part, was commonly very susceptible to attentions of that kind.

He made me a sign of thanks, but pushed my hand away.

Finally, I bent over to light the cigarette for myself: Anthony stopped me.

'Alexandre,' he said to me, 'listen, I beg of you.'

'But you have been already a quarter of an hour and have not told me anything.'

'Oh! it is a most strange adventure.'

I got up, placed my cigarette on the mantelpiece, and crossed my arms like a man resigned; only I began to believe, as he did, that he was fast becoming mad.

'You remember the ball at the Opéra, where I met you?' he said to me after a moment's silence.

'The last one, where there were at least two hundred people?'

'The very same. I left you with the intention of abandoning myself to one of those varieties of which they spoke to me as being a curiosity even in the midst of our curious times; you wished to dissuade me from going; a fatality drove me on. Oh! you, why did you not see it all, you who have the knack of observation? Why were not Hoffman or Callot there to paint the picture as the fantastic burlesque thing kept unrolling itself beneath my eyes? Unsatisfied and in melancholy mood I walked away, about to quit the Opéra; I came to a hall that was overflowing and in high spirits: corridors, boxes, parterre. Everything was obstructed. I made a tour of the room; twenty masks called me by name and told me theirs.

'These were all leaders – aristocrats and merchants – in the undignified disguise of pierrots, of postilions, of merry-andrews, or of fishwives. They were all young people of family, of culture, of talent; and there, forgetful of family, talent, breeding, they were resurrecting in the midst of our sedate and serious times a soirée of the Regency. They had told me about it, and yet I could not have believed it! – I mounted a few steps, and leaning against a pillar, half hidden by it, I fixed my eyes on that sea of human beings surging beneath me. Their dominoes, of all colours, their motley costumes, their grotesque disguises formed a spectacle resembling nothing human. The music began to play. Oh, it was then these gargoyle creatures stirred themselves to the sound of that orchestra whose harmony reached me only in the midst of cries, of laughs, of hootings; they hung on to each other by their hands, by their arms, by their necks; a long coil formed itself, beginning with a circular motion, the dancers, men and women, stamping with their feet, made the dust break forth with a noise, the atoms of which were rendered visible by the wan light of the lustres; turning at ever-increasing speed with bizarre postures, with unseemly gestures, with cries full of abandonment; turning always faster and still faster, swaying and swinging like drunken men, yelling like lost women, with more delirium than delight, with more passion than pleasure; resembling a coil of the damned doing infernal penance under the scourge of demons!

'All this passed beneath my eyes, at my feet. I felt the wind of their whirling past; as they rushed by each one whom I knew flung a word at me that made me blush. All this noise, all this humming, all this confusion, all this music went on in my brain as well as in the room! I soon came to the point of no longer knowing whether that which I had before my eyes was a dream or reality; I came to the point of asking myself whether it was not I who was mad and they who were sane; I was seized with a weird temptation to throw myself into the midst of this pandemonium, like Faust through the Witches' Sabbath, and I felt that I, too, would then have cries, postures, laughs like theirs. Oh! from that to madness there is but one step. I was appalled; I flung myself out of the room, followed even to the street door by shrieks that were like those cries of passion that come out of the caverns of the fallow deer.

'I stopped a moment under the portico to collect myself; I did not wish to venture into the street; with such confusion still in my soul I might not be able to find my way; I might, perhaps, be thrown under the wheels of some carriage I had not seen coming. I was as a drunken man might be who begins to recover sufficient reason in his clouded brain to recognize his condition, and who, feeling the will return but not the power, with fixed eyes and staring, leans motionless against some street post or some tree on the public promenade.

'At that moment a carriage stopped before the door, a woman alighted or rather shot herself from the doorway.

'She entered beneath the peristyle, turning her head from right to left like one who had lost her way; she was dressed in a black domino, had her face covered by a velvet mask. She presented herself at the door.

' "Your ticket," said the door-keeper.

' "My ticket?" she replied. "I have none."

' "Then get one at the box-office."

'The domino came back under the peristyle, fumbled nervously about in all her pockets.

' "No money!" she cried. "Ah! this ring – a ticket of admission for this ring," she said.

' "Impossible," replied the woman who was distributing the cards; "we do not make bargains of that kind."

'And she pushed away the brilliant, which fell to the ground and rolled to my side.

'The domino remained still without moving, forgetting the ring, sunk in thought.

'I picked up the ring and handed it to her.

'Through her mask I saw her eyes fixed on mine.

' "You must help me to get in," she said to me; "you must, for pity's sake."

' "But I am going out, madame," I said to her.

' "Then give me six francs for this ring, and you will render me a service for which I shall bless you my life long."

'I replaced the ring on her finger; I went to the box-office, I took two tickets. We re-entered together.

'As we arrived within the corridor I felt that she was tottering. Then with her second hand she made a kind of ring around my arm.

' "Are you in pain?" I asked her.

' "No, no, it is nothing," she replied, "a dizziness, that is all."

'She hurried me into the hall.

'We re-entered into that giddy madhouse.

'Three times we made the tour, breaking our way with great difficulty through the waves of masks that were hurling themselves one upon the other; she trembling at every unseemly word that came to her ear; I blushing to be seen giving my arm to a woman who would thus put herself in the way of such words; then we returned to the end of the hall.

'She fell upon a sofa. I remained standing in front of her, my hand leaning on the back of her seat.

'"Oh! this must seem to you very bizarre," she said, "but not more so than to me, I swear to you. I have not the slightest idea of all this" (she looked at the ball), "for even in my dreams I could not imagine such things. But they wrote me, you see, that he would be here with a woman, and what sort of woman should it be who could come to a place like this?"

'I made a gesture of surprise; she understood.

'"But *I* am here, you wish to ask, do you not? Oh! but for me that is another thing: I, I am looking for him; I, I am his wife. As for these people, it is madness and dissipation that drives them hither. But I, I, it is jealousy infernal! I have been everywhere looking for him; I have been all night in a cemetery; I have been to a public execution; and yet, I swear to you, as a young girl I have never once gone into the street without my mother; as a wife I have never taken one step out of doors without being followed by a lackey; and yet here I am, the same as all these women who are so familiar with the way; here I am giving my arm to a man whom I do not know, blushing under my mask at the opinion he ought to have of me! I know all this! – Have you ever been jealous, monsieur?"

'"Unhappily," I replied to her.

'"Then you will forgive me, for you understand. You know that voice that cries out to you 'Do!' as in the ear of a madman; you have felt that arm that pushes one into shame and crime, like the arm of fate. You know that at such a moment one is capable of everything, if one can only get vengeance."

'I was about to reply; all at once she rose, her eyes fastened on two dominoes that were passing in front of us at that moment.

'"Silence!" she said.

'And she hurried me on following in their footsteps. I was thrown into the middle of an intrigue of which I understood nothing;

I could feel all the threads vibrating, but could take hold of none of them by the end; but this poor wife seemed so troubled that she became interesting. I obeyed like a child, so imperious is real feeling, and we set ourselves to follow the two masks, one of which was evidently a man, the other a woman. They spoke in a low voice; the sounds reached our ears with difficulty.

'"It is he!" she murmured; "it is his voice; yes, yes, that is his figure..."

'The latter of the two dominoes began to laugh.

'"That is his laugh," said she; "it is he, monsieur, it is he! The letter said true, O, *mon Dieu, mon Dieu!*"

'In the meanwhile the two masks kept on, and we followed them always. They went out of the hall, and we went out after them; they took the stairs leading to the boxes, and we ascended in their footsteps; they did not stop till they came to the boxes in the centre; we were like their two shadows. A little closed box was opened; they entered it; the door again closed upon them.

'The poor creature I was supporting on my arm frightened me by her excitement. I could not see her face, but crushed against me as she was, I could feel her heart beating, her body shivering, her limbs trembling. There was something uncanny in the way there came to me such knowledge of unheard of suffering, the spectacle of which I had before my very eyes, of whose victim I knew nothing, and of the cause of which I was completely ignorant. Nevertheless, for nothing in this world would I have abandoned that woman at such a moment.

'As she saw the two masks enter the box and the box close upon them, she stopped still a moment, motionless, and as if overwhelmed. Then she sprang forward to the door to listen. Placed as she was, her slightest movement would betray her presence and ruin her; I dragged her back violently by the arm, I lifted the latch of the adjoining box, I drew her in after me, I lowered the grille and pulled the door to.

'"If you wish to listen," I said to her, "at least listen from here."

'She fell upon one knee and flattened her ear against the partition, and I – I held myself erect on the opposite side, my arms crossed, my head bent and thoughtful.

'All that I had been able to observe of that woman seemed to me to indicate a type of beauty. The lower part of her face, which was not concealed by her mask, was youthful, velvety, and round; her lips were scarlet and delicate; her teeth, which the black velvet mask falling just above them made appear still whiter, were small, separated, and glistening; her hand was one to be modelled, her figure to be held between the fingers; her black hair, silky, escaped in profusion from beneath the hood of her domino, and the foot of a child, that played in and out under her skirt, looked as if it should have trouble in balancing her body, all lithe, all graceful, all airy as it was.

'Oh! what a marvellous piece of perfection must she be! Oh! he that should hold her in his arms, that should see every faculty of that spirit absorbed in loving him, that should feel the beating of her heart against his, her tremblings, her nervous palpitations, and that should be able to say, "All of this, all of this, comes of love, of love for me, for me alone among all the millions of men, for me, angel predestined! Oh! that man! – that man!"

'Such were my thoughts, when all at once I saw that woman rise, turn toward me, and say to me in a voice broken and fierce:

' "Monsieur, I am beautiful, I swear it; I am young, I am but nineteen. Until now I have been white as an angel of the Creation – ah, well – " she threw both arms about my neck, " – ah, well, I am yours – take me!"

'At the same instant I felt her lips pressed close to mine, and the effect of a bite, rather than that of a kiss, ran shuddering and dismayed through my whole body; over my eyes passed a cloud of flame.

'Ten minutes later I was holding her in my arms, in a swoon, half dead and sobbing.

'Slowly she came to herself; through her mask I made out how haggard were her eyes; I saw the lower part of her pale face, I heard her teeth chatter one upon the other, as in the chill of a fever. I see it all once more.

'She remembered all that had taken place, and fell at my feet.

' "If you have any compassion," she said, to me, sobbing, "any pity, turn away your eyes from me, never seek to know me; let me go and forget me. I will remember for two!"

'At these words she rose again; quickly, like a thought that escapes us, she darted toward the door, opened it, and coming back again, "Do not follow me, in heaven's name, monsieur, do not follow me!" she said.

'The door pushed violently open, closed again between her and me, stole her from my sight, like an apparition. I have never seen her more!

'I have never seen her more! And ever since, ever since the six months that have glided by, I have sought her everywhere, at balls, at spectacles, at promenades. Every time I have seen from a distance a woman with a lithe figure, with a foot like a child's, with black hair, I have followed her, I have drawn near to her, I have looked into her face, hoping that her blushes would betray her. Nowhere have I found her again, in no place have I seen her again – except at night, except in my dreams! Oh! there, there she reappears; there I feel her, I feel her embraces, her biting caresses so ardent, as if she had something of the devil in her; then the mask has fallen and a face more grotesque appeared to me at times blurred as if veiled in a cloud; sometimes brilliant, as if circled by an aureole; sometimes pale, with skull white and naked, with eyes vanished from the orbits, with teeth chattering and few.

'In short, ever since that night, I have ceased to live; burning with mad passion for a woman I do not know, hoping always, and always disappointed at my hopes. Jealous without the right to be so, without knowing of whom to be jealous, not daring to avow such madness, and all the time pursued, preyed upon, wasted away, consumed by her.'

As he finished these words he tore a letter from his breast.

'Now that I have told you everything,' he said to me, 'take this letter and read it.'

I took the letter and read:

'Have you perhaps forgotten a poor woman who has forgotten nothing and who dies because she cannot forget?

'When you receive this letter I shall be no more. Then go to the cemetery of Père-Lachaise, tell the concierge to let you see among the newest graves one that bears on its stone the simple name "Marie", and when you are face to face with that grave, fall on your knees and pray.'

'Ah, well!' continued Anthony, 'I received that letter yesterday, and I went there this morning. The concierge conducted me to the grave, and I remained two hours on my knees there, praying and weeping. Do you understand? She was there, that woman. Her flaming spirit had stolen away; the body consumed by it had bowed, even to breaking, beneath the burden of jealousy and of remorse; she was there, under my feet, and she had lived, and she had died for me unknown; unknown! – and taking a place in my life as she had taken one in the grave: unknown! – and burying in my heart a corpse, cold and lifeless, as she had buried one in the sepulchre – Oh! Do you know anything to equal it? Do you know any event so appalling? Therefore, now, no more hope. I will see her again never. I would dig up her grave that I might recover, perhaps, some traces wherewithal to reconstruct her face; and I love her always! Do you understand, Alexandre? I love her like a madman; and I would kill myself this instant in order to rejoin her, if she were not to remain unknown to me for eternity, as she was unknown to me in this world.'

With these words he snatched the letter from my hands, kissed it over and over again, and began to weep like a little child.

I took him in my arms, and not knowing what to say to him, I wept with him.

THE MORTAL IMMORTAL

Mary Shelley

Mary Shelley's novel Frankenstein *is a beautifully constructed work and one cannot help being impressed that she was only nineteen years old when she created such an enduring masterpiece. Of course virtually all my Frankenstein roles have only drawn a little from the original novel, but I have always tried to give the part the dignity and dedication of Miss Shelley's conception. She also wrote a number of short stories, including this strange and original tale of a man cursed with immortality – a subject which would surely have fascinated Baron Frankenstein himself!*

16 July 1833 – this is a memorable anniversary for me; on it I complete my three hundred and twenty-third year!

The Wandering Jew? – certainly not. More than eighteen centuries have passed over his head. In comparison with him, I am a very young Immortal.

Am I, then, immortal? This is a question which I have asked myself, by day and night, for now three hundred and three years, and yet cannot answer it. I detected a grey hair amidst my brown locks this very day – that surely signifies decay. Yet it may have remained concealed there for three hundred years – for some persons have become entirely white-headed before twenty years of age.

I will tell my story, and my reader shall judge for me. I will tell my story, and so contrive to pass some few hours of a long eternity, become so wearisome to me. For ever! Can it be? to live for ever! I have heard of enchantments, in which the victims were plunged into a deep sleep, to wake, after a hundred years, as fresh as ever: I have heard of the Seven Sleepers – thus to be immortal would not be so burthensome: but, oh! the weight of never-ending time – the tedious passage of the still-succeeding hours! How happy was the fabled Nourjahad! – But to my task.

All the world has heard of Cornelius Agrippa. His memory is as immortal as his arts have made me. All the world has also heard of his scholar, who, unawares, raised the foul fiend during his master's absence, and was destroyed by him. The report, true or false, of this accident, was attended with many inconveniences to the renowned philosopher. All his scholars at once deserted him – his servants disappeared. He had no one near him to put coals on his ever-burning fires while he slept, or to attend to the changeful colours of his medicines while he studied. Experiment after experiment failed, because one pair of hands was insufficient to complete them: the dark spirits laughed at him for not being able to retain a single mortal in his service.

I was then very young – very poor – and very much in love. I had been for about a year the pupil of Cornelius, though I was absent when this accident took place. On my return, my friends implored me not to return to the alchemist's abode. I trembled as I listened to the dire tale they told; I required no second warning; and when Cornelius came and offered me a purse of gold if I would remain under his roof, I felt as if Satan himself tempted me. My teeth chattered – my hair stood on end – I ran off as fast as my trembling knees would permit.

My failing steps were directed whither for two years they had every evening been attracted – a gently bubbling spring of pure living water, beside which lingered a dark-haired girl, whose beaming eyes were fixed on the path I was accustomed each night to tread. I cannot remember the hour when I did not love Bertha; we had been neighbours and playmates from infancy – her parents, like mine, were of humble life, yet respectable – our attachment had been a source of pleasure to them. In an evil hour, a malignant fever carried off both her father and mother, and Bertha became an orphan. She would have found a home beneath my paternal roof, but, unfortunately, the old lady of the near castle, rich, childless, and solitary, declared her intention to adopt her. Henceforth Bertha was clad in silk – inhabited a marble palace – and was looked on as being highly favoured by fortune. But in her new situation among her new associates, Bertha remained true to the friend of her humbler days; she often visited the cottage of my father, and when forbidden to go thither, she would stray towards the neighbouring wood, and meet me beside its shady fountain.

She often declared that she owed no duty to her new protectress equal in sanctity to that which bound us. Yet still I was too poor to marry, and she grew weary of being tormented on my account. She had a haughty but an impatient spirit, and grew angry at the obstacles that prevented our union. We met now after an absence, and she had been sorely beset while I was away; she complained bitterly, and almost reproached me for being poor. I replied hastily, 'I am honest, if I am poor! – were I not, I might soon become rich!' This exclamation produced a thousand questions. I feared to shock her by owning the truth, but she drew it from me; and then, casting a look of disdain on me, she said,

'You pretend to love, and you fear to face the Devil for my sake!' I protested that I had only dreaded to offend her – while she dwelt on the magnitude of the reward that I should receive. Thus encouraged – shamed by her – led on by love and hope, laughing at my late fears, with quick steps and a light heart, I returned to accept the offers of the alchemist, and was instantly installed in my office.

A year passed away. I became possessed of no insignificant sum of money. Custom had banished my fears. In spite of the most painful vigilance, I had never detected the trace of a cloven foot; nor was the studious silence of our abode ever disturbed by demoniac howls. I still continued my stolen interviews with Bertha, and Hope dawned on me – Hope – but not perfect joy; for Bertha fancied that love and security were enemies, and her pleasure was to divide them in my bosom. Though true of heart, she was somewhat of a coquette in manner; and I was jealous as a Turk. She slighted me in a thousand ways, yet would never acknowledge herself to be in the wrong. She would drive me mad with anger, and then force me to beg her pardon. Sometimes she fancied that I was not sufficiently submissive, and then she had some story of a rival, favoured by her protectress. She was surrounded by silk-clad youths – the rich and gay. What chance had the sad-robed scholar of Cornelius compared with these?

On one occasion, the philosopher made such large demands upon my time, that I was unable to meet her as I was wont. He was engaged in some mighty work, and I was forced to remain, day and night, feeding his furnaces and watching his chemical preparations. Bertha waited for me in vain at the fountain. Her haughty spirit fired at this neglect; and when at last I stole out during the few short minutes alloted to me for slumber, and hoped to be consoled by her, she received me with disdain, dismissed me in scorn, and vowed that any man should possess her hand rather than he who could not be in two places at once for her sake. She would be revenged! And truly she was. In my dingy retreat I heard that she had been hunting, attended by Albert Hoffer. Albert Hoffer was favoured by her protectress, and the three passed in cavalcade before my smoky window. Methought that they mentioned my name; it was followed by a laugh of derision, as her dark eyes glanced contemptuously towards my abode.

Jealousy, with all its venom and all its misery, entered my breast. Now I shed a torrent of tears, to think that I should never call her mine; and, anon, I imprecated a thousand curses on her inconstancy. Yet, still I must stir the fires of the alchemist, still attend on the changes of his unintelligible medicines.

Cornelius had watched for three days and nights, nor closed his eyes. The progress of his alembics was slower than he expected: in spite of his anxiety, sleep weighed upon his eyelids. Again and again he threw off drowsiness with more than human energy; again and again it stole away his senses. He eyed his crucibles wistfully. 'Not ready yet,' he murmured; 'will another night pass before the work is accomplished? Winzy, you are vigilant – you are faithful – you have slept, my boy – you slept last night. Look at that glass vessel. The liquid it contains is of a soft rose-colour: the moment it begins to change its hue, awaken me – till then I may close my eyes. First, it will turn white, and then emit golden flashes; but wait not till then; when the rose-colour fades, rouse me.' I scarcely heard the last words, muttered, as they were, in sleep. Even then he did not quite yield to nature. 'Winzy, my boy,' he again said, 'do not touch the vessel – do not put it to your lips; it is a philtre – a philtre to cure love; you would not cease to love your Bertha – beware to drink!'

And he slept. His venerable head sunk on his breast, and I scarce heard his regular breathing. For a few minutes I watched the vessel – the rosy hue of the liquid remained unchanged. Then my thoughts wandered – they visited the fountain, and dwelt on a thousand charming scenes never to be renewed – never! Serpents and adders were at my heart as the word 'Never!' half formed itself on my lips. False girl! – false and cruel! Never more would she smile on me as that evening she smiled on Albert. Worthless, detested woman! I would not remain unrevenged – she should see Albert expire at her feet – she should die beneath my vengeance. She had smiled in disdain and triumph – she knew my wretchedness and her power. Yet what power had she? – the power of exciting my hate – my utter scorn – my – oh, all but indifference! Could I attain that – could I regard her with careless eyes, transferring my rejected love to one fairer and more true, that were indeed a victory!

A bright flash darted before my eyes. I had forgotten the medicine of the adept; I gazed on it with wonder: flashes of admirable beauty, more bright than those which the diamond emits when the sun's rays are on it, glanced from the surface of the liquid; an odour the most fragrant and grateful stole over my sense; the vessel seemed one globe of living radiance, lovely to the eye, and most inviting to the taste. The first thought, instinctively inspired by the grosser sense, was, I will – I must drink. I raised the vessel to my lips. 'It will cure me of love – of torture!' Already I had quaffed half of the most delicious liquor ever tasted by the palate of man, when the philosopher stirred. I started – I dropped the glass – the fluid flamed and glanced along the floor, while I felt Cornelius's gripe at my throat, as he shrieked aloud, 'Wretch! you have destroyed the labour of my life!'

The philosopher was totally unaware that I had drunk any portion of his drug. His idea was, and I gave a tacit assent to it, that I had raised the vessel from curiosity, and that, frighted at its brightness, and the flashes of intense light it gave forth, I had let it fall. I never undeceived him. The fire of the medicine was quenched – the fragrance died away – he grew calm, as a philosopher should under the heaviest trials, and dismissed me to rest.

I will not attempt to describe the sleep of glory and bliss which bathed my soul in paradise during the remaining hours of that memorable night. Words would be faint and shallow types of my enjoyment, or of the gladness that possessed my bosom when I woke. I trod air – my thoughts were in heaven. Earth appeared heaven, and my inheritance upon it was to be one trance of delight. 'This it is to be cured of love,' I thought; 'I will see Bertha this day, and she will find her lover cold and regardless; too happy to be disdainful, yet how utterly indifferent to her!'

The hours danced away. The philosopher, secure that he had once succeeded, and believing that he might again, began to concoct the same medicine once more. He was shut up with his books and drugs, and I had a holiday. I dressed myself with care; I looked in an old but polished shield, which served me for a mirror; methought my good looks had wonderfully improved. I hurried beyond the precincts of the town, joy in my soul, the beauty of heaven and earth around me. I turned my steps towards the castle – I could look on its lofty turrets with lightness of heart, for I was cured of love. My Bertha saw me afar off, as I came up the avenue. I know not what sudden impulse animated her bosom, but at the sight, she sprung with a light fawn-like bound down the marble steps, and was hastening towards me. But I had been perceived by another person. The old high-born hag, who called herself her protectress, and was her tyrant, had seen me also; she hobbled, panting, up the terrace; a page, as ugly as herself, held up her train, and fanned her as she hurried along, and stopped my fair girl with a 'How, now, my bold mistress? whither so fast? Back to your cage – hawks are abroad!'

Bertha clasped her hands – her eyes were still bent on my approaching figure. I saw the contest. How I abhorred the old crone who checked the kind impulses of my Bertha's softening heart. Hitherto, respect for her rank had caused me to avoid the lady of the castle; now I disdained such trivial considerations. I was cured of love, and lifted above all human fears; I hastened forwards, and soon reached the terrace. How lovely Bertha looked! her eyes flashing fire, her cheeks glowing with impatience and anger, she was a thousand time more graceful and charming than ever. I no longer loved – Oh no! I adored – worshipped – idolized her!

She had that morning been persecuted, with more than usual vehemence, to consent to an immediate marriage with my rival. She was reproached with the encouragement that she had shown him – she was threatened with being turned out of doors with disgrace and shame. Her proud spirit rose in arms at the threat; but when she remembered the scorn that she had heaped upon me, and how, perhaps, she had thus lost one whom she now regarded as her only friend, she wept with remorse and rage. At that moment I appeared. 'Oh, Winzy!' she exclaimed, 'take me to your mother's cot; swiftly let me leave the detested luxuries and wretchedness of this noble dwelling – take me to poverty and happiness.'

I clasped her in my arms with transport. The old dame was speechless with fury, and broke forth into invective only when we were far on our road to my natal cottage. My mother received the fair fugitive, escaped from a gilt cage to nature and liberty, with tenderness and joy; my father, who loved her, welcomed her heartily; it was a day of rejoicing, which did not need the addition of the celestial potion of the alchemist to steep me in delight.

Soon after this eventful day, I became the husband of Bertha. I ceased to be the scholar of Cornelius, but I continued his friend. I always felt grateful to him for having, unawares, procured me that delicious draught of a divine elixir, which, instead of curing me of love (sad cure! solitary and joyless remedy for evils which seem blessings to the memory), had inspired me with courage and resolution, thus winning for me an inestimable treasure in my Bertha.

I often called to mind that period of trance-like inebriation with wonder. The drink of Cornelius had not fulfilled the task for which he affirmed that it had been prepared, but its effects were more potent and blissful than words can express. They had faded by degrees, yet they lingered long – and painted life in hues of splendour. Bertha often wondered at my lightness of heart and unaccustomed gaiety; for, before, I had been rather serious, or even sad, in my disposition. She loved me the better for my cheerful temper, and our days were winged by joy.

Five years afterwards I was suddenly summoned to the bedside of the dying Cornelius. He had sent for me in haste, conjuring my instant presence. I found him stretched on his pallet, enfeebled even to death; all of life that yet remained animated his piercing eyes, and they were fixed on a glass vessel, full of a roseate liquid. 'Behold,' he said, in a broken and inward voice, 'the vanity of human wishes! a second time my hopes are about to be crowned, a second time they are destroyed. Look at that liquor – you remember five years ago I had prepared the same, with the same success – then, as now, my thirsting lips expected to taste the immortal elixir – you dashed it from me! and at present it is too late.'

He spoke with difficulty, and fell back on his pillow. I could not help saying,

'How, revered master, can a cure for love restore you to life?'

A faint smile gleamed across his face as I listened earnestly to his scarcely intelligible answer.

'A cure for love and for all things – the Elixir of Immortality. Ah! if now I might drink, I should live for ever!'

As he spoke, a golden flash gleamed from the fluid; a well-remembered fragrance stole over the air; he raised himself, all weak as he was – strength seemed miraculously to re-enter his frame – he stretched forth his hand – a loud explosion startled me – a ray of fire shot up from the elixir, and the glass vessel which contained it was shivered to atoms! I turned my eyes towards the philosopher; he had fallen back – his eyes were glassy – his features rigid – he was dead!

But I lived, and was to live for ever! So said the unfortunate alchemist, and for a few days I believed his words. I remembered the glorious intoxication that had followed my stolen draught. I reflected on the change I had felt in my frame – in my soul. The bounding elasticity of the one – the buoyant lightness of the other. I surveyed myself in a mirror, and could perceive no change in my features during the space of the five years which had elapsed. I remembered the radiant hues and grateful scent of that delicious beverage – worthy the gift it was capable of bestowing – I was, then, IMMORTAL!

A few days after I laughed at my credulity. The old proverb, that 'a prophet is least regarded in his own country,' was true with respect to me and my defunct master. I loved him as a man – I respected him as a sage – but I derided the notion that he could command the powers of darkness, and laughed at the superstitious fears with which he was regarded by the vulgar. He was a wise philosopher, but had no acquaintance with any spirits but those clad in flesh and blood. His science was simply human; and human science, I soon persuaded myself, could never conquer nature's laws so far as to imprison the soul for ever within its carnal habitation. Cornelius had brewed a soul-refreshing drink – more inebriating than wine – sweeter and more fragrant than any fruit: it possessed probably strong medicinal powers, imparting gladness to the heart and vigour to the limbs; but its effects would wear out; already were they diminished in my frame. I was a lucky fellow to have quaffed health and joyous spirits, and perhaps long life, at my master's hands; but my good fortune ended there: longevity was far different from immortality.

I continued to entertain this belief for many years. Sometimes a thought stole across me – was the alchemist indeed deceived? But my habitual credence was, that I should meet the fate of all the children of Adam at my appointed time – a little late, but still at a natural age. Yet it was certain that I retained a wonderfully youthful look. I was laughed at for my vanity in consulting the mirror so often, but I consulted it in vain – my brow was untrenched – my cheeks – my eyes – my whole person continued as untarnished as in my twentieth year.

I was troubled. I looked at the faded beauty of Bertha – I seemed more like her son. By degrees our neighbours began to make similar observations, and I found at last that I went by the name of the Scholar Bewitched. Bertha herself grew uneasy. She became jealous and peevish, and at length she began to question me. We had no children; we were all in all to each other; and though, as she grew older, her vivacious spirit became a little allied to ill-temper, and her beauty sadly diminished, I cherished her in my heart as the mistress I had idolized, the wife I had sought and won with such perfect love.

At last our situation became intolerable: Bertha was fifty – I twenty years of age. I had, in very shame, in some measure adopted the habits of a more advanced age; I no longer mingled in the dance among the young and gay, but my heart bounded along with them while I restrained my feet; and a sorry figure I cut among the Nestors of our village. But before the time I mention, things were altered – we were universally shunned; we were – at least, I was – reported to have kept up an iniquitous acquaintance with some of my former master's supposed friends. Poor Bertha was pitied, but deserted. I was regarded with horror and detestation.

What was to be done? we sat by our winter fire – poverty had made itself felt, for none would buy the produce of my farm; and often I had been forced to journey twenty miles, to some place where I was not known, to dispose of our property. It is true, we had saved something for an evil day – that day was come.

We sat by our lone fireside – the old-hearted youth and his antiquated wife. Again Bertha insisted on knowing the truth; she recapitulated all she had ever heard said about me, and added her own observations. She conjured me to cast off the spell; she described how much more comely grey hairs were than my chestnut locks; she descanted on the reverence and respect due to age – how preferable to the slight regard paid to mere children: could I imagine that the despicable gifts of youth and good looks outweighed disgrace, hatred, and scorn? Nay, in the end I should be burnt as a dealer in the black art, while she, to whom I had not deigned to communicate any portion of my good fortune, might be stoned as my accomplice. At length she insinuated that I must share my secret with her, and bestow on her like benefits to those I myself enjoyed, or she would denounce me – and then she burst into tears.

Thus beset, methought it was the best way to tell the truth. I revealed it as tenderly as I could, and spoke only of a *very long life*, not of immortality – which representation, indeed, coincided best with my own ideas. When I ended, I rose and said,

'And now, my Bertha, will you denounce the lover of your youth? – You will not, I know. But it is too hard, my poor wife, that you should suffer from my ill-luck and the accursed arts of Cornelius. I will leave you – you have wealth enough, and friends will return in my absence. I will go; young as I seem, and strong as I am, I can work and gain my bread among strangers, unsuspected and unknown. I loved you in youth; God is my witness that I would not desert you in age, but that your safety and happiness require it.'

I took my cap and moved towards the door; in a moment Bertha's arms were round my neck, and her lips were pressed to mine. 'No, my husband, my Winzy,' she said, 'you shall not go alone – take me with you; we will remove from this place, and, as you say, among strangers we shall be unsuspected and safe. I am not so very old as quite to shame you, my Winzy; and I daresay the charm will soon wear off, and, with the blessing of God, you will become more elderly-looking, as is fitting; you shall not leave me.'

I returned the good soul's embrace heartily. 'I will not, my Bertha; but for your sake I had not thought of such a thing. I will be your true, faithful husband while you are spared to me, and do my duty by you to the last.'

The next day we prepared secretly for our emigration. We were obliged to make great pecuniary sacrifices – it could not be helped. We realized a sum sufficient, at least, to maintain us while Bertha lived; and, without saying adieu to any one, quitted our native country to take refuge in a remote part of western France.

It was a cruel thing to transport poor Bertha from her native village, and the friends of her youth, to a new country, new language, new customs. The strange secret of my destiny rendered this removal immaterial to me; but I compassionated her deeply, and was glad to perceive that she found compensation for her misfortunes in a variety of little ridiculous circumstances. Away from all tell-tale chroniclers, she sought to decrease the apparent disparity of our ages by a thousand feminine arts – rouge, youthful dress, and assumed juvenility of manner. I could not be angry. Did not I myself wear a mask? Why quarrel with hers, because it was less successful? I grieved deeply when I remembered that this was my Bertha, whom I had loved so fondly, and won with such transport – the dark-eyed, dark-haired girl, with smiles of enchanting archness and a step like a fawn – this mincing, simpering, jealous old woman. I should have revered her grey locks and withered cheeks; but thus! – It was my work, I knew; but I did not the less deplore this type of human weakness.

Her jealousy never slept. Her chief occupation was to discover that, in spite of outward appearances, I was myself growing old. I verily believe that the poor soul loved me truly in her heart, but never had woman so tormenting a mode of displaying fondness. She would discern wrinkles in my face and decrepitude in my walk, while I bounded along in youthful vigour, the youngest looking of twenty youths. I never dared address another woman. On one occasion, fancying that the belle of the village regarded me with favouring eyes, she brought me a grey wig. Her constant discourse among her acquaintances was, that though I looked so young, there was ruin at work within my frame; and she affirmed that the worst symptom about me was my apparent health. My youth was a disease, she said, and I ought at all times to prepare, if not for a sudden and awful death, at least to awake some morning white-headed and bowed down with all the marks of advanced years. I let her talk – I often joined in her conjectures. Her warnings chimed in with my never-ceasing speculations concerning my state, and I took an earnest, though painful, interest in listening to all that her quick wit and excited imagination could say on the subject.

Why dwell on these minute circumstances? We lived on for many long years. Bertha became bedrid and paralytic; I nursed her as a mother might a child. She grew peevish, and still harped upon one string – of how long I should survive her. It has ever been a source of consolation to me, that I performed my duty scrupulously towards her. She had been mine in youth, she was mine in age; and at last, when I heaped the sod over her corpse, I wept to feel that I had lost all that really bound me to humanity.

Since then how many have been my cares and woes, how few and empty my enjoyments! I pause here in my history – I will pursue it no further. A sailor without rudder or compass, tossed on a stormy sea – a traveller lost on a widespread heath, without landmark or stone to guide him – such have I been: more lost, more hopeless than either. A nearing ship, a gleam from some far cot, may save them; but I have no beacon except the hope of death.

Death! mysterious, ill-visaged friend of weak humanity! Why alone of all mortals have you cast me from your sheltering fold? Oh, for the peace of the grave! the deep silence of the iron-bound tomb! that thought would cease to work in my brain, and my heart beat no more with emotions varied only by new forms of sadness!

Am I immortal? I return to my first question. In the first place, is it not more probable that the beverage of the alchemist was fraught rather with longevity than eternal life? Such is my hope. And then be it remembered, that I only drank *half* of the potion prepared by him. Was not the whole necessary to complete the charm? To have drained half the Elixir of Immortality is but to be half-immortal – my Forever is thus truncated and null.

But again, who shall number the years of the half of eternity? I often try to imagine by what rule the infinite may be divided. Sometimes I fancy age advancing upon me. One grey hair I have found. Fool! do I lament? Yes, the fear of age and death often creeps coldly into my heart; and the more I live, the more I dread death, even while I abhor life. Such an enigma is man – born to perish – when he wars, as I do, against the established laws of his nature.

But for this anomaly of feeling surely I might die: the medicine of the alchemist would not be proof against fire – sword – and the strangling waters. I have gazed upon the blue depths of many a placid lake, and the tumultuous rushing of many a mighty river, and have said, peace inhabits those waters; yet I have turned my steps away, to live yet another day. I have asked myself, whether suicide would be a crime in one to whom thus only the portals of the other world could be opened. I have done all, except presenting myself as a soldier or duellist, an object of destruction to my – no, *not* my fellow-mortals, and therefore I have shrunk away. They are not my fellows. The inextinguishable power of life in my frame, and their ephemeral existence, places us wide as the poles asunder. I could not raise a hand against the meanest or the most powerful among them.

Thus I have lived on for many a year – alone, and weary of myself – desirous of death, yet never dying – a mortal immortal. Neither ambition nor avarice can enter my mind, and the ardent love that gnaws at my heart, never to be returned – never to find an equal on which to expend itself – lives there only to torment me.

This very day I conceived a design by which I may end all – without self-slaughter, without making another man a Cain – an expedition, which mortal frame can never survive, even endued with the youth and strength that inhabits mine. Thus I shall put my immortality to the test, and rest for ever – or return, the wonder and benefactor of the human species.

Before I go, a miserable vanity has caused me to pen these pages. I would not die, and leave no name behind. Three centuries have passed since I quaffed the fatal beverage; another year shall not elapse before, encountering gigantic dangers – warring with the powers of frost in their home – beset by famine, toil, and tempest – I yield this body, too tenacious a cage for a soul which thirsts for freedom, to the destructive elements of air and water; or, if I survive, my name shall be recorded as one of the most famous among the sons of men; and, my task achieved, I shall adopt more resolute means, and, by scattering and annihilating the atoms that compose my frame, set at liberty the life imprisoned within, and so cruelly prevented from soaring from this dim earth to a sphere more congenial to its immortal essence.

DRACULA'S GUEST
Bram Stoker

Bram Stoker's Dracula *is, like* Frankenstein, *a superbly constructed book, and one can well understand when reading it why it appeals to each new generation. I have always enjoyed playing the courageous Dr Van Helsing, and I think the Dracula films have the same appeal as the old morality plays with the struggle of good over evil and good always triumphing in the end. Because the first publisher of* Dracula *thought the manuscript was too long, he asked Bram Stoker to leave an episode out, and it is this bizarre little story which I have selected here to represent my vampire hunting!*

When we started for our drive the sun was shining brightly on Munich, and the air was full of the joyousness of early summer. Just as we were about to depart, Herr Delbrück (the *maître d'hôtel* of the Quatre Saisons, where I was staying) came down, bareheaded, to the carriage and, after wishing me a pleasant drive, said to the coachman, still holding his hand on the handle of the carriage door:

'Remember to come back by nightfall. The sky looks bright but there is a shiver in the north wind that says there may be a sudden storm. But I am sure you will not be late.' Here he smiled, and added, 'For you know what night it is.'

Johann answered with an emphatic, '*Ja, mein Herr,*' and touching his hat, drove off quickly. When we had cleared the town, I said, after signalling him to stop:

'Tell me, Johann, what is tonight?'

He crossed himself, as he answered laconically: '*Walpurgis Nacht.*' Then he took out his watch, a great, old-fashioned German silver thing as big as a turnip, and looked at it, with his eyebrows gathered together and a little impatient shrug of his shoulders. I realized that this was his way of respectfully protesting against the unnecessary delay, and sank back in the carriage, merely motioning him to proceed. He started off rapidly, as if to make up for lost time. Every now and then the horses seemed to throw up their heads and sniff the air suspiciously. On such occasions I often looked round in alarm. The road was pretty bleak, for we were traversing a sort of high, wind-swept plateau. As we drove, I saw a road that looked but little used, and which seemed to dip through a little, winding valley. It looked so inviting that, even at the risk of offending him, I called Johann to stop – and when he had pulled up, I told him I would like to drive down that road. He made all sorts of excuses, and frequently crossed himself as he spoke. This somewhat piqued my curiosity, so I asked him various questions. He answered fencingly, and repeatedly looked at his watch in protest. Finally I said:

'Well, Johann, I want to go down this road. I shall not ask you to come unless you like; but tell me why you do not like to go, that is all I ask.' For answer he seemed to throw himself off the box, so quickly did he reach the ground. Then he stretched out his hands appealingly to me, and implored me not to go. There was just enough of English mixed with the German for me to understand the drift of his talk. He seemed always just about to tell me something – the very idea of which evidently frightened him; but each time he pulled himself up, saying, as he crossed himself: '*Walpurgis Nacht!*'

I tried to argue with him, but it was difficult to argue with a man when I did not know his language. The advantage certainly rested with him, for although he began to speak in English, of a very crude and broken kind, he always got excited and broke into his native tongue – and every time he did so, he looked at his watch. Then the horses became restless and sniffed the air. At this he grew very pale, and, looking around in a frightened way, he suddenly jumped forward, took them by the bridles and led them on some twenty feet. I followed, and asked why he had done this. For answer he crossed himself, pointed to the spot we had left and drew his carriage in the direction of the other road, indicating a cross, and said, first in German, then in English: 'Buried him – him what killed themselves.'

I remembered the old custom of burying suicides at crossroads: 'Ah! I see, a suicide. How interesting!' But for the life of me I could not make out why the horses were frightened.

While we were talking, we heard a sort of sound between a yelp and a bark. It was far away; but the horses got very restless, and it took Johann all his time to quiet them. He was pale, and said: 'It sounds like a wolf – but yet there are no wolves here now.'

'No?' I said, questioning him; 'isn't it long since the wolves were so near the city?'

'Long, long,' he answered, 'in the spring and summer; but with the snow the wolves have been here not so long.'

While he was petting the horses and trying to quiet them, dark clouds drifted rapidly across the sky. The sunshine passed away, and a breath of cold wind seemed to drift past us. It was only a breath, however, and more in the nature of a warning than a fact, for the sun came out brightly again. Johann looked under his lifted hand at the horizon and said:

'The storm of snow, he comes before long time.' Then he looked at his watch again, and, straightway holding his reins firmly – for the horses were still pawing the ground restlessly and shaking their heads – he climbed to his box as though the time had come for proceeding on our journey.

I felt a little obstinate and did not at once get into the carriage.

'Tell me,' I said, 'about this place where the road leads,' and I pointed down.

Again he crossed himself and mumbled a prayer, before he answered: 'It is unholy.'

'What is unholy?' I inquired.

'The village.'

'Then there is a village?'

'No, no. No one lives there hundreds of years.' My curiosity was piqued: 'But you said there was a village.'

'There was.'

'Where is it now?'

Whereupon he burst out into a long story in German and English, so mixed up that I could not quite understand exactly what he said, but roughly I gathered that long ago, hundreds of years, men had died there and been buried in their graves; and sounds were heard under the clay, and when the graves were opened, men and women were found rosy with life, and their mouths red with blood. And so, in haste to save their lives (aye, and their souls! – and here he crossed himself) those who were left fled away to other places, where the living lived, and the dead were dead and not – not something. He was evidently afraid to speak the last words. As he proceeded with his narration, he grew more and more excited. It seemed as if his imagination had got hold of him, and he ended in a perfect paroxysm of fear – white-faced, perspiring, trembling and looking round him, as if expecting that some dreadful presence would manifest itself there in the bright sunshine on the open plain. Finally, in an agony of desperation he cried:

'*Walpurgis Nacht!*' and pointed to the carriage for me to get in. All my English blood rose at this, and standing back, I said:

'You are afraid, Johann, you are afraid. Go home; I shall return alone; the walk will do me good.' The carriage door was open. I took from the seat my oak walking-stick – which I always carry on my holiday excursions – and closed the door, pointing back to Munich, and said, 'Go home, Johann – Walpurgis Nacht doesn't concern Englishmen.'

The horses were now more restive than ever, and Johann was trying to hold them in, while excitedly imploring me not to do anything so foolish. I pitied the poor fellow, he was so deeply in earnest; but all the same I could not help laughing. His English was quite gone now. In his anxiety he had forgotten that his only means of making me understand was to talk my language, so he jabbered away in his native German. It began to be a little tedious. After giving the direction, 'Home!' I turned to go down the crossroad into the valley.

With a despairing gesture, Johann turned his horses towards Munich. I leaned on my stick and looked after him. He went slowly along the road for a while: then there came over the crest of the hill a man tall and thin. I could see so much in the distance. When he drew near the horses, they began to jump and kick about, then to scream with terror. Johann could not hold them in; they bolted down the road, running away madly. I watched him out of sight, then looked for the stranger, but I found that he, too, was gone.

With a light heart I turned down the side road through the deepening valley to which Johann had objected. There was not the slightest reason, that I could see, for his objection; and I daresay I tramped for a couple of hours without thinking of time or distance, and certainly without seeing a person or a house. So far as the place was concerned, it was desolation itself. But I did not notice this particularly till, on turning a bend in the road, I came upon a scattered fringe of wood; then I recognized that I had been impressed unconsciously by the desolation of the region through which I had passed.

I sat down to rest myself, and began to look around. It struck me it was considerably colder than it had been at the commencement of my walk – a sort of sighing sound seemed to be around me, with, now and then, high overhead, a sort of muffled roar. Looking upwards I noticed that great thick clouds were drifting rapidly across the sky from north to south at a great height. There were signs of coming storm in some lofty stratum of the air. I was a little chilly, and thinking that it was the sitting still after the exercise of walking, I resumed my journey.

The ground I passed over was now much more picturesque. There were no striking objects that the eye might single out; but in all there was a charm of beauty. I took little heed of time and it was only when the deepening twilight forced itself upon me that I began to think of how I should find my way home. The brightness of the day had gone. The air was cold, and the drifting of clouds high overhead was more marked. They were accompanied by a sort of faraway rushing sound, through which seemed to come at intervals that mysterious cry which the driver had said came from a wolf. For a while I hesitated. I had said I would see the deserted village, so on I went, and presently came on a wide stretch of open country, shut in by hills all around. Their sides were covered with trees which spread down to the plain, dotting, in clumps, the gentler slopes and hollows which showed here and there. I followed with my eye the winding of the road, and saw that it curved close to one of the densest of these clumps and was lost behind it.

As I looked there came a cold shiver in the air, and the snow began to fall. I thought of the miles and miles of bleak country I had passed, and then hurried on to seek the shelter of the wood in front. Darker and darker grew the sky, and faster and heavier fell the snow, till the earth before and around me was a glistening white carpet the further edge of which was lost in misty vagueness. The road was here but crude, and when on the level its boundaries were not so marked, as when it passed through the cuttings; and in a little while I found that I must have strayed from it, for I missed underfoot the hard surface, and my feet sank deeper in the grass and moss. Then the wind grew stronger and blew with ever increasing force, till I was fain to run before it. The air became icy-cold, and in spite of my exercise I began to suffer. The snow was now falling so thickly and whirling around me in such rapid eddies that I could hardly keep my eyes open. Every now and then the heavens were torn asunder by vivid lightning, and in the flashes I could see ahead of me a great mass of trees, chiefly yew and cypress all heavily coated with snow.

I was soon amongst the shelter of the trees, and there, in comparative silence, I could hear the rush of the wind high overhead. Presently the blackness of the storm had become merged in the darkness of the night. By-and-by the storm seemed to be passing away: it now only came in fierce puffs or blasts. At such moments the weird sound of the wolf appeared to be echoed by many similar sounds around me.

Now and again, through the black mass of drifting cloud, came a straggling ray of moonlight, which lit up the expanse, and showed me that I was at the edge of a dense mass of cypress and yew trees. As the snow had ceased to fall, I walked out from the shelter and began to investigate more closely. It appeared to me that, amongst so many old foundations as I had passed, there might be still standing a house in which, though in ruins, I could find some sort of shelter for a while. As I skirted the edge of the copse, I found that a low wall encircled it, and following this I presently found an opening. Here the cypresses formed an alley leading up to a square mass of some kind of building. Just as I caught sight of this, however, the drifting clouds obscured the moon, and I passed up the path in darkness. The wind must have grown colder, for I felt myself shiver as I walked; but there was hope of shelter, and I groped my way blindly on.

I stopped, for there was a sudden stillness. The storm had passed; and, perhaps in sympathy with nature's silence, my heart seemed to cease to beat. But this was only momentarily; for suddenly the moonlight broke through the clouds, showing me that I was in a graveyard, and that the square object before me was a great massive tomb of marble, as white as the snow that lay on and all around it. With the moonlight there came a fierce sigh of the storm, which appeared to resume its course with a long, low howl, as of many dogs or wolves. I was awed and shocked, and felt the cold perceptibly grow upon me till it seemed to grip me by the heart. Then while the flood of moonlight still fell on the marble tomb, the storm gave further evidence of renewing, as though it were returning on its track. Impelled by some sort of fascination, I approached the sepulchre to see what it was, and why such a thing stood alone in such a place. I walked around it, and read, over the Doric door in German:

COUNTESS DOLINGEN OF GRATZ
IN STYRIA
SOUGHT AND FOUND DEATH.
1801.

On the top of the tomb, seemingly driven through the solid marble – for the structure was composed of a few vast blocks of stone – was a great iron spike or stake. On going to the back I saw, graven in great Russian letters:

'The dead travel fast.'

There was something so weird and uncanny about the whole thing that it gave me a turn and made me feel quite faint. I began to wish, for the first time, that I had taken Johann's advice. Here a thought struck me, which came under almost mysterious circumstances and with a terrible shock. This was Walpurgis Night!

Walpurgis Night, when, according to the belief of millions of people, the devil was abroad – when the graves were opened and the dead came forth and walked. When all evil things of earth and air and water held revel. This very place the driver had specially shunned. This was the depopulated village of centuries ago. This was where the suicide lay; and this was the place where I was alone – unmanned, shivering with cold in a shroud of snow with a wild storm gathering again upon me! It took all my philosophy, all the religion I had been taught, all my courage, not to collapse in a paroxysm of fright.

And now a perfect tornado burst upon me. The ground shook as though thousands of horses thundered across it; and this time the storm bore on its icy wings, not snow, but great hailstones which drove with such violence that they might have come from the thongs of Balearic slingers – hailstones that beat down leaf and branch and made the shelter of the cypresses of no more avail than though their stems were standing corn. At the first I had rushed to the nearest tree; but I was soon fain to leave it and seek the only spot that seemed to afford refuge, the deep Doric doorway of the marble tomb. There, crouching against the massive bronze door, I gained a certain amount of protection from the beating of the hailstones, for now they only drove against me as they ricocheted from the ground and the side of the marble.

As I leaned against the door, it moved slightly and opened inwards. The shelter of even a tomb was welcome in that pitiless tempest, and I was about to enter it when there came a flash of forked lightning that lit up the whole expanse of the heavens. In the instant, as I am a living man, I saw, as my eyes were turned into the darkness of the tomb, a beautiful woman, with rounded cheeks and red lips, seemingly sleeping on a bier. As the thunder broke overhead, I was grasped as by the hand of a giant and hurled out into the storm. The whole thing was so sudden that, before I could realize the shock, moral as well as physical, I found the hailstones beating me down. At the same time I had a strange, dominating feeling that I was not alone. I looked toward the tomb. Just then there came another blinding flash, which seemed to strike the iron stake that surmounted the tomb and to pour through to the earth, blasting and crumbling the marble, as in a burst of flame. The dead woman rose for a moment of agony, while she was lapped in the flame, and her bitter scream of pain was drowned in the thundercrash. The last thing I heard was this mingling of dreadful sound, as again I was seized in the giant grasp and dragged away, while the hailstones beat on me, and the air around seemed reverberant with the howling of wolves. The last sight that I remembered was a vague, white, moving mass, as if all the graves around me had sent out the phantoms of their sheeted dead, and that they were closing in on me through the white cloudiness of the driving hail.

Gradually there came a sort of vague beginning of consciousness; then a sense of weariness that was dreadful. For a time I remembered nothing; but slowly my senses returned. My feet seemed positively racked with pain, yet I could not move them. They seemed to be numbed. There was an icy feeling at the back of my neck and all down my spine, and my ears, like my feet, were dead, yet in torment; but there was in my breast a sense of warmth which was, by comparison, delicious. It was a nightmare – a physical nightmare, if one may use such an expression; for some heavy weight on my chest made it difficult for me to breathe.

This period of semi-lethargy seemed to remain a long time, and as it faded away I must have slept or swooned. Then came a sort of loathing, like the first stage of sea-sickness, and a wild desire to be free from something – I knew not what. A vast stillness enveloped me, as though all the world were asleep or dead – only broken by the low panting, as of some animal, close to me. I felt a warm rasping at my throat, then came a consciousness of the awful truth, which chilled me to the heart and sent the blood surging up through my brain. Some great animal was lying on me and now licking my throat. I feared to stir, for some instinct of prudence bade me lie still; but the brute seemed to realize that there was now some change in me, for it raised its head. Through my eyelashes I saw above me the two great flaming eyes of a gigantic wolf. Its sharp white teeth gleamed in the gaping red mouth, and I could feel its hot breath fierce and acrid upon me.

For another spell of time I remembered no more. Then I became conscious of a low growl, followed by a yelp, renewed again and again. Then, seemingly very far away, I heard a 'Holloa! holloa!' as of many voices calling in unison. Cautiously I raised my head and looked in the direction whence the sound came; but the cemetery blocked my view. The wolf still continued to yelp in a strange way, and a red glare began to move round the grove of cypresses, as though following the sound. As the voices drew closer, the wolf yelped faster and louder. I feared to make either sound or motion. Nearer came the red glow, over the white pall which stretched into the darkness around me. Then all at once from beyond the trees there came at a trot a troop of horsemen bearing torches. The wolf rose from my breast and made for the cemetery. I saw one of the horsemen (soldiers by their caps and their long military cloaks) raise his carbine and take aim. A companion knocked up his arm, and I heard the ball whizz over my head. He had evidently taken my body for that of the wolf. Another sighted the animal as it slunk away, and a shot followed. Then, at a gallop, the troop rode forward – some towards me, others following the wolf as it disappeared amongst the snow-clad cypresses.

As they drew nearer I tried to move, but was powerless, although I could see and hear all that went on around me. Two or three of the soldiers jumped from their horses and knelt beside me. One of them raised my head, and placed his hand over my heart.

'Good news, comrades!' he cried. 'His heart still beats!'

Then some brandy was poured down my throat; it put vigour into me, and I was able to open my eyes fully and look around. Lights and shadows were moving among the trees, and I heard men call to one another. They drew together, uttering frightened exclamations; and the lights flashed as the others came pouring out of the cemetery pell-mell, like men possessed. When the further ones came close to us, those who were around me asked them eagerly:

'Well, have you found him?'

The reply rang out hurriedly:

'No! no! Come away quick – quick! This is no place to stay, and on this of all nights!'

'What was it?' was the question, asked in all manner of keys. The answer came variously and all indefinitely as though the men were moved by some common impulse to speak, yet were restrained by some common fear from uttering their thoughts.

'It – it – indeed!' gibbered one, whose wits had plainly given out for the moment.

'A wolf – and yet not a wolf!' another put in shudderingly.

'No use trying for him without the sacred bullet,' a third remarked in a more ordinary manner.

'Serves us right for coming out of this night! Truly we have earned our thousand marks!' were the ejaculations of a fourth.

'There was blood on the broken marble,' another said after a pause – 'the lightning never brought that there. And for him – is he safe? Look at his throat! See, comrades, the wolf has been lying on him and keeping his blood warm.'

The officer looked at my throat and replied:

'He is all right; the skin is not pierced. What does it all mean? We should never have found him but for the yelping of the wolf.'

'What became of it?' asked the man who was holding up my head, and who seemed the least panic-stricken of the party, for his hands were steady and without tremor. On his sleeve was the chevron of a petty officer.

'It went to its home,' answered the man, whose long face was pallid, and who actually shook with terror as he glanced around him fearfully. 'There are graves enough there in which it may lie. Come, comrades – come quickly! Let us leave this cursed spot.'

The officer raised me to a sitting posture, as he uttered a word of command; then several men placed me upon a horse. He sprang to the saddle behind me, took me in his arms, gave the word to advance;

and, turning our faces away from the cypresses, we rode away in swift, military order.

And yet my tongue refused its office, and I was perforce silent. I must have fallen asleep; for the next thing I remembered was finding myself standing up, supported by a soldier on each side of me. It was almost broad daylight, and to the north a red streak of sunlight was reflected, like a path of blood, over the waste of snow. The officer was telling the men to say nothing of what they had seen, except that they had found an English stranger, guarded by a large dog.

'Dog! that was no dog,' cut in the man who had exhibited such fear. 'I think I know a wolf when I see one.'

The young officer answered calmly: 'I said a dog.'

'Dog!' reiterated the other ironically. It was evident that his courage was rising with the sun; and, pointing to me, he said, 'Look at his throat. Is that the work of a dog, master?'

Instinctively I raised my hand to my throat, and as I touched it I cried out in pain. The men crowded round to look, some stooping down from their saddles; and again there came the calm voice of the young officer:

'A dog, as I said. If ought else were said we should only be laughed at.'

I was then mounted behind a trooper, and we rode on into the suburbs of Munich. Here we came across a stray carriage, into which I was lifted, and it was driven off to the Quatre Saisons – the young officer accompanying me, while a trooper followed with his horse, and the others rode off to their barracks.

When we arrived, Herr Delbrück rushed so quickly down the steps to meet me, that it was apparent he had been watching within. Taking me by both hands he solicitously led me in. The officer saluted me and was turning to withdraw, when I recognized his purpose, and insisted that he should come to my rooms. Over a glass of wine I warmly thanked him and his brave comrades for saving me. He replied simply that he was more than glad, and that Herr Delbrück had at the first taken steps to make all the searching party pleased; at which ambiguous utterance the *maître d'hôtel* smiled, while the officer pleaded duty and withdrew.

'But Herr Delbrück,' I inquired, 'how and why was it that the soldiers searched for me?'

He shrugged his shoulders, as if in depreciation of his own deed, as he replied:

'I was so fortunate as to obtain leave from the commander of the regiment in which I served, to ask for volunteers.'

'But how did you know I was lost?' I asked.

'The driver came hither with the remains of his carriage, which had been upset when the horses ran away.'

'But surely you would not send a search party of soldiers merely on this account?'

'Oh, no!' he answered; 'but even before the coachman arrived, I had this telegram from the Boyar whose guest you are,' and he took from his pocket a telegram which he handed to me, and I read.

BISTRITZ

Be careful of my guest – his safety is most precious to me. Should aught happen to him, or if he be missed, spare nothing to find him and insure his safety. He is English and therefore adventurous. There are often dangers from snow and wolves and night. Lose not a moment if you suspect harm to him. I answer your zeal with my fortune – Dracula.

As I held the telegram in my hand, the room seemed to whirl around me; and, if the attentive *maître d'hôtel* had not caught me, I think I should have fallen. There was something so strange in all this, something so weird and impossible to imagine, that there grew on me a sense of my being in some way the sport of opposite forces – the mere vague idea of which seemed in a way to paralyze me. I was certainly under some form of mysterious protection. From a distant country had come, in the very nick of time, a message that took me out of the danger of the snow-sleep and the jaws of the wolf.

IN THE FOOTSTEPS OF THE ABOMINABLE SNOWMAN

Josef Nesvadba

I first really learned about the legend of the Abominable Snowman when I appeared in the BBC television play, The Creature in 1955. This was later made into a film, The Abominable Snowman (1957) and I think it was very clever the way the script-writer, Nigel Kneale, made it more than just the story of a hunt for a monster. I played a Dr John Rollason, the sole survivor of a party that went searching for the Yeti, and he escaped death because he was more anxious to learn the truth about the creature than capturing it for commercial gain. I am of the opinion the legend is rather like that of the Loch Ness Monster, and there is something there, but perhaps not in the form it is popularly presented. It could be an essence, or a spirit, or something of the kind, just as the Loch Ness Monster might be some sort of creature that only surfaces perhaps every twenty years when it needs a fresh supply of oxygen. We are always discovering life forms thought to be extinct, too, and I gather even scientists who used to have an axiom 'we believe what we see' are beginning to realize that there are things in existence that we don't always see. I believe very strongly in another world, in the unseen, and the Yeti may well be a part of that.

January last year the papers were full of the tragic end of Lord Esdale, whose expedition was said to have been swept away in a snowstorm when crossing an open mountain plateau in the Himalayas. I declare on my word of honour and in good faith that this is untrue and contrary to the facts of the case. For I am the only man who knows why Lord Esdale disappeared in the Himalayas, and I am prepared to swear on oath to the following:

I first met Lord Esdale in the thirties, when he came to see me, secretly, in Markvartice. I was teaching art in the school there and looking after the local museum collections. Markvartice is practically next door to Věstonice, where Professor Absolon found the ivory figure of a woman buried in diluvial strata; later it became famous as the Věstonice Venus. On historical expeditions in the vicinity I had found many old caves between Markvartice and Věstonice, caves that were half buried, with relics of various Stone Age animals in them. I once managed to find a broken mammoth tusk (*Elephas primigenius*) which I intended to give the place of honour in the school collection. At that time my father-in-law had come to visit us; his name is Josef Žabka, and he comes from Mikulov, where he had a chocolate factory. Žabka talked me into keeping the tusk for myself and then came to the point.

'You're clever at carving and painting things. It wouldn't be hard for you to carve a figure like the one they found in Věstonice, and then I'll rub clay and old soil into it.'

'Whatever for?'

'Do you want to sit in this country school all your days for a couple of hundred crowns a month? My daughter is used to more comfort than that...'

They kept on at me for weeks. I loved my wife. To make matters worse the headmaster accused me of spending more time on my collections than on my pupils. We came to words and he threatened to report me and have me dismissed from the teaching profession. My father-in-law declared that two nice prehistoric figures would see us in comfort to the end of our days, because the traveller who sold him cocoa was in touch with a collector in London who bought things like that. The traveller was in Brno at that very moment. I had to carve a second Věstonice Venus in a single night. The tusk kept crumbling and I kept having to start over and over again. I'd got an illustrated book on the Quaternary era, and from that I copied the figure of a mammoth and a long-haired rhinoceros (*Coelodonta antiquitatis*). I gave my carvings to my father-in-law and he showed them to the cocoa traveller. Then we sat back and waited a few months. No news came from London, although we had sent photographs of my works of art, and my father-in-law got hold of a Viennese professor who gave him a certificate to say they really were the work of Stone Age artists. I began to think I'd better soothe the headmaster's feelings and I swore I'd turn my father-in-law out next time he came, and reserve my friendship for the workers in his Mikulov factory, who'd been my companions at school. Then suddenly one morning, I think it was a Saturday, a car of foreign make drew up in front of our school and an elegant gentleman got out, dressed in homespun and a stitched hat such as you don't see round our way. He had to bend down to get through the door of my Natural History room. He shook hands with his left hand.

'I'm Lord Esdale,' he said in poor German. I touched his right hand and found it was artificial. 'Lions,' said Esdale laconically and sat down right under my rare sand viper. 'I've come about your forgeries . . .'

'I assure you they are genuine figures,' I said rudely.

'The ivory is genuine enough, and that's why I'm here. There's no point in denying it. They're quite nice little figures and I'm glad in this age of reason to meet a man with as much feeling for form as man had in the Ice Age . . .' He was not flattering me; I looked at myself in the mirror; my face is cheesy white and my ginger hair is thinning, there are times when I find myself ugly; but not as ugly as our hairy ancestors. 'I'll buy your figures, but only on one condition,' he said quickly, seeing that I was softening. 'You must take me into the caves where you found the mammoth tusk. And explore them thoroughly with me.' Just then the cheerful Viennese chauffeur came into the room with mountaineering equipment and a travelling bag in his arms. He told Esdale he had arranged a room for him at the inn, and asked for his money. Esdale gave him a cheque and the man thanked him politely and withdrew, with a puzzled look at me and my collections. He got in the car and drove off.

'Nobody explores the caves round Markvartice,' I told his lordship miserably. I wanted the money, but I wanted to stay alive to enjoy it. 'A lot of people got lost in them and either died of hunger or fell into terrible abysses. I write to Prague regularly every month to get them to send a proper expedition. There may be even more beautiful stalactite caves here than in Damänov. Two is not enough for that, Mr Lord.'

'Are you afraid? How much money do you want?' He thought

I was trying to drive his price up. He probably thought Markvartice was like darkest Africa and started dealing with me as he would with a native medicine-man. I felt like saying I wanted a kilogramme of pretty beads and a pound of gunpowder, to put a match to under his chair, but I thought better of it and sent him off to bed at the Post Inn. All that night I tried to decide which of the caves would be the least dangerous. It was a long time before I could get to sleep. Next morning we set out. I thought I'd lead him round a bit in the dark, give him a soaking in the underground river, show him a hearth that had long since been robbed of everything of interest when the local boys got at it; and satisfy him with some bones of domestic animals nobody was interested in because they had obviously been brought into the cave by some nineteenth-century fox – they're good enough to scare off trippers. The trouble was, Lord Esdale hadn't been born yesterday.

'A large cave,' he said, as he nibbled the roast chicken I'd brought with me, 'a very large cave, indeed, but you ought to install electric light here,' he gazed without interest at a whitened horse skull that frightens all visitors away. 'Then you could safely bring school-children in here ...' He got to his feet and marched off with such long steps I could hardly keep pace with him. I felt ashamed, and I was furious with my father-in-law. It was all his doing. I told Lord Esdale I was not going into any caves with him because I was scared and had never dared to go further than just inside before. Two of my pals who were willing to risk more were somewhere in the deep caves, as ghostly as that whitened horse skull, and I had not the slightest desire to end up in some museum as the remarkably well-preserved skeleton of a prehistoric man. I am *homo sapiens*, a man of reason, and I want my mortal remains buried decently in a cemetery and not in diluvial deposits.

He did not take offence in the least. Quite the reverse; he waited for me to catch up with him, took me by the arm, and lit his pipe.

'That's the best proof, my goodness, that's the best proof. Do you really believe your friends were killed down there?' For the first time I began to wonder whether he wasn't mad.

'What would they be doing there all this time? It's five years since Tonda Kopecky went.'

'Just like my wife,' said his lordship and puffed furiously at his pipe. 'That's proof. You're coming into those caves with me, even if I have to play hell,' he said determinedly.

He took me back to the inn, where he had rented the whole of one floor, and ordered two half-pound steaks off Müller, who couldn't bow low enough. From his travelling bag he took a bottle of Black and White, the special brand of Buchanan's choice old whisky, Glasgow and London. By morning we had finished off two bottles. And by morning I had heard the story of Lady Esdale, to which I am also prepared to swear in my deposition.

Lady Esdale disappeared five years ago when taking part in the first Himalayan expedition organized by Prince Paul of L. She was Lord Esdale's second wife.

'We wanted to go abroad somewhere for our honeymoon, and I happened to receive this invitation from Paul; we were old Monte Carlo acquaintances. You know, Paul was a strange creature. He looked like a goalkeeper, with shoulders like an orang-outang; when he spoke he had such a high squeaky voice that you felt instead of Prince Paul there was a scared little cry-baby Paul tucked away inside that hefty body. He had married a Portuguese noblewoman of sorts, whose family just managed to keep going because they owned a horse-meat shop in Oporto. They lived together for two years and then there was a dreadful scandal. At the roulette table, one of her cast-off lovers started reciting a list of his predecessors ... Perhaps he was jealous, heaven only knows – but it was a terrific scandal. Of course everybody knows that women change their lovers from time to time, but it isn't usual for the public to hear about it like that, and all at once, too.

'Paul almost killed the man, but he wanted to go on living with his wife. His family were against the idea, he had his obligations to his rank in life, they said, and he would have to divorce her. Paul didn't agree with them and so he started studying polyandry. He set off on his travels to visit all the tribes where polyandry was still practised – that is to say, tribes where every woman can have more than one husband. He wanted to write a scientific study of the subject that would break down the social prejudices of his class. For the time being, his wife, whom he left behind in Europe, studied polyandry effectively in practice.

'It was well known that until not long before, Tibet had been the land where polyandry was commonest. Paul settled there for a couple of years and invited us to spend our honeymoon with him. I had no fear that my wife might be influenced by the example of the women of Tibet, and so two days after the wedding we set off.

At that time I knew nothing of the Himalayas and still less about the Abominable Snowman.'

'The abominable what?' I asked, for Europe had heard nothing of this phenomenon as yet, in the thirties.

'The Abominable Snowman,' said Esdale 'Yeti, the natives call him. We came across his tracks when we were making for an out-of-the-way mountain village where one young woman was said to have a ration of thirty husbands; they all lived in peace and friendliness without any signs of jealousy, apparently, and paternity was attributed to the men in order of seniority. Paul thought that in this village high up in the mountains we could study polyandry in practically laboratory conditions, if I may use the term. It was very difficult to get there, though. Three times the native bearers wanted to turn back. We had to make our own rope bridge across an abyss that was narrow enough, it is true, but apparently bottomless. It was frightfully risky and the landscape round us was so strangely beautiful that my wife was quite happy at the thought that not one of her friends had had such a magnificent honeymoon. All her friends were stupid narrow-minded geese. Helen was the only one of them who had been to a university; she had worked in my Manchester firm as a machine designer. That was a sign of her noble mind, and my marriage to her was certainly not the *mésalliance* some of my friends persisted in calling it. She was the perfect wife, beautiful and clever. I still love her dearly ...' Lord Esdale poured himself a double whisky and swallowed it at one gulp. Whenever he recalled his wife he talked more loudly, as though he felt the need to convince himself of something.

'Helen was the first to notice the tracks. She had been on two shooting trips with me in Africa before that, and I had always admired her acute powers of observation; she could read tracks better than my Somali boy. The last time we were in the Congo she shot three male gorillas herself, and all next day the niggers danced round her in the village as if she were one of their idols. And now she noticed that these tracks in the Himalayas were like gorilla tracks. How could they possibly have got up there into those frozen mountains? I asked the bearers what they thought, but they swore they could see nothing, it was all a mistake, there were no tracks there at all. Later on, though, when we got to a snow-covered plateau, you would have had to be blind not to see those tracks. The natives took counsel; we could see they were scared.

' "It's the yeti," the eldest of them said at last. "The only thing to do is to take no notice and then he'll leave us alone."

' "What's the yeti?" They told us it was a spirit. I couldn't help laughing. What spirit could leave tracks like that behind? It was clearly some large kind of monkey that inhabited these high mountains. Helen fetched my gun. I have a very accurate big game gun that I bought in Germany, and I had never yet missed with it. We set off to follow those strange tracks. Prince Paul had to go with us, although he did not feel like it. We were his guests, after all.

' "We have warned you," the eldest of the bearers said, and put his burden down on the ground. "We will not follow the yeti!"

' "Why?" I snapped and turned my gun on him. "I do not like discontent and disobedience when I am hunting big game. The first essential is to have one's rear covered."

' "Whoever goes in his tracks, never returns ..." he said it over and over again in that singsong Yahoo of theirs and the others murmured after him as though it were a religious ceremony.

' "The tracks are quite fresh," said Helen, "they can wait here until we get back. We shan't be long."

' "You will never get back," the old man said with a sad smile, looking into her eyes. "You will never come back!"

'He was right.'

'We almost ran along those tracks. Paul was carrying our ammunition, he himself did not like killing game. He really was a strange creature. Helen was leading the way as though frantic with impatience. After an hour had passed we saw drops of blood; the creature we were tracking must be wounded. Then the blood stains grew bigger, and when the tracks seemed to halt, about half an hour later, we found a bone. The shoulder-blade of some small animal. Gnawed clean. We stopped too; what could it mean? If it was a monkey of some kind we were tracking, as we had assumed so far, then it was unthinkable that it might be feeding on raw meat. Or were there such strange monkeys here that their menu resembled that of man? It occurred to us for the first time that we had perhaps happened upon a real mystery, and that we might bring back to Europe not only rare furs, but perhaps fame among the scientists of the world, for the discovery of a new species of animal, carnivorous Himalayan monkeys. It looked as though we were bound to come on the creature at any moment, and to be on the safe side I released the safety catch of my gun.

'That was when it began. Out of a clear sky, 6,500 feet above sea level, with the temperature far below zero a fantastic thunderstorm burst upon us. Lightning was flashing all round us and then snow began to fall. We could not see each other, it was so thick. We made for a rock to shelter under but it was even worse there. I wanted to give Helen my arm in that white darkness, but my hand grasped a great big paw. I thought it was Paul and shook it off angrily. Then something struck me on the head, I fell flat on my back and lost consciousness.

'When I came to myself everything was calm. But we were no longer under the shelter of a rock; we were high up in the mountains, on the threshold of a strange cave with big rocks barring the way out. Naturally I wanted to climb over them and get out.

' "Wait!" Helen screamed in anguish. "There's a drop of at least three thousand feet!" I scrambled up the boulders and saw that she was right. The cave opened in a sheer rock face lost in the abyss below and towering into the clouds above. We could not get out of there without mountaineering equipment.

' "All I've got is a flashlamp," said Paul miserably. "They've taken everything away from us. They didn't leave me a single cartridge. Not even matches and cigarettes." I searched my pockets too. All I had left was a handkerchief. There could be no doubt that we had been attacked in the storm by a band of mountain robbers such as were said to exist here, living in quite feudal conditions. It was not so long ago that some of them sent a demand for ransom to a lawyer I knew in London, and as a proof that they really held his client they sent the man's right thumb in a box. I looked at Helen. She had such lovely hands.

' "We've got to get away from here, and the sooner the better..."

' "Do you know how to fly?" Paul asked, "or do you intend to use your handkerchief as a parachute?"

' "We must use your flashlamp to explore the interior of the cave. Don't expect me to believe that the bandits brought us up that cliff face in a thunderstorm. They must have come from in here..." and I pointed into the darkness behind us.

' "I've been to look," said Paul, "and the cave ends in a low, crooked passage. We haven't got a rope and every step we take in the darkness may mean death. There are sure to be ups and downs and pits in the floor. I can't shine the lamp all the time, it only lasts two hours at the best."

'Nevertheless we set off to explore the interior of the cave. We held hands like children playing a game, and went very slowly and carefully. From time to time we hit our heads on overhanging rocks, but after we had been going about half an hour we found the passage getting wider, and soon we were able to stand upright and look round. There was light coming from somewhere high up and making the sort of twilight you get in Gothic cathedrals. Paul switched the flashlamp off and we gazed round. He was the first to see them.'

'The abominable snow ...' I asked stupidly.

'The paintings,' he replied sternly, because he did not like to be interrupted.

'There were paintings on the wall of that cave that made the Altamira paintings look like child's play, although in some ways they were very similar. For a while we forgot that we were trying to save our lives and that we would probably have to try and climb up the way the light was coming in, up that narrow chimney over our heads. We forgot everything in our excitement as we examined the paintings on the cave wall as if it was a museum we were in. Most of them were of animals. The prehistoric bison the naturalists call *Bison priscus*, that looks more like the Lithuanian aurochs than the American bison, the hairy rhinoceros, reindeer, a horse that looked something like the Przewalski horse, some small deer or chamois, strange birds and small game. The paintings were wonderful. If only we could get out of here alive, they would make our reputation for us. How on earth were we going to get out, though? I tried to clamber up the chimney, but each time I fell back on top of my companions. To make matters worse, we began to suffer the pangs of hunger. We managed to keep our thirst down by licking the moisture off the walls, but there was nothing we could eat. In a few days we should be so weak and starved that we would slowly die. Perhaps it would be better after all to try the cliff face; at least that death would be quicker and more merciful. We sat down in that prehistoric cathedral and took counsel.

' "I suggest ..." said Helen, and forgot to close her mouth. She was looking over my shoulder in amazement, in the direction from which we had come. I had experienced something similar once before, when I was leopard-hunting in the territory of the Drobo tribe. My boy looked round with the same horror. I doubt whether any man can be as treacherous as a leopard. The only hope is to do the unexpected. If the bandit behind me expected me to get up, and was holding his sabre at the ready, then what I had to do was to fall to the ground, turn round to face him, and throw my coat over his weapon – having taken it off for that purpose as I dropped. I did not put my plan into action, however, for another figure appeared, behind my wife. They were not bandits, nor did they look like natives, because they were practically naked and were much bigger. It was two men, one older and one younger, with long hair on their backs, chest and legs, and with somewhat longer arms than we have. One of them was carrying some scraggy dead animal, and the other had a couple of spears resting on his shoulder. They looked like monkeys with intelligent human eyes. They uttered some sounds. We wanted to protest and explain, but the first figure pushed me along in front of him. He was tremendously strong, and lifted me to shoulder height like a feather. I recognized the paw. That was how we had been brought here, then. How had they climbed that cliff face with bare feet, and no ropes, and us in their arms? We could not bother about that now, running along in front of them like dogs, or like prisoners taken in battle.

'The passage went further into the rock, and after a while we came to a smaller cave where there was a fire-place. A well-built young woman emerged from the darkness and began to light a fire. Although they had taken matches from our pockets, she was trying to strike a spark from a stone. They paid no attention to us. Were they going to roast us alive? The beast they had killed seemed very lean. When the fire got started an even older man appeared, covered in grey hair; he was carrying a joint of frozen meat. It was then that I realized what a blessing the Ice Age was, really; it was true that they had to run about barefoot in the frost and snow, but on the other hand they could keep their food fresh in the snow for as long as they liked. In fact, that appeared to me to be the explanation of why they had climbed right up here to the eternal snows, for hunting, which provided their sustenance, is – *experto crede!* – an irregular and dangerous business. In the African jungle with its wealth of prey there are even families which own rifles and cannot secure their whole year's food that way. Here the success of the hunt is certainly even less sure.

'They threw us a piece of raw meat rubbed in ash, which seemed to serve them in place of salt. I was starving, and the meat had been kept until it was tender. No roast beef ever had a better flavour! So they were not going to eat us, but to feed us. Apart from that they did not bother about us overmuch. They must have been used to armed hunters, but why did they not use the weapons they had secured from us? I wanted to suggest it to them, I was an experienced hunter and I would have liked to talk it over with them. I wondered how they used their spears. After all, they could not go close enough to use them on larger animals. It was a very dangerous way of doing it. I remembered the Eskimo tribe that did not believe there was such a thing as natural death; they had not yet acquired the use of bows and arrows, and most of the tribe fell victim to infuriated animals. The only death they knew was a hunter's death, and for that they had seventeen different words in their language. Did that explain why all the inhabitants of the village were strong and healthy? I remembered the cliff face and the sudden storm. How did the old man get along, then? He was not even able to eat unaided. I watched the woman chewing mouthfuls of food and spitting them carefully into the old man's mouth; why did they go to such lengths to preserve an individual who was so helpless?

' "Polyandry," said Prince Paul by my side with shining eyes, "this is a far better example than that village. Look at the way the female looks after the old one, and neither of the hunters would dream of feeling jealous. This must be the purest form of polyandrous living in the world."

'I doubted whether his Portuguese wife would be willing to chew his food up for him, but that was not the point at the moment.

' "Listen!" said Helen in a strangely soft voice.

' "What to? Nobody's saying anything."

' "I can hear them," she replied. "They're singing a funny sort of song, and they're arguing about something." She looked as though she was listening to something.

' "You'd better try and talk to them then," I suggested. "I can't hear a sound." She went and sat near the fire and the younger of the two hunters broke open a bone; he gave her the marrow to suck. In hunting societies that is a mark of favour. Then she went off with them into the big cave, and they all began to dance. The old man thumped the hollow rock wall with rhythmic blows of his hand. From time to time the hunters pointed to one or other of the animals and uttered cries that represented the creatures. After a little while they started hurling their spears against the cliff wall, hitting the painted animals in their weakest spots. That was when I realized what these paintings were for in the lives of our ancestors. It was a sort of training for the hunt. These men were daily learning how to kill mammoths, although they would never meet one now. I could not help smiling. The primitive creatures! I glanced at Paul; the good fellow was swaying to the rhythm of the old man's drumming, as though he were having convulsions.

' "Paul!" I said loudly, "Your Royal Highness!" And then a woman's voice added to the general confusion. I recognized it at once; Helen had joined in the dance. I could not understand her behaviour; in that African village she had never even thought of such a thing. Of course it was out of the question to knock them all down. I returned to the smaller cave with all the dignity at my command, and fell asleep on the rocky floor, with my jacket over my face.

'Paul woke me next morning. He looked unhappy.

' "I've been talking to my wife," he said.

' "What did you say?"

' "Just imagine – she has renounced polyandry. Now she is living with an old toreador in Madrid and even cooks his meals for him. She no longer wants to live with more than one man at a time. She has become monyandrous. I would never have thought it of her. Now I shall have to stay in the Himalayas until I die. With my ridiculous research programme and all ..."

' "I did not know there was a telephone in this cave. I'd like to speak to my agent in London. I'm worried about my factories in Manchester ..."

' "There is no telephone."

' "Wake up, man! You couldn't have spoken to your wife whether she's in Madrid, Oporto or Nice. You've just been dreaming ..."

' "I really did talk to her." Paul looked surprised, as though he had never had cause to doubt his dreams before. He was really very childish in some ways. Whenever he got excited or wanted to convince you of something urgently, he always squeaked in such a high voice too.

' "Where is Helen?" We went to look for her, but the hunters had disappeared and so had Helen. There was nobody but the old man in the big cave, painting the picture of a small animal on the wall of the cave. It was the animal they had brought in for his supper the evening before. I observed that he used only three colours, Venetian red, black, and yellow ochre. What were his brushes made of, I wondered? He did not bother to look at us, we might just as well not have been there. I felt like pushing into him on purpose. Who knows, though, what strength he might still possess, even in old age? We hurried towards the main entrance to the cave and I scrambled up on the boulders. There was a three-quarter-length quilted lady's coat lying there.

' "What have the beasts done with her?"

'I leaned over the precipice. Surely she had not dared to go down that sheer rock face? She suffered from dizziness and hated mountain climbing. I thought I could see a smashed skull lying at the foot of the cliff.

' "She went out to hunt with the others," I heard a voice behind me. I turned round.

' "Did you see her go?" I asked Paul.

' "No."

' "Then how do you know she went hunting with them?"

' "I don't. And I never said she went, either. I didn't hear anybody saying anything."

'The old man was still standing there at the back of the cave, bent over his painting.

' "I'm beginning to understand. They communicate without words, like animals and insects."

' "You don't understand anything at all yet," I heard the voice again.'

'My comparison was unjust. They were neither animals nor insects. They were people. But they were people who had taken a different path from *homo sapiens*. They were not reasonable in our sense of the word, they did not use their reason for logical analysis, for deduction or abstract calculation. They were *homines sensuosi*; they had developed their senses further than any of the other animals – their sight, smell, hearing and touch. They perceived better and more accurately than we did. That was why they could paint such wonderful likenesses, that was why they could communicate over great distances by a sort of telepathy which I believe is a peculiarity of human perception; it enabled them to foretell the weather at any moment, to evade even my accurate big game gun, and meant that they could catch their pursuers whenever they liked. These were essential characteristics for life in their conditions. They did not build homes or tame animals; they had only the most primitive instruments. They did not live outside the bounds of nature, they did not try to adapt nature even to the primitive degree the local natives did, but lived in nature as a part of it, as the highest form of carnivorous animals. How I regretted that I could not watch them hunt! I was sure that even if someone brought leopards all the way up here they would be able to kill them off as they had the great bears whose bones we found by the fire in the cave.

'In a few days a strange apathy took hold of me. Paul called it happiness. I felt as though all my problems had been solved and that I had become a permanent member of the tribe I intended to help, although I did not know how; I was delighted when Helen brought home her first prey, and I thought it was silly to bother my head about my English factories, my wealth and estates, my friends and relations. I literally had a bird's eye view of life, partly because the snow people's eyrie was so high up, and partly because I felt strangely content and happy; it was like the opium dreams I used to enjoy in Hongkong before the war. Paul had the same feeling. We were happy just to sit still all day dreaming or watching the old man at work, looking at his paintings or at those his forefathers had adorned the cave with in the age of mammoths.

'I was the only one to realize how dangerous this state was. Long ago I had left the opium den although the Chinese girl who served us there was the most delightful creature on earth and was not yet thirteen. I left resolutely, and I smashed her pipe. I knew that I must do the same now; the apathy that Paul blessed with the name of happiness might be nothing but the result of living in that high mountain retreat, where the air was rarified and acted like a drug. I did not believe drugs could make a man happy. I believed in the brain and human reason. My family set up manufactories near Manchester before the age of steam arrived. We were the first to introduce machinery into the region. I had always been against religion and supported science, for science held the key to the prosperity of our family, of England, and of the whole world. I believed in reason, which in the long run would transform nature; and in man, who would master his environment and come up to his age-old fantasy of an all-powerful god. He would become that god. If anybody doubted me they had only to visit Manchester or the Ruhr, Silesia or the Don Basin. Once they saw the miracles of modern technique they would no longer doubt the future open to man. My factories were going to be modernized, I was going to introduce new methods and machines. I could not stay there in the Himalayas happily lying on my back while everybody else was working.

'Helen refused to return with me. Naturally, I assumed she had fallen in love with the younger hunter, but she explained that it was nothing like love. It was contentment and peace, she said, that she got out of this kind of life. It was much more restful than hunting hippoes in Africa. She had always been a creature of feeling and sensibility, given to sudden enthusiasms; she had even painted in water-colours at home, in secret; it was an accident that I found out. She even seemed to believe in some sort of supernatural being, in some sort of deist religion of her own creation, suitably adapted to her technical education. She always felt she was one of the creations of nature and that she had to observe the laws of nature.

' "Our civilization is doomed to die," she said that day, the blood of her prey still clinging to her hands. "People are succumbing to mass hysteria, they believe political claptrap, they are inconstant and capricious and cannot endure to be cut off from nature. The whole of our species has developed along bad lines. We have overdeveloped brains and underdeveloped senses; that is why we are unhappy, sick, and desperate. We cannot live life to the full. Yet we want to live the way these people do."

' "These disgusting creatures?" I was angry. "You've less common sense than the worst of the natives."

' "I don't want to have anything to do with common sense. It's never done me any good. I married you out of common sense, because I wanted to get on in the social world. I didn't love you. I know what went wrong with your first marriage. I married you out of common sense. That's what we civilized people are like, we let our common sense violate even our sex . . ."

'I could find no answer. I was brought up in Victorian ideas and I find it impossible to discuss sex as though it were toothache. Not to mention the fact that she had insulted me profoundly.

'So it was the hunter, after all. She had fallen in love with a monkey. Wooing a wild beast.

'How could that possibly happen? How could a woman who had been educated at the university, who had always behaved sensibly and whose intelligence I had always admired, do a thing like that?

Was I to believe that we were not men of reason, then? Was I to believe that those creatures round us were the only truly reasonable beings, while we down there in the valleys were monsters with overdeveloped skulls? Was it possible?

' "We've got to get away," I said to Paul, who listened to the whole conversation with a miserable expression on his face. "We've got to get away from here, and don't start persuading me to study polyandry with you. I'd rather make a study of crimes of passion. There is probably more material on the subject in our human history. What do you call jealousy, though? Is it reasonable to feel anything of the sort? Is it a useful feeling? Is it not rather a ridiculous and useless habit? I am going back to England," I concluded, "I have important business to attend to in Manchester."

' "What about Helen?"

' "My wife is dead. She has chosen the diluvial existence."

' "Wait till tomorrow," said the voice of the old man, but Paul could not hear him. That made me even angrier. There was a strong wind blowing outside, though, and so we waited till morning. I believe that sometimes, just because they are reasonable beings, reasonable people can make use of non-reasonable advice.

'The advice was no good to Paul, any more than was the primitive rope the old man gave us to start on our way. Thirty feet above the ground Prince Paul of L. slipped and fell head first on an enormous boulder, and was swept away by the torrential mountain stream swirling round it. I had never in my life done a more fatiguing descent, not even after we had climbed Gross Glockner. The death of my friend saddened me greatly. The moment I reached the foot of the cliff I fell on my knees and wept like a child; my legs were trembling right up to the thigh from the dreadful effort, and my hands were torn and bleeding.

'Perhaps it was all for the best that the Prince died; he would never have got over his wife's treachery. How was I going to get over my disillusionment? I dried my eyes and made my way down the valley. Not until the second day did I find a hovel inhabited by real human beings. One of our bearers opened the door to me and shrieked in astonishment; he thought he was looking at my ghost.

'Everyone in London naturally thought Helen had died on a shooting trip. Their condolences were touched with respect. In the circles in which I move death out hunting is something to be viewed with respect. In that respect, at least, we resemble the abominable snow-people. I bribed all the publishers and travellers and instructed my lawyer to censor any mention of the yeti. I did not want attention drawn to them. I bribed everybody who wanted to write about them and hired two glib journalists to ridicule a young Norwegian who had referred to the snow people in the *International Geographic Magazine*. The whole world was laughing at the fellow, and several of the most famous naturalists were prepared to swear that the figures he had seen in the distance were two bears, although only he had been present at the moment referred to. Later on I met the young man at dinner at Lady Astor's, and by then he was convinced himself that they were bears he had seen.

'I wanted to keep the abominable people to myself. It was a battle between my family and their tribe, a bitter fight like those between Scottish highland clans. I invested a good deal of my wealth in research into wireless communication and by the end of a year I was in possession of a gadget the size of a despatch case, by means of which I could communicate with the owner of another such gadget at a distance of five kilometres. It was an expensive toy and it had batteries that needed charging, but at least you were not required to dance round a fire or concentrate your thoughts on your dear ones. It was a telepathy gadget, a telepathy machine; a way of communicating over long distances with the help of the intellect. I realize it will seem ridiculous, that although I was able to achieve more than the abominable rabble in trifles like that, yet I was hardly likely to be able to prove during my lifetime that reason and intellect were victorious, that the great ideas of Newton and Darwin had freed mankind, and that we had mastered nature. It would be good enough for Helen, though. I would take with me photographs of the new machinery I had installed in my factories, real miracles of human ingenuity; she would appreciate that. I would prove to her . . . yes, my friend. You will surely have guessed by now that there was nothing else in my thoughts but to return. That I wanted to prove reason victorious, because I thought I could win Helen back that way; she would be fed up with her hunter, like a dog. I was preparing to make another expedition to the Himalayas. At first, of course, I had tried to forget. Friends came to keep me company, I lost money at the gambling tables, I paid huge sums to mediums of all kinds so as to be able to watch their occult practices; I was a constant visitor to brothels and I broke the hearts of the wives of my employees. Yet all the time I was making love to others I was thinking of her; in the midst of the wild shrieks of the mediums I was hoping to hear her voice; and with my friends I spoke of nothing but her. They could all see how I was suffering, and my relatives stopped being catty about her; nobody accused me of having made a *mésalliance*, now. That year I lost ten pounds in weight. In May I was already telegraphing to Katamanda, to say I was on my way. All through the winter my agent had been making preparations for a grand expedition the like of which had never been financed before. Officially we were supposed to be attempting to climb Nangu Barbat, but in fact my team included the best big game hunters I knew, men who were accustomed to catching their prey alive. In my frustrated dreams I imagined how, if my wife refused to return to me of her own accord, I would carry her off to London as a female yeti and put her in a cage in the Zoo, with her young hunter; they would be on show, a pair of snow-monkeys, and every day reformatories for fallen girls would send their charges to look at them.

'When the expedition reached the place where we had last camped, however, there was not a soul in the mountain village. We were told the people had moved lower down the valley because the yeti had started molesting them; they no longer avoided the villagers. They carried some of them off; when they did not come back from the mountains, the rest fled in panic down to the valley. That was the first thing that delayed us. We had to go back to find bearers. Then the weather deteriorated. Snowstorms and blizzards blew up, the like of which the local people had never seen. There was heavy frost and in many places avalanches broke loose. It was with the greatest difficulty that we moved forward. When the blizzards calmed down the pass where we had first come upon the tracks of the snowmen was completely snowed up. It had disappeared, and nobody could find the way through the cliffs. It looked as though we should have to make a detour right round the shoulder of the mountain, which would take us another two months.

'I was determined not to give in. I ordered a single-engined plane from Delhi – we should not be delayed a single day. I would air-lift the whole expedition, and at the same time I would get a bird's eye view of the whole kingdom of my victims. It was a terrific expense, but I was a rich man in those days. I was so intent on collecting information about the yeti, I was so passionately taken up with my expedition, that those around me began to doubt my sanity.

'One day a Buddhist monk appeared in our camp and invited me to the nearby monastery to rest, and to talk to their wisest holy man. I was not interested in the monastery when the monk declared the yeti did not exist and that it was nothing but the invention of the villagers' fevered imaginations. He said he had been wandering round this countryside alone for years, and never seen anything of the kind. I turned him out. Either he was blind, or he was a liar. Nothing would turn me from my purpose, or at least, that was what I thought then.

'The aeroplane did not arrive. Instead I received an urgent telegram from Delhi to say that my cheques were not being honoured. The London banks had refused to pay anything over my signature. I hurried to Katamanda. As if on purpose, the weather that day was wonderful; but I had other things to worry about. I did not understand the change of weather at home. On the Stock Exchange. I expect you remember the catastrophe. Men were shooting themselves and jumping out of windows, and yesterday's millionaires were selling oranges in the streets. All at once I found that my faith in reason had been betrayed; my factories were no more mine than Trafalgar Square. All my life I had believed in something that was nonsense. Man is too far from perfect, and his pretence at reason is only a game. Human beings are dangerously capricious apes whom only their own shameless arrogance has tried to make out the lords of creation. The yeti now appeared to me far more sensible than man. Even more furious blizzards and catastrophes were shaking our civilization than those I had experienced in the Himalayas. How proud I had been! How I had been ready to bring Helen home in chains, what a triumph my wireless receiver had seemed to me then! I felt like a small boy boasting about the car he has got, and then finding out that it is only a pedal push-car. I had been cheated. I was poor.

'All I had left was the ancient family seat and a little land. My lawyer gassed himself and his family. Shortly before the crash came he had invested all my money – without my knowledge – in worthless shares. I had to give pieces of furniture to the servants in lieu of wages, as long as I could find no buyer for the land. On the first of the month they got Louis xv chairs or an old gown. They were faithful servants, and not one of them left me. I remembered them all in my will. I decided to end my life in the oldest wing of the house, beneath the portrait of my grandfather, a hero of the Boer

War, who shot himself on that very spot because he had neglected to present arms to the queen at a military parade. It was the dead of night and I had just finished cleaning the pistol that had saved my life in Africa on two occasions. Now it would save my honour. I could not live a beggar; the Esdales had always been rich. I was slowly loading the gun; the bullets were new, well oiled; I hoped they would not make too much of a mess of my appearance. The barrel of the pistol was pleasantly cool. It was like Paul, I suddenly thought; perhaps he had not slipped by accident that day when we were climbing down the cliff – perhaps he had deliberately flung himself head first, because he could not bear to live without his wife. His dream had been true, you see; his wife really had fallen in love with that toreador from Madrid. I would meet Paul now.

' "Santillane del Mar," I heard a voice say by my side. It was late at night and that wing of the house was quite deserted. The roof leaked and the windows fitted badly, and none of the servants ever dared to go into the room where my grandfather had died by his own hand. "Santillane del Mar," I heard it say again, right close to my ear, as if the voice were coming out of the barrel of the pistol. It was a woman's voice, a beloved voice; Helen's voice. "Santillane del Mar," she said for the last time, and I had the feeling she was going away. So she had thought of me after all. Perhaps she was following my fate, up there in her mountain eyrie, although she had neither a wireless set nor a television screen. I, fool that I was, had wanted to chase her and revenge myself, and all the time she really loved me, maybe. Maybe it was she who had chosen the right way to live in our world of hypocrisy and half-sense. I dashed into the library, which was in the opposite wing of the house. An elderly lady's maid met me and screamed, because she thought I was chasing a thief. I had to tuck the pistol out of sight.

'Santillane is in Spain, in the province of Santander. First thing in the morning I rang my cousin in the Foreign Office.

' "Santillane del Mar? Yes, of course; it's not far from the famous Altamira caves. You can't go there now, though."

' "Why not?"

' "Don't you read the papers? General Liro, or some such name, has started a civil war there." My cousin had no head for foreign names, and even got the different currencies mixed up.

'I borrowed money for the journey and left that very day. Helen must know why she was sending me there. They took me through the caves; I was the only tourist in the place. M. l'Abbé Neuil and Professor Untermaler, who had given the world the results of their researches in the local caves, and a great deal of information about prehistoric man, were just leaving. They warned me anxiously about the strong anarchist movement in Santander; the fascists would have a difficult job there, there would certainly be bloodshed, and I ought not to stay. I was not interested in the Civil War, though. I let the local guides take me through the Altamira cave; they were glad to have any customer in that dead season, and showed me things they did not bother about at other times. There were paintings in low passages that could only be entered on all fours.

' "M. l'Abbé Neuil believes that prehistoric man thought the bison was a gift from the gods, that it was born in the heart of the rocks. The paintings in these low passages, deep in the cliff, were meant to call the bison forth."

' "That's nonsense," I replied. "What a pity the Abbé has gone. I would have explained to him that prehistoric man needed a lot of practice before he could kill a bison at close quarters, with those short spears of his. In these low passages they prepared themselves to face the moment when they had to let the bison get within a few feet of them before they could tear at his underbelly with their flint spears. Look at this," and I pointed to a long cut drawn across the beast's belly. In these caves the prehistoric artists had used a pale mauve colour I had never seen in the Himalayas.

' "You're right!" my guide was amazed. That made my reputation as a scholar who had solved the mystery of why the paintings were so scratched. Nobody was in the least surprised after that to see me wandering about looking for other caves and looking for entrances to underground passages. If Helen had told me to come here she must have had some reason. She certainly would not have suggested our meeting in the Altamira cave; we might just as well have met in Trafalgar Square. She did not say Altamira, either; she said Santillane del Mar. I spent a week searching the neighbourhood but it was not until the next week that I found the cave I was looking for. It was in a quarry not far away, and some children led me to it. They used to go there to play. I had to exercise great care climbing down the cliff. This eyrie, too, was higher than the country round, even if only by a few feet. The children did not dare to go further than the stones at the entrance, which had never been disturbed.

I soon saw that the cave was really only a kind of entrance hall like the one that led into the labyrinth in the Himalayas. I had to move forward cautiously, although I was equipped for mountaineering and had a powerful light with me. I was alone, you see. A broken leg here underground would mean certain death, for nobody knew where I had gone, not even the children. I had set out late in the evening, not wanting to attract more attention than was necessary. The whole business might be a miserable fiasco; perhaps I had heard Helen's voice, there beneath that portrait, simply because when death is near we always hear the voices of those we love best.

'At last I was rewarded. I had had to wade across an underground stream, crawl on my belly and avoid sleeping bats, but at last I stood in a shadowy underground place, vaulted like a Gothic cathedral. The paintings on the wall were more beautiful and more perfectly executed even than those in Altamira. There was not a sign of Helen, though, nor of any news of her. I wanted to have something to eat.

' "It's taken you long enough to get here," I heard a woman's voice whisper.

'Here too there was a second, smaller cave. There I found a shrivelled, weak old man, nothing but skin and bone, with bald patches on his thick skin. He was barely breathing. I wanted to give him some food.

' "I've just had a haunch of reindeer, I'm not hungry," I heard a voice say. I looked round. On the walls I saw paintings of rabbits, wild ducks, partridges, and even cats, dogs and rats. Had these local yeti sunk so low as to eat rats, I wondered.

' "You can have whatever you wish; all you need to do is to wish for it truly . . ." I heard the voice again. I looked at the living corpse that still grasped a paintbrush between its fingers. The bowls of paint stood near. Was he really happy? How had his tribe held on here for thousands and thousands of years, unnoticed, while our life went on nearby? It must have been a very obstinate tribe indeed, that had not followed the retreating ice-fields. Perhaps they were priests dedicated to the protection of this temple; who could tell? It is a fact that no priest is ever found in these paintings of theirs.

' "Don't go away . . ." I heard Helen's voice. I was not going to hang round here in a cave, waiting for this creature to die. "Stay here. You must see what happiness is . . ." It made me want to laugh. There was I expecting to meet her alone here, expecting her to come herself or at least to tell me through some medium where she was and how I could get to her. I did not care for spiritualist nonsense and I had no intention of taking part in any. I began packing my stuff. Next morning I intended to bring the local archaeologists in here, we might be in time to save the old man's life. He was an absolutely unique specimen.

'As I went out of the cave, though, I tripped over his clothes. How could a yeti have worn clothes? I never saw them in as much as a rag. And here was a pile of garments dating from the beginning of the century, and even a dilapidated bowler hat. Was this dying creature one of our species, then? Was he a mad fellow who had wandered into these caves on purpose and carried on in the tradition of the prehistoric painters? Why should he have bothered? What reason could he have?

'A week later there was I, holding his brush and trying my hand at drawing on the wall too. I could never explain why; it's a feeling you have to experience for yourself. I stayed in the cave the first night because I was exhausted and felt like going to sleep. I had an extraordinarily vivid dream in which Helen and I were running down a strange valley, among glaciers, drinking the raw blood of wild animals. I dreamed that we were in love with each other, that we were happy, and that it was no dream, but the most real reality.

'Again I fell a prey to that strange apathy, but I did not call it apathy because no memories disturbed me and my faith in the power of reason to achieve great things had been cruelly disillusioned. I did not care what was happening out there in the daylight, I did not bother about cold or hunger, just as I spared no thought for my family, humanity, England or the world. My machinery at home now seemed ridiculous. The only important thing was the degree of perfection to be achieved in the pictures on the wall; that was the only thing worthy of man's time to create. I felt calm. I was happy. And at last I realized why those who fall in with the yeti never come back. Even I no longer wanted to come back.

'A few days later I was roused from my dreams by a strange rhythmical vibration of the earth that could not have been caused by any super-reasonable force. It was the thunder of artillery, and towards evening the sound of small arms came through, too. The front was moving in on our caves. I did not know then, of course, that the fascists had brought up heavy artillery and were preparing to blow Santillane del Mar sky-high. The defenders of the town wanted to use the underground passages to surprise the enemy. All the tourist guides turned out to be anarchists, and they all knew the locality blindfold. One particularly ardent lad thought he could use my cave to bring him to the enemy's rear; he used to play there as a child. And so here, in our underground retreat, we were in the thick of the fighting, because the fascists got news of the anarchists' plan and sent a force ahead to meet them. The main body of men met in the big cave that had so fascinated me with its mauve colours. The shooting lasted for about five hours. There were big losses on both sides because they were shooting at random in the shadowy cave, and as often as not it was falling rock that wounded the men, and not the hand grenades themselves. Many lay buried under falls of rock, including the old man who had not wanted to die yet. An enormous boulder decorated with his own paintings fell on him. I watched the whole battle from a small niche in one of the walls, where I lay on my belly on a ledge thinking of the scene in the Himalayas, long before, and the abominable snow people dancing round the fire to the strange rhythmic sound made by the old man on the wall of the cave, so different from the barking of machine guns, and remembering Helen's cries of joy, so different from the groans of the wounded and the dying that now echoed throughout the caves.

'In the end the fascists were pushed back. They had to retreat, anyway, for the republican forces had found another passage leading right to the rear of their Moroccan units, and had killed them to a man. The attack on Santillane del Mar had been repulsed, and the whole province rejoiced.

'I was carried off with the rest of the wounded to the local military hospital. They thought I was the English poet who was said to be fighting in the anarchist ranks here. My friend the old man was buried with their dead. They were still very polite to me, even when I told them who I was. It is true that they called me Mr Esdale, because after all it was an anarchist hospital, but except for that their behaviour was correct and they were attentive to my needs. I must say that all the stories you hear about the anarchists are highly coloured exaggerations, although of course it is clear that soldiers who do not recognize the authority of their officers must lose any war. They told me they gave themselves orders, and they were in the habit of baring their chests when they went into the attack. I heard later that the whole unit had been wiped out near Barcelona. They were men of courage and I remember them often. Naturally they had no idea that reason and intellect would get them nowhere. I did not understand what their fighting was really all about, nor were the aims of the Spanish Republic at all clear to me. Men of reason show strange ways of trying to achieve their ends. By force of arms. It was not possible, either, to go on searching for prehistoric happiness right in the front line. I was forced to return to London. My cousin had a lot of bother over the whole business, because the means of communication were interrupted and in the end he had to send a special plane for me.

'Fortunately a few days later I was visited by the agent who offered me your very successful creations, under the names of a second Věstonice Venus, the Markvartice bison, and the Mikulov rhinoceros. I saw at a glance that they were frauds, but at the same time I realized that there must be as rich deposits in Moravia as in Spain, and that here there was the possibility of exploring the caves more or less at our leisure and undisturbed, to get at the secret no one has yet found.'

'I'm a married man,' I told him, 'and I want to have children. It's my job to teach other people's children to use their minds. I am a schoolteacher, Mr Esdale, and you could not have found a less suitable audience for your attacks on reason. I'm used to arguing with the village priest here; I believe we are living in a great age, when there will soon be abundance of all things for everybody. Man will fly through the universe, the earth will be used to far better advantage, and people will be happy because they will have confidence in the power of their minds.'

'They will not be happy.'

'They will not be happy the way your prehistoric hunters see it. They will not be drinking raw animal blood.'

'They will not know love.'

'They will know love under a different guise. No, no, Mr Esdale, I am all for this civilization of ours. I like it. I certainly would not like to exchange it for a slow death in any cave, even if Rembrandt himself had painted the walls.'

'Do you mean to say you like society as it is?'

'I was never the owner of any factories and I never gambled on the Stock Exchange. I've always been pretty hard up.'

'That's not going to help you when the guns get here from Santillane del Mar. I've been in Vienna and seen them marching through the streets. Brown shirts and jackboots. They will come here one day, too. Do you want to convince me that these creatures are the product of reason? Yet they are definitely a part of the civilization you like so much. Your friends were more sensible.'

'What friends?'

'The chaps who stayed down in the caves.'

'You mean Tonda and Mirek? They didn't stay down in any caves, my dear lord. Both of them were football fans, they played for the Mikulov team, and I've never seen either of them draw a line in their lives. They'd be more convincing than I am in explaining what's wrong with our civilization. They learned a lot, working in my father-in-law's factory. It's reason and common sense that's lacking in our civilization, we've got too little of it, not too much. The crisis and fascism and all the rest of the mess have come on us because people act the way you do. They give up reason, they want to get out while the train's in motion. That's suicide. Tonda and Mirek would explain it better than I can. They went into those caves because they were starving, not for fun. Because they hoped they'd find something that somebody would buy!'

'I shall meet them soon.'

'You are drunk, Mr Lord.' He was insulted; he got up and opened the door.

'You are ill bred, young man.' He swayed in the doorway and I thought he was going to fall.

'I beg your pardon. Perhaps drunk is not the right word, but you ought to order a strong coffee.' He turned me out. Nobody would have made him coffee at that hour, anyway. It was nearly three and everybody was asleep in the inn. I heard the first cocks crow as I went home.

What was it that attracted him most, I wondered, the apathy or the idea of happiness? What did he mean by either of them? It was really strange, the way all kinds of people longed to get back to nature. There had been some spiritualists when I was teaching in Železný Brod; the nonsense they talked sounded like pure reason after what I'd been listening to that night. It was almost easier to believe their tales than his. Telepathy and all that nonsense would certainly be explained some day, like electricity. If there was anything of the sort, of course. But what had that got to do with art? The kids I taught in school could tell me what a poem we'd been doing was about, or describe a picture they'd seen at an exhibition, without needing to spend day after day in an underground cave, shut up in grim meditation ...

The whole village was plunged in darkness, except for the light shining in our place. Žabka was sitting at the table with my wife, papers everywhere. They had been calculating all night. What should we buy, to make best use of the money?

'How much?' they both said at once before I was half in through the door.

'What's he offering?'

'Nothing.' I sat down heavily and took a long drink of cold black coffee straight from the pot. 'Nothing at all. He knew they were forgeries.'

'How did he guess?' my father-in-law was astounded.

'What did he come here for, then?' my wife asked. She is cleverer than her father. 'He could have written if that was all. What's he after?'

I didn't want to tell them, because I know what that family's like, but they wouldn't leave me alone. In the end they might even have thought I'd done a bit of business on the sly.

'He wants to organize an expedition into the caves here.'

'Alone?' they gasped, knowing how dangerous it was.

'Not at all, my nearest and dearest. He wanted to organize the expedition in my company. When I say "wanted" to, I say so deliberately in the past tense, because I refused to have anything at all to do with the suggestion. Now either I get a cup of hot, freshly made coffee, or we're going to bed. My head's swimming, what with one thing and another.'

'Didn't he offer to pay you in pounds sterling?' asked my father-in-law.

'I have no intention of selling my life for sterling, father. Neither did I bargain over it.'

'You coward!' he leaped to his feet as though he'd been stung. 'How often have I risked my life for the family. Just you ask her ...'

'I know all about that. You made chocolate out of chaff. At the worst you might have got hard labour. Alas, it is no longer a hanging offence in this country. But you're sending *me* into the bowels of the earth. Have you ever seen the Macocha precipice? There can be just as steep a drop in our caves here. Even deeper, maybe. When I feel like that particular way of committing suicide I shall leap down Macocha, because at least I'll be able to see what I'm doing ...'

Žabka began to get excited. He showed me how he'd worked it all out; he could expand production, he'd make me his manager, I'd be able to design all his advertising posters since I was such an artist. He'd thought of making chocolate figures of the Věstonice Venus, that was bound to be a hit. He got all worked up trying to talk me round; he even promised to find another guide for his lordship himself, but I shook my head.

'I don't want to have any death on my conscience. Let his lordship burn his fingers all by himself – I'm fed up with your swindling.'

'My swindling?' he shouted, and the insult brought the blood to his face.

'Was it me that carved an idiotic rhinoceros when the smallest child can tell you there's never been a rhinoceros seen near the place? If it had been my work nobody would ever have found it out, because I'm used to working thoroughly and honestly. That applies to swindling too, but you're a bungler. You'll bungle your whole life. If she's got any sense my girl'll see the last of you tomorrow.'

He dashed out as though there were something at stake. He even forgot to shut the door behind him.

I adore my wife and I admire her legs above all. Her figure is perfect and most exciting. The trouble is she will never take her clothes off in front of me. I don't know why, but she's dreadfully puritanical.

She was lying naked on the bed when I went into the room. She welcomed me with the kisses that rouse me most quickly. I was still a bit drunk, and I had never seen her look so lovely. Never had I loved her so much ...

Then, as she put on her long nightgown and let her hair down, she picked up the alarm clock and said firmly:

'What time shall I set it for? What time do you leave?'

I thought I'd burst into tears there and then. Outside day was breaking and the birds were singing in the garden. They sing fit to burst every day at sunrise. I wondered whether the abominable snow people worshipped the sun, too, if they were so damned natural?

'There's no need to wake me at all.' I got unsteadily to my feet. 'I'm going now.'

She did nothing to hold me back and said nothing to dissuade me. She offered to make me some coffee.

'No,' I said, 'I don't want anything. And I think I'm the only member of your family who doesn't ...'

I remembered Lord Esdale talking about his wife and how she distorted her natural feelings in the name of reason. I had just experienced the same thing. She had behaved like a slut, knowing she would gain more that way than her father with his excited talk. She had acted with more reason than he had.

She was a clever girl. A slut. I ran back to the inn and woke his lordship from his first sleep. I had to kick at the door.

'I'm going with you. Tomorrow,' I said.

'All right,' he agreed. 'I knew you'd come to your senses and see reason – I mean, see beyond reason ...' he corrected himself, and fell asleep on his feet. 'It will be my fourth expedition,' he still managed to get out.

We set out before midday. I considered telling the innkeeper where we were going, but then I remembered that they could never get together a rescue party, far and wide, and that nobody would dare to go far into the caves anyway. All I did was to bargain for my terms; I fixed them pretty high, but his lordship merely laughed. He was ready to pay whatever I asked. He must have put his financial matters on a better footing than when he used to pay his servants with pieces of furniture. He was convinced, of course, that once we found his cave I would not dream of going back.

'I'm not going to argue about that now, but I want my money even if we find nothing.' He promised me everything, and we even put it down on paper in some form or other.

I knew very well why I was insisting on the money. When he told me all about his travels, the evening before, it made me think of a little cave in a cliff not far away, hidden in the woods. I had never been inside because it meant going down a rope to get there. The local keeper told me about it; he said there was a special variety of owl that nested there. In this cave his lordship would feel quite at home. He was better shod for such an undertaking than I was. I could never afford to buy mountain climbing boots, and had never even saved enough for ski boots. I slid down his rope with ordinary Bata shoes on my feet and thought about Prince Paul. Fortunately there were no giant boulders beneath us, only soft clay. How ridiculous it all was! Here was I playing servant to an eccentric; I'd turned into a 'boy', as he called his natives. It was humiliating. What was the point of the whole business? He declared that the snow people had left Spain and got as far as the Himalayas because they needed glaciers to preserve their food caught in the hunt; what did he think the people in our local caves used? Refrigerators, or ice-boxes? Did he want me to believe these were fairytale places that cast a spell on you and nobody ever got away? That everyone who went in turned into a prehistoric man! I had heard there were a lot of degenerate minds among the aristocracy. But his lordship did not look in the least half-witted. And he knew how to climb a rope, too. I could hardly keep pace with him all the way there. He showed no signs of degeneration. Inside the cave we could see as well as in broad daylight, because he brought a strong flashlamp with him, an enormous thing the size of my forearm; and a Davy lamp as well. He had clearly acquired a great deal of experience of this sort of thing. The trouble here was that the passage was very low indeed, and finally we could not get through with our rucksacks on our backs. We had to take them off and push them along in front of us; that meant that we could not see what was beyond them; we had good lighting with us but could not see a thing. We shoved ourselves forward blindly, inch by inch, and I thought the passage would come to a dead end and we should have to go back. Esdale was in his element, and would not hear of return. Indeed, he was sure it was the right cave, he could tell for certain; and he could hear a voice. All I could hear was an underground stream somewhere to the right of us. In the end we should be drowned like rats. There was no trace of any drawings on the walls, and not even the usual bones lying about. I kept trying to discover something of interest; I felt all over the walls and ventured into the little tunnels that led off our passage, but in every case I found after a yard or two that they were blind alleys. Esdale had a remarkable sense of direction. One such venture into a side passage sealed my fate.

I suddenly put my weight on nothingness, lost my balance and hurtled into space. For several seconds I flew through the air, fortunately landing on my feet. Then I found I could not stand. There was a sharp pain in my ankle.

'Help!' I yelled. 'Mr Esdale!' His flashlamp gleamed far above my head. I had not realized I had fallen so far. Everything went black and I lost consciousness.

'You must think about your rescuers, you must really wish for rescue...' I thought I could hear Esdale's voice and that I was meant to imagine the innkeeper with a rope, my headmaster in climbing boots and the whole expedition that was never going to come from Prague. When I came to myself I was alone in the half darkness. Lord Esdale did not seem to have had the slightest qualms about leaving me here. Probably he thought that with a broken leg I was likely to find happiness even sooner than he was. I did not experience apathy, though; I was afraid, afraid of dying in a deserted underground abyss. I concentrated my mind on how to get out of there. I wanted to escape.

I decided that if I were to scratch a way out parallel to the path we had followed inside the cave, I was bound to reach daylight. I tore at the earth with bleeding fingers, reminding myself of a mole. The pain in my ankle and the hunger in my belly drove me on. I did not rely on any wishes; it was by sense and reason alone that I saved my life. After a few hours of that I saw the first glimmer of light and dragged myself out. I crawled on hands and knees to the nearest cottage and from there they took me to hospital. I had my leg put in plaster and they gave me pills to cure my pneumonia. I spent a long time in that hospital. If I had relied on pious hopes and nothing else I should be a dead man today.

They said Lord Esdale had found nothing. Two days later he had turned up in Věstonice and then left for Vienna. Nobody heard any more of him and of course I never got my reward. I was thankful my leg got all right again. And I parted ways with Žabka for good and all. To this very day the broken mammoth tusk (*Elephas primigenius*) adorns my school collections. My wife dares not say a word. There is no stepping aside from the path of reason our civilization has undertaken to follow. The alternative is death in the darkness. Tonda and Mirek were right. I remember them whenever I feel that pain in my ankle. That is pretty often, especially when the weather is about to change.

This explains why I am prepared to swear that Lord Esdale did not die in the Himalayas. He evidently set off to find his wife and joined the community of abominable snowmen, which is where he belonged, anyway. I have my doubts, though, whether he will be happy there.

THE RING OF THOTH

Sir Arthur Conan Doyle

I think Sherlock Holmes is the most complex character I have had to play – having appeared in the film, The Hound of the Baskervilles *in 1959 and made a television series based on the short adventures in 1967. I have always been a great admirer of Conan Doyle's work and possess a collection of material relating to Holmes, including copies of the* Strand *magazine in which the stories were first published. I should certainly relish the opportunity to play the Master again if the occasion arose, particularly because of the kind things which people have said about my interpretation of the part. I may, of course, be too old now! As the Holmes' stories are easily obtainable, I have instead selected another Conan Doyle story about an 'investigator'. There are two reasons for this: firstly, because it is a rattling good yarn, and, secondly, because it is about a mummy, that strange Egyptian creation which was the subject of the third of my breakthrough Hammer pictures,* The Mummy (1959).

Mr John Vansittart Smith, FRS, of 147A Gower Street, was a man whose energy of purpose and clearness of thought might have placed him in the very first rank of scientific observers. He was the victim, however, of a universal ambition which prompted him to aim at distinction in many subjects rather than pre-eminence in one. In his early days he had shown an aptitude for zoology and for botany which caused his friends to look upon him as a second Darwin, but when a professorship was almost within his reach he had suddenly discontinued his studies and turned his whole attention to chemistry. Here his researches upon the spectra of the metals had won him his fellowship in the Royal Society; but again he played the coquette with his subject, and after a year's absence from the laboratory he joined the Oriental Society, and delivered a paper on the 'Hieroglyphic and Demotic inscriptions of El Kab', thus giving a crowning example both of the versatility and of the inconstancy of his talents.

The most fickle of wooers, however, is apt to be caught at last, and so it was with John Vansittart Smith. The more he burrowed his way into Egyptology the more impressed he became by the vast field which it opened to the inquirer, and by the extreme importance of a subject which promised to throw a light upon the first germs of human civilization and the origin of the greater part of our arts and sciences. So struck was Mr Smith that he straightway married an Egyptological young lady who had written upon the sixth dynasty, and having thus secured a sound base of operations he set himself to collect materials for a work which should unite the research of Lepsius and the ingenuity of Champollion. The preparation of this *magnum opus* entailed many hurried visits to the magnificent Egyptian collections of the Louvre, upon the last of which, no longer ago than the middle of last October, he became involved in a most strange and noteworthy adventure.

The trains had been slow and the Channel had been rough, so that the student arrived in Paris in a somewhat befogged and feverish condition. On reaching the Hôtel de France, in the Rue Laffitte, he had thrown himself upon a sofa for a couple of hours, but finding that he was unable to sleep, he determined, in spite of his fatigue, to make his way to the Louvre, settle the point which he had come to decide, and take the evening train back to Dieppe. Having come to this conclusion, he donned his greatcoat, for it was a raw rainy day, and made his way across the Boulevard des Italiens and down the Avenue de l'Opéra. Once in the Louvre he was on familiar ground, and he speedily made his way to the collection of papyri which it was his intention to consult.

The warmest admirers of John Vansittart Smith could hardly claim for him that he was a handsome man. His high-beaked nose and prominent chin had something of the same acute and incisive character which distinguished his intellect. He held his head in a birdlike fashion, and birdlike, too, was the pecking motion with which, in conversation, he threw out his objections and retorts. As he stood, with the high collar of his greatcoat raised to his ears, he might have seen from the reflection in the glass case before him that his appearance was a singular one. Yet it came upon him as a sudden jar when an English voice behind him exclaimed in very audible tones, 'What a queer-looking mortal!'

The student had a large amount of petty vanity in his composition which manifested itself by an ostentatious and overdone disregard of all personal considerations. He straightened his lips and looked rigidly at the roll of papyrus, while his heart filled with bitterness against the whole race of travelling Britons.

'Yes,' said another voice, 'he really is an extraordinary fellow.'

'Do you know,' said the first speaker, 'one could almost believe that by the continual contemplation of mummies the chap has become half a mummy himself?'

'He has certainly an Egyptian cast of countenance,' said the other.

John Vansittart Smith spun round upon his heel with the intention of shaming his countrymen by a corrosive remark or two. To his surprise and relief, the two young fellows who had been conversing had their shoulders turned towards him, and were gazing at one of the Louvre attendants who was polishing some brass-work at the other side of the room.

'Carter will be waiting for us at the Palais Royal,' said one tourist to the other, glancing at his watch, and they clattered away, leaving the student to his labours.

'I wonder what these chatterers call an Egyptian cast of countenance,' thought John Vansittart Smith, and he moved his position slightly in order to catch a glimpse of the man's face. He started as his eyes fell upon it. It was indeed the very face with which his studies had made him familiar. The regular statuesque features, broad brow, well-rounded chin, and dusky complexion were the exact counterpart of the innumerable statues, mummy-cases, and pictures which adorned the walls of the apartment. The thing was beyond all coincidence. The man must be an Egyptian. The national angularity of the shoulders and narrowness of the hips were alone sufficient to identify him.

John Vansittart Smith shuffled towards the attendant with some intention of addressing him. He was not light of touch in conversation, and found it difficult to strike the happy mean between the brusqueness of the superior and the geniality of the equal. As he came nearer, the man presented his side face to him, but kept his gaze still bent upon his work. Vansittart Smith, fixing his eyes upon the fellow's skin, was conscious of a sudden impression that there was something inhuman and preternatural about its appearance. Over the temple and cheek-bone it was as glazed and as shiny as varnished parchment. There was no suggestion of pores. One could not fancy a drop of moisture upon that arid surface. From brow to chin, however, it was cross-hatched by a million delicate wrinkles, which shot and interlaced as though Nature in some Maori mood had tried how wild and intricate a pattern she could devise.

'*Où est la collection de Memphis?*' asked the student, with the awkward air of a man who is devising a question merely for the purpose of opening a conversation.

'*C'est là,*' replied the man brusquely, nodding his head at the other side of the room.

'*Vous êtes un Egyptien, n'est-ce pas?*' asked the Englishman.

The attendant looked up and turned his strange dark eyes upon his questioner. They were vitreous, with a misty dry shininess, such as Smith had never seen in a human head before. As he gazed into them he saw some strong emotion gather in their depths, which rose and deepened until it broke into a look of something akin both to horror and to hatred.

'*Non, monsieur; je suis français.*' The man turned abruptly and bent low over his polishing. The student gazed at him for a moment in astonishment, and then turning to a chair in a retired corner behind one of the doors he proceeded to make notes of his researches among the papyri. His thoughts, however, refused to return into their natural groove. They would run upon the enigmatical attendant with the sphinx-like face and the parchment skin.

'Where have I seen such eyes?' said Vansittart Smith to himself. 'There is something saurian about them, something reptilian. There's the *membrana nictitans* of the snakes,' he mused, bethinking himself of his zoological studies. 'It gives a shiny effect. But there was something more here. There was a sense of power, of wisdom – so I read them – and of weariness, utter weariness, and ineffable despair. It may be all imagination, but I never had so strong an impression. By Jove, I must have another look at them!' He rose and paced round the Egyptian rooms, but the man who had excited his curiosity had disappeared.

The student sat down again in his quiet corner, and continued to work at his notes. He had gained the information which he required from the papyri, and it only remained to write it down while it was still fresh in his memory. For a time his pencil travelled rapidly over the paper, but soon the lines became less level, the words more blurred, and finally the pencil tinkled down upon the floor, and the head of the student dropped heavily forward upon his chest. Tired out by his journey, he slept so soundly in his lonely post behind the door that neither the clanking civil guard, nor the footsteps of sightseers, nor even the loud hoarse bell which gives the signal for closing, were sufficient to arouse him.

Twilight deepened into darkness, the bustle from the Rue de Rivoli waxed and then waned, distant Notre Dame clanged out the hour of midnight, and still the dark and lonely figure sat silently in the shadow. It was not until close upon one in the morning that, with a sudden gasp and an intaking of the breath, Vansittart Smith returned to consciousness. For a moment it flashed upon him that he had dropped asleep in his study-chair at home. The moon was shining fitfully through the unshuttered window, however, and as his eyes ran along the lines of mummies and the endless array of polished cases, he remembered clearly where he was and how he came there. The student was not a nervous man. He possessed that love of a novel situation which is peculiar to his race. Stretching out his cramped limbs, he looked at his watch, and burst into a chuckle as he observed the hour. The episode would make an admirable anecdote to be introduced into his next paper as a relief to the graver and heavier speculations. He was a little cold, but wide awake and much refreshed. It was no wonder that the guardians had overlooked him, for the door threw its heavy black shadow right across him.

The complete silence was impressive. Neither outside nor inside was there a creak or a murmur. He was alone with the dead men of a dead civilization. What though the outer city reeked of the garish nineteenth century! In all this chamber there was scarce an article, from the shrivelled ear of wheat to the pigment-box of the painter, which had not held its own against four thousand years. Here was the flotsam and jetsam washed up by the great ocean of time from that far-off empire. From stately Thebes, from lordly Luxor, from the great temples of Heliopolis, from a hundred rifled tombs, these relics had been brought. The student glanced round at the long-silent figures who flickered vaguely up through the gloom, at the busy toilers who were now so restful, and he fell into a reverent and thoughtful mood. An unwonted sense of his own youth and insignificance came over him. Leaning back in his chair, he gazed dreamily down the long vista of rooms, all silvery with the moonshine, which extend through the whole wing of the widespread building. His eyes fell upon the yellow glare of a distant lamp.

John Vansittart Smith sat up on his chair with his nerves all on edge. The light was advancing slowly towards him, pausing from time to time, and then coming jerkily onwards. The bearer moved noiselessly. In the utter silence there was no suspicion of the pat of a footfall. An idea of robbers entered the Englishman's head. He snuggled up farther into the corner. The light was two rooms off. Now it was in the next chamber, and still there was no sound. With something approaching to a thrill of fear the student observed a face, floating in the air as it were, behind the flare of the lamp. The figure was wrapped in shadow, but the light fell full upon the strange eager face. There was no mistaking the metallic, glistening eyes and the cadaverous skin. It was the attendant with whom he had conversed.

Vansittart Smith's first impulse was to come forward and address him. A few words of explanation would set the matter clear, and lead doubtless to his being conducted to some side-door from which he might make his way to his hotel. As the man entered the chamber, however, there was something so stealthy in his movements, and so furtive in his expression, that the Englishman altered his intention. This was clearly no ordinary official walking the rounds. The fellow wore felt-soled slippers, stepped with a rising chest, and glanced quickly from left to right, while his hurried, gasping breathing thrilled the flame of his lamp. Vansittart Smith crouched silently back into the corner and watched him keenly, convinced that his errand was one of secret and probably sinister import.

There was no hesitation in the other's movements. He stepped lightly and swiftly across to one of the great cases, and, drawing a key from his pocket, he unlocked it. From the upper shelf he pulled down a mummy, which he bore away with him, and laid it with much care and solicitude upon the ground. By it he placed his lamp, and then squatting down beside it in Eastern fashion he began with long, quivering fingers to undo the cerecloths and bandages

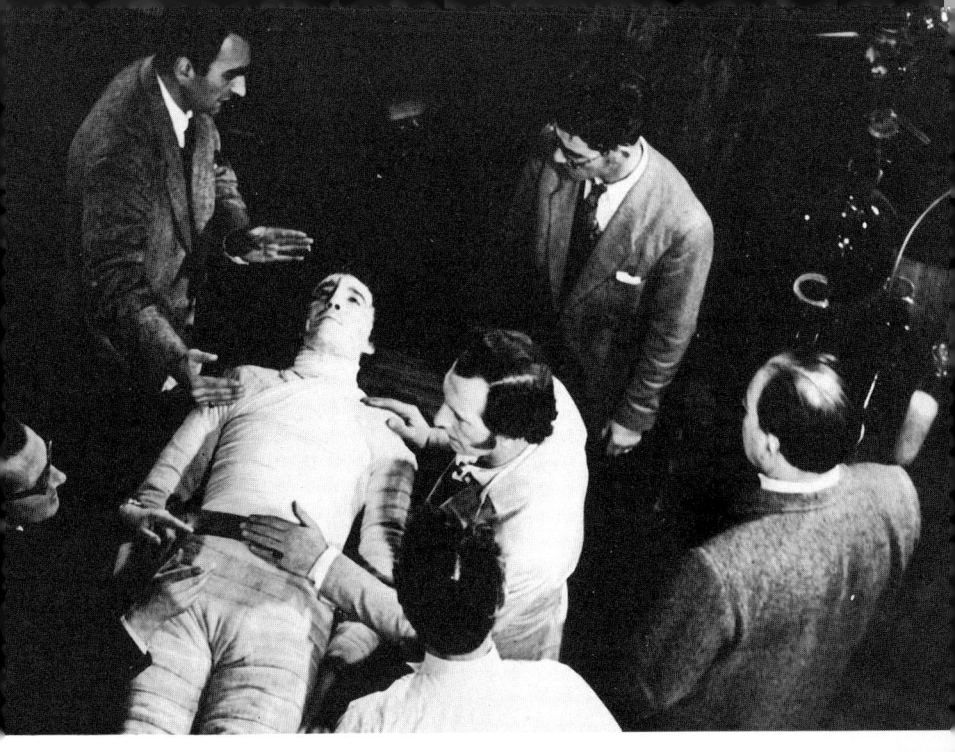

Two rare photographs from my first horror film, *The Curse of Frankenstein* (1957), when I made my début as Baron Victor Frankenstein.
(Above) Rehearsing a scene on the set with director Terence Fisher and my co-star, Christopher Lee.
(Right) Looking rather pensive before giving a meal to my creation!

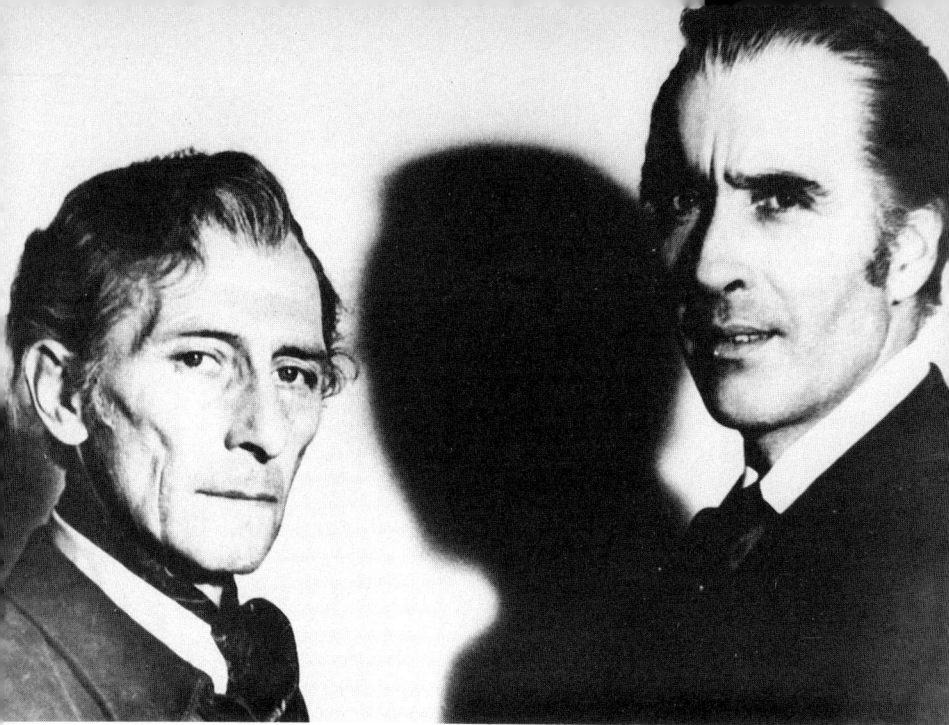

My good friend Christopher Lee whom I often opposed in the Dracula films with him playing the Undead Count to my Dr Van Helsing. In this publicity still for *The Satanic Rites of Dracula* (1973) he is casting a most un-vampiric shadow! *(Below)* Only a crucifix can stop Valerie Gaunt – one of the vampires in Hammer's first film of the Dracula series, *Horror of Dracula* (1958)

Trying to keep cool and look cold on the set of *The Abominable Snowman* (1957) with my co-star Forrest Tucker

Christopher Lee gets a stranglehold on me in *The Mummy* (1959)

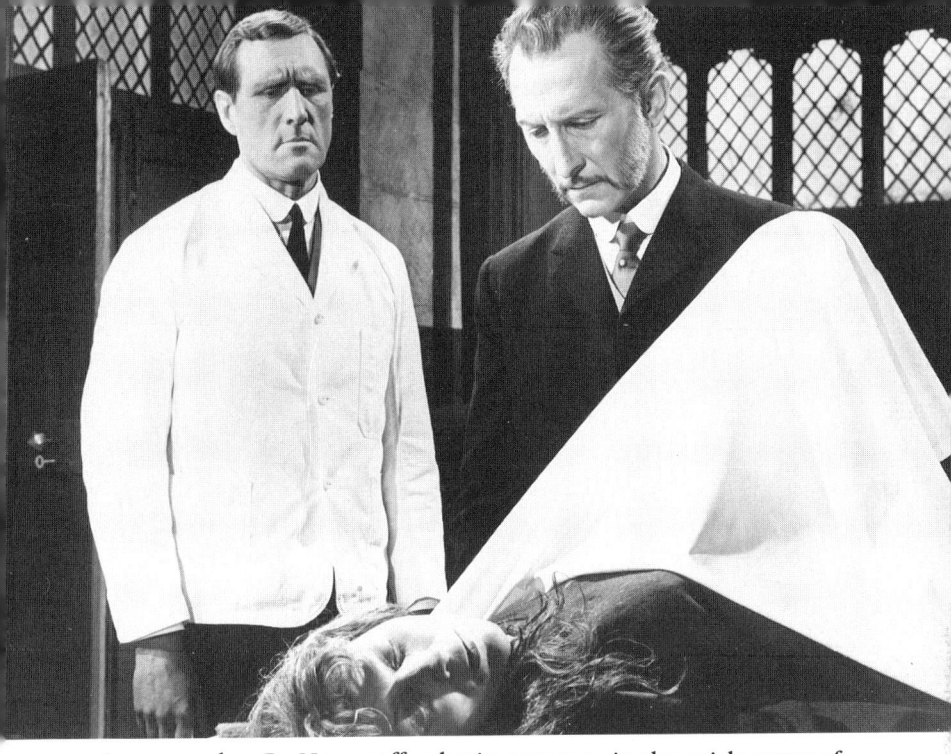

I appeared as Dr Namaroff, a brain surgeon, in the grisly story of *The Gorgon* (1964) *(Below)* A happy scene with Jack Palance in *Torture Garden* (1967) in which I played the obsessive collector of Edgar Allan Poe memorabilia in the story by Robert Bloch

Not all my creations were monsters – here I am with the lovely Susan Denberg in *Frankenstein Created Woman* (1967)

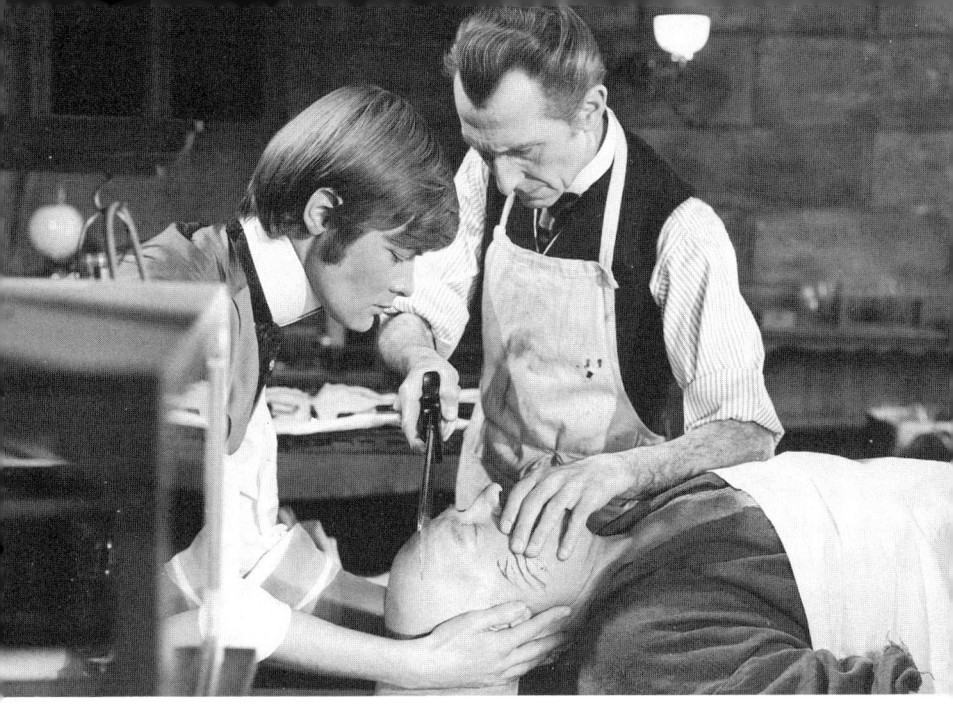

Another of my ghoulish operations in *Frankenstein Must Be Destroyed* (1969) with Simon Ward as my assistant and George Pravda about to have his brain removed!

I was also a bedevilled collector in *The Skull* (1966) based on another story by Robert Bloch, *The Skull of the Marquis de Sade*

I finally became a monster myself in *Tales From The Crypt* (1979) when the luckless Grimsdyke was turned into a walking corpse

which girt it round. As the crackling rolls of linen peeled off one after the other, a strong aromatic odour filled the chamber, and fragments of scented wood and of spices pattered down upon the marble floor.

It was clear to John Vansittart Smith that this mummy had never been unswathed before. The operation interested him keenly. He thrilled all over with curiosity, and his bird-like head protruded farther and farther from behind the door. When, however, the last roll had been removed from the four-thousand-year-old head, it was all that he could do to stifle an outcry of amazement. First, a cascade of long, black, glossy tresses poured over the workman's hands and arms. A second turn of the bandage revealed a low, white forehead, with a pair of delicately arched eyebrows. A third uncovered a pair of bright, deeply-fringed eyes, and a straight, well-cut nose, while a fourth and last showed a sweet, full, sensitive mouth, and a beautifully curved chin. The whole face was one of extraordinary loveliness, save for the one blemish that in the centre of the forehead there was a single, irregular, coffee-coloured splotch. It was a triumph of the embalmer's art. Vansittart Smith's eyes grew larger and larger as he gazed upon it, and he chirruped in his throat with satisfaction.

Its effect upon the Egyptologist was as nothing, however, compared with that which it produced upon the strange attendant. He threw his hands up into the air, burst into a harsh clatter of words, and then, hurling himself down upon the ground beside the mummy, he threw his arms round her, and kissed her repeatedly upon the lips and brow. '*Ma petite!*' he groaned in French, '*Ma pauvre petite!*' His voice broke with emotion, and his innumerable wrinkles quivered and writhed, but the student observed in the lamp-light that his shining eyes were still dry and tearless as two beads of steel. For some minutes he lay, with a twitching face, crooning and moaning over the beautiful head. Then he broke into a sudden smile, said some words in an unknown tongue, and sprang to his feet with the vigorous air of one who has braced himself for an effort.

In the centre of the room there was a large, circular case which contained, as the student had frequently remarked, a magnificent collection of early Egyptian rings and precious stones. To this the attendant strode, and, unlocking it, threw it open. On the ledge at the side he placed his lamp, and beside it a small, earthenware jar which he had drawn from his pocket. He then took a handful of rings from the case, and with a most serious and anxious face he proceeded to smear each in turn with some liquid substance from the earthen pot, holding them to the light as he did so. He was clearly disappointed with the first lot, for he threw them petulantly back into the case and drew out some more. One of these, a massive ring with a large crystal set in it, he seized and eagerly tested with the contents of the jar. Instantly he uttered a cry of joy, and threw out his arms in a wild gesture which upset the pot and set the liquid streaming across the floor to the very feet of the Englishman. The attendant drew a red handkerchief from his bosom, and, mopping up the mess, he followed it into the corner, where in a moment he found himself face to face with his observer.

'Excuse me,' said John Vansittart Smith, with all imaginable politeness; 'I have been unfortunate enough to fall asleep behind this door.'

'And you have been watching me?' the other asked in English, with a most venomous look on his corpse-like face.

The student was a man of veracity. 'I confess,' said he, 'that I have noticed your movements, and that they have aroused my curiosity and interest in the highest degree.'

The man drew a long, flamboyant, bladed knife from his bosom. 'You have had a very narrow escape,' he said; 'had I seen you ten minutes ago, I should have driven this through your heart. As it is, if you touch me or interfere with me in any way you are a dead man.'

'I have no wish to interfere with you,' the student answered. 'My presence here is entirely accidental. All I ask is that you will have the extreme kindness to show me out through some side-door.' He spoke with great suavity, for the man was still pressing the tip of his dagger against the palm of his left hand, as though to assure himself of its sharpness, while his face preserved its malignant expression.

'If I thought . . .' said he. 'But no, perhaps it is as well. What is your name?'

The Englishman gave it.

'Vansittart Smith,' the other repeated. 'Are you the same Vansittart Smith who gave a paper in London upon El Kab? I saw a report of it. Your knowledge of the subject is contemptible.'

'Sir!' cried the Egyptologist.

'Yet it is superior to that of many who make even greater pretensions. The whole keystone of our old life in Egypt was not the inscriptions or monuments of which you make so much, but was our hermetic philosophy and mystic knowledge of which you say little or nothing.'

'Our old life!' repeated the scholar, wide-eyed; and then suddenly, 'Good God, look at the mummy's face!'

The strange man turned and flashed his light upon the dead woman, uttering a long, doleful cry as he did so. The action of the air had already undone all the art of the embalmer. The skin had fallen away, the eyes had sunk inwards, the discoloured lips had writhed away from the yellow teeth, and the brown mark upon the forehead alone showed that it was indeed the same face which had shown such youth and beauty a few short minutes before.

The man flapped his hands together in grief and horror. Then mastering himself by a strong effort he turned his hard eyes once more upon the Englishman.

'It does not matter," he said, in a shaking voice. 'It does not really matter. I came here tonight with the fixed determination to do something. It is now done. All else is as nothing. I have found my quest. The old curse is broken. I can rejoin her. What matter about her inanimate shell so long as her spirit is awaiting me at the other side of the veil!'

'These are wild words,' said Vansittart Smith. He was becoming more and more convinced that he had to do with a madman.

'Time presses, and I must go,' continued the other. 'The moment is at hand for which I have waited this weary time. But I must show you out first. Come with me.'

Taking up the lamp, he turned from the disordered chamber, and led the student swiftly through the long series of the Egyptian, Assyrian, and Persian apartments. At the end of the latter he pushed open a small door let into the wall and descended a winding, stone stair. The Englishman felt the cold, fresh air of the night upon his brow. There was a door opposite him which appeared to communicate with the street. To the right of this another door stood ajar, throwing a spurt of yellow light across the passage. 'Come in here!' said the attendant shortly.

Vansittart Smith hesitated. He had hoped that he had come to the end of his adventure. Yet his curiosity was strong within him. He could not leave the matter unsolved, so he followed his strange companion into the lighted chamber.

It was a small room, such as is devoted to a concierge. A wood fire sparkled in the grate. At one side stood a truckle bed, and at the other a coarse, wooden chair, with a round table in the centre, which bore the remains of a meal. As the visitor's eye glanced round he could not but remark with an ever-recurring thrill that all the small details of the room were of the most quaint design and antique workmanship. The candlesticks, the vases upon the chimney-piece, the fire-irons, the ornaments upon the walls, were all such as he had been wont to associate with the remote past. The gnarled, heavy-eyed man sat himself down upon the edge of the bed, and motioned his guest into the chair.

'There may be design in this,' he said, still speaking excellent English. 'It may be decreed that I should leave some account behind as a warning to all rash mortals who would set their wits up against workings of Nature. I leave it with you. Make such use as you will of it. I speak to you now with my feet upon the threshold of the other world.

'I am, as you surmised, an Egyptian – not one of the down-trodden race of slaves who now inhabit the Delta of the Nile, but a survivor of that fiercer and harder people who tamed the Hebrew, drove the Ethiopian back into the southern deserts, and built those mighty works which have been the envy and the wonder of all after generations. It was in the reign of Tuthmosis, sixteen hundred years before the birth of Christ, that I first saw the light. You shrink away from me. Wait, and you will see that I am more to be pitied than to be feared.

'My name was Sosra. My father had been the chief priest of Osiris in the great temple of Abaris, which stood in those days upon the Bubastic branch of the Nile. I was brought up in the temple and was trained in all those mystic arts which are spoken of in your own Bible. I was an apt pupil. Before I was sixteen I had learned all which the wisest priest could teach me. From that time on I studied nature's secrets for myself, and shared my knowledge with no man.

'Of all the questions which attracted me there were none over which I laboured so long as over those which concern themselves with the nature of life. I probed deeply into the vital principle. The aim of medicine had been to drive away disease when it appeared. It seemed to me that a method might be devised which should so fortify the body as to prevent weakness or death from ever taking hold of it. It is useless that I should recount my researches. You would scarce comprehend them if I did. They were carried out partly upon animals, partly upon slaves, and partly on myself. Suffice it that their result was to furnish me with a substance which, when injected into the blood, would endow the body with strength to resist the effects of time, of violence, or of disease. It would not indeed confer immortality, but its potency would endure for many thousands of years. I used it upon a cat, and afterwards drugged the creature with the most deadly poisons. That cat is alive in Lower Egypt at the present moment. There was nothing of mystery or magic in the matter. It was simply a chemical discovery, which may well be made again.

'Love of life runs high in the young. It seemed to me that I had broken away from all human care now that I had abolished pain and driven death to such a distance. With a light heart I poured the accursed stuff into my veins. Then I looked round for someone whom I could benefit. There was a young priest of Thoth, Parmes by name, who had won my goodwill by his earnest nature and his devotion to his studies. To him I whispered my secret, and at his request I injected him with my elixir. I should now, I reflected, never be without a companion of the same age as myself.

'After this grand discovery I relaxed my studies to some extent, but Parmes continued his with redoubled energy. Every day I could see him working with his flasks and his distiller in the temple of Thoth, but he said little to me as to the result of his labours. For my own part, I used to walk through the city and look around me with exultation as I reflected that all this was destined to pass away, and that only I should remain. The people would bow to me as they passed me, for the fame of my knowledge had gone abroad.

'There was war at this time, and the Great King had sent down his soldiers to the eastern boundary to drive away the Hyksos. A governor, too, was sent to Abaris, that he might hold it for the king. I had heard much of the beauty of the daughter of this governor, but one day as I walked out with Parmes we met her, borne upon the shoulders of her slaves. I was struck with love as with lightning. My heart went out from me. I could have thrown myself beneath the feet of her bearers. This was my woman. Life without her was impossible. I swore by the head of Horus that she should be mine. I swore it to the priest of Thoth. He turned away from me with a brow which was as black as midnight.

'There is no need to tell you of our wooing. She came to love me even as I loved her. I learned that Parmes had seen her before I did, and had shown her that he, too, loved her, but I could smile at his passion, for I knew that her heart was mine. The white plague had come upon the city and many were stricken, but I laid my hands upon the sick and nursed them without fear or scathe. She marvelled at my daring. Then I told her my secret, and begged her that she would let me use my art upon her.

' "Your flower shall then be unwithered, Atma," I said. "Other things may pass away, but you and I, and our great love for each other, shall outlive the tomb of King Chefru."

'But she was full of timid, maidenly objections. "Was it right?" she asked, "was it not a thwarting of the will of the gods? If the great Osiris had wished that our years should be so long, would he not himself have brought it about?"

'With fond and loving words I overcame her doubts, and yet she hesitated. It was a great question, she said. She would think it over for this one night. In the morning I should know of her resolution. Surely one night was not too much to ask. She wished to pray to Isis for help in her decision.

'With a sinking heart and a sad foreboding of evil I left her with her tirewomen. In the morning, when the early sacrifice was over, I hurried to her house. A frightened slave met me upon the steps. Her mistress was ill, she said, very ill. In a frenzy I broke my way through the attendants, and rushed through hall and corridor to my Atma's chamber. She lay upon her couch, her head high upon the pillow, with a pallid face and a glazed eye. On her forehead there blazed a single angry, purple patch. I knew that hell-mark of old. It was the scar of the white plague, the sign-manual of death.

'Why should I speak of that terrible time? For months I was mad, fevered, delirious, and yet I could not die. Never did an Arab thirst after the sweet wells as I longed after death. Could poison or steel have shortened the thread of my existence, I should soon have rejoined my love in the land with the narrow portal. I tried, but it was of no avail. The accursed influence was too strong upon me. One night as I lay upon my couch, weak and weary, Parmes, the priest of Thoth, came to my chamber. He stood in the circle of the lamp-light, and he looked down upon me with eyes which were bright with a mad joy.

' "Why did you let the maiden die?" he asked; "why did you not strengthen her as you strengthened me?"

' "I was too late," I answered. "But I had forgot. You also loved her. You are my fellow in misfortune. Is it not terrible to think of the centuries which must pass ere we look upon her again? Fools, fools, that we were to take death to be our enemy!"

' "You may say that," he cried with a wild laugh; "the words come well from your lips. For me they have no meaning."

' "What mean you?" I cried, raising myself upon my elbow. "Surely, friend, this grief has turned your brain." His face was aflame with joy, and he writhed and shook like one who hath a devil.

' "Do you know whither I go?" he asked.

' "Nay," I answered, "I cannot tell."

' "I go to her," said he. "She lies embalmed in the farther tomb by the double palm-tree beyond the city wall."

' "Why do you go there?" I asked.

' "To die!" he shrieked, "to die! I am not bound by earthen fetters."

' "But the elixir is in your blood," I cried.

' "I can defy it," said he; "I have found a stronger principle which will destroy it. It is working in my veins at this moment, and in an hour I shall be a dead man. I shall join her, and you shall remain behind."

'As I looked upon him I could see that he spoke words of truth. The light in his eye told me that he was indeed beyond the power of the elixir.

' "You will teach me!" I cried.

' "Never!" he answered.

' "I implore you, by the wisdom of Thoth, by the majesty of Anubis!"

' "It is useless," he said coldly.

' "Then I will find it out," I cried.

' "You cannot," he answered; "it came to me by chance. There is one ingredient which you can never get. Save that which is in the ring of Thoth, none will ever more be made."

' "In the ring of Thoth!" I repeated, "where then is the ring of Thoth?"

' "That also you shall never know," he answered. "You won her love. Who has won in the end? I leave you to your sordid earth life. My chains are broken. I must go!" He turned upon his heel and fled from the chamber. In the morning came the news that the Priest of Thoth was dead.

'My days after that were spent in study. I must find this subtle poison which was strong enough to undo the elixir. From early dawn to midnight I bent over the test-tube and the furnace. Above all, I collected the papyri and the chemical flasks of the priest of Thoth. Alas! they taught me little. Here and there some hint or stray expression would raise hope in my bosom, but no good ever came of it. Still, month after month, I struggled on. When my heart grew faint I would make my way to the tomb by the palm-trees. There, standing by the dead casket from which the jewel had been rifled, I would feel her sweet presence, and would whisper to her that I would rejoin her if mortal wit could solve the riddle.

'Parmes had said that his discovery was connected with the ring of Thoth. I had some remembrance of the trinket. It was a large and weighty circlet, made, not of gold, but of a rarer and heavier metal brought from the mines of Mount Harbal. Platinum, you call it. The ring had, I remembered, a hollow crystal set in it, in which some few drops of liquid might be stored. Now, the secret of Parmes could not have to do with the metal alone, for there were many rings of that metal in the temple. Was it not more likely that he had stored his precious poison within the cavity of the crystal? I had scarce come to this conclusion before, in hunting through his papers, I came upon one which told me that it was indeed so, and that there was still some of the liquid unused.

'But how to find the ring? It was not upon him when he was stripped for the embalmer. Of that I made sure. Neither was it among his private effects. In vain I searched every room that he had entered, every box and vase and chattel that he had owned. I sifted the very sand of the desert in the places where he had been wont to walk; but, do what I would, I could come upon no traces of the ring of Thoth. Yet it may be that my labours would have overcome all obstacles had it not been for a new and unlooked-for misfortune.

'A great war had been waged against the Hyksos, and the captains of the great king had been cut off in the desert, with all their bowmen and horsemen. The shepherd tribes were upon us like the locusts in a dry year. From the wilderness of Shur to the great, bitter lake there was blood by day and fire by night. Abaris was the bulwark of Egypt, but we could not keep the savages back. The city fell. The governor and the soldiers were put to the sword, and I, with many more, was led away into captivity.

'For years and years I tended cattle in the great plains by the Euphrates. My master died, and his son grew old, but I was still as far from death as ever. At last I escaped upon a swift camel, and made my way back to Egypt. The Hyksos had settled in the land which they had conquered, and their own King ruled over the country. Abaris had been torn down, the city had been burned, and of the great Temple there was nothing left save an unsightly mound. Everywhere the tombs had been rifled and the monuments destroyed. Of my Atma's grave no sign was left. It was buried in the sands of the desert, and the palm trees which marked the spot had long disappeared. The papers of Parmes and the remains of the temple of Thoth were either destroyed or scattered far and wide over the deserts of Syria. All search after them was vain.

'From that time I gave up all hope of ever finding the ring or discovering the subtle drug. I set myself to live as patiently as might be until the effect of the elixir should wear away. How can you understand how terrible a thing time is, you who have experience only of the narrow course which lies between the cradle and the grave! I know it to my cost, I who have floated down the whole stream of history. I was old when Ilium fell. I was very old when Herodotus came to Memphis. I was bowed down with years when the new gospel came upon earth. Yet you see me much as other men are, with the cursed elixir still sweetening my blood, and guarding me against that which I would court. Now, at last, at last I have come to the end of it!

'I have travelled in all lands and I have dwelt with all nations. Every tongue is the same to me. I learned them all to help pass the weary time. I need not tell you how slowly they drifted by, the long dawn of modern civilization, the dreary middle years, the dark times of barbarism. They are all behind me now. I have never looked with the eyes of love upon another woman. Atma knows that I have been constant to her.

'It was my custom to read all that the scholars had to say upon Ancient Egypt. I have been in many positions, sometimes affluent, sometimes poor, but I have always found enough to enable me to buy the journals which deal with such matters. Some nine months ago I was in San Francisco, when I read an account of some discoveries made in the neighbourhood of Abaris. My heart leapt into my mouth as I read it. It said that the excavator had busied himself in exploring some tombs recently unearthed. In one there had been found an unopened mummy with an inscription upon the outer case setting forth that it contained the body of the daughter of the governor of the city in the days of Tuthmosis. It added that on removing the outer case there had been exposed a large platinum ring set with a crystal, which had been laid upon the breast of the embalmed woman. This, then, was where Parmes had hid the ring of Thoth. He might well say that it was safe, for no Egyptian would ever stain his soul by moving even the outer case of a buried friend.

'That very night I set off from San Francisco, and in a few weeks I found myself once more at Abaris, if a few sand-heaps and crumbling walls may retain the name of the great city. I hurried to the Frenchmen who were digging there and asked them for the ring. They replied that both the ring and the mummy had been sent to the Boulak Museum at Cairo. To Boulak I went, but only to be told that Mariette Bey had claimed them and had shipped them to the Louvre. I followed them, and there, at last, in the Egyptian chamber, I came, after close upon four thousand years, upon the remains of my Atma, and upon the ring for which I had sought so long.

'But how was I to lay hands upon them? How was I to have them for my very own? It chanced that the office of attendant was vacant. I went to the Director. I convinced him that I knew much about Egypt. In my eagerness I said too much. He remarked that a professor's chair would suit me better than a seat in the conciergerie. I knew more, he said, than he did. It was only by blundering, and letting him think that he had over-estimated my knowledge, that I prevailed upon him to let me move the few effects which I have retained into this chamber. It is my first and my last night here.

'Such is my story, Mr Vansittart Smith. I need not say more to a man of your perception. By a strange chance you have this night looked upon the face of the woman whom I loved in those far-off days. There were many rings with crystals in the case, and I had to test for the platinum to be sure of the one which I wanted. A glance at the crystal has shown me that the liquid is indeed within it, and that I shall at last be able to shake off that accursed health which has been worse to me than the foulest disease. I have nothing more to say to you. I have unburdened myself. You may tell my story or you may withhold it at your pleasure. The choice rests with you. I owe you some amends, for you have had a narrow escape of your life this night. I was a desperate man, and not to be baulked in my purpose. Had I seen you before the thing was done, I might have put it beyond your power to oppose me or to raise an alarm. This is the door. It leads into the Rue de Rivoli. Good-night.'

The Englishman glanced back. For a moment the lean figure of Sosra the Egyptian stood framed in the narrow doorway. The next the door had slammed, and the heavy rasping of a bolt broke on the silent night.

It was on the second day after his return to London that Mr John Vansittart Smith saw the following concise narrative in the Paris correspondence of *The Times*:

> *Curious Occurrence in the Louvre.* Yesterday morning a strange discovery was made in the principal Eastern chamber. The *ouvriers* who are employed to clean out the rooms in the morning found one of the attendants lying dead upon the floor with his arms round one of the mummies. So close was his embrace that it was only with the utmost difficulty that they were separated. One of the cases containing valuable rings had been opened and rifled. The authorities are of opinion that the man was bearing away the mummy with some idea of selling it to a private collector, but that he was struck down in the very act by long-standing disease of the heart. It is said that he was a man of uncertain age and eccentric habits, without any living relations to mourn over his dramatic and untimely end.

THE GORGON
Gertrude Bacon

The Gorgon (1964) was one of the very few films in which I played an evil man, although to be fair even this character, Dr Namaroff, had a secret reason for behaving as he did. Again I was teamed up with Christopher Lee in an orginal screen story which drew on the old Greek legend of the hideous female monster who had snakes instead of hair on her head and turned anyone foolish enough to look at her into stone. The tale here by the Victorian writer Gertrude Bacon also makes use of the tradition and is interesting in being one of the very few short stories written on this topic.

'They that go down to the sea in ships' see strange things, but what they tell is oft-times stranger still. A faculty for romancing is imparted by a seafaring life as readily and surely as a rolling gait and a weather-beaten countenance. A fine imagination is one of the gifts of the ocean – witness the surprising and unlimited power of expression and epithet possessed by the sailor. And a fine imagination will frequently manifest itself in other ways besides swear words.

Captain Brander is one of the most gifted men in this way in the whole merchant service. His officers say of him with pride that he possesses the largest vocabulary in the great steamship company of which he is one of the oldest and most respected skippers, and his yarns are only equalled in their utter impossibility by the genius he displays in furnishing them with minute detail and all the outward circumstance of truth.

I first learned this fact from the second engineer the evening of the sixth day of our voyage, as we leant across the bulwarks and watched the sunset. The second engineer was a bit of a liar – or I should say romancer – himself. The day he took me down into the engine-room he told me, as personal experiences, tales of mutinous Lascar firemen, unpopular officers who disappeared suddenly into the fiery maw of blazing furnaces, and so forth, which, whatever foundation of fact they may have possessed, certainly did not lose in the telling. As a humble aspirant in the same branch of art he naturally was quick to recognize the genius of that past master, the captain, and his admiration for his chief was as boundless as it was sincere.

'I say, Miss Baker,' he said apropos of nothing, 'have you had the skipper "on" yet?'

'Not that I am aware of,' I said. 'What do you mean?'

'Why, has he been spinning you any yarns yet? There isn't a man in the service can touch him for stories. I don't deny that he has seen some service, and been in some tight places, but for a real out-and-out lie, commend me to old Monkey Brand!' (It was by this sobriquet, I regret to say, suggested partly by his name, and mostly by his undoubted resemblance to a well-known advertisement, that the worthy captain was known in the unregenerate engine-room.)

'Oh, I should just love to hear him,' I cried. 'There is nothing I should like better. Do tell me how I can manage to draw him.'

'Well, he doesn't want much drawing as a rule,' said the engineer. 'He likes to give vent to his imagination. Let me see,' he continued; 'tomorrow afternoon we shall be about passing the Grecian Islands. Ask him about them, and try and get him on the subject of Gorgons.'

'Gorgons!' I said. 'What a strange topic! Why, since I've left school I have almost forgotten what they were. Weren't they mythological creatures who turned people into stone when they looked at them?'

'That's about it, I believe,' said the engineer, 'and a fellow called Perseus cut off their heads, or something of that kind. It's a lie anyhow, but you ask the skipper.'

It was the custom of Captain Brander every afternoon to make a kind of royal progress among his passengers. Going the entire circuit of the ship; passing slowly from group to group, with a joke here and a chat there, and bestowing his favours in lordly and impartial fashion – especially among the ladies. I have watched him often coming the whole length of the promenade deck, making some outrageous compliment to one girl, patting another on the shoulder, even chucking a third under the chin; a sense of supreme self-satisfaction animating his red cheeks, curling his grey hair, and suffusing his whole short, portly person. Eccentric he was; indifferent to his personal appearance – his battered old cap had seen almost as much service as he had – but a more popular man or an abler officer never walked the bridge. On this particular occasion I was at the end of the deck, and had so arranged that an inviting deck chair stood vacant beside me. Wearied by his progress by the time he reached me, he fell at once into my little trap, and sat down on the empty chair, leant back, and spread his legs. He and I were fast friends, and had been since the day when I tried to photograph him, and he had frustrated my design by unscrewing the front lens of my camera and keeping it in his pocket for the rest of the morning.

'Captain,' I said, pointing to a cloudy grey outline faintly visible against the eastern horizon, 'what land is that?'

'My dear young lady,' said he, 'I am quite sick of answering that question! If I have been asked it once I have been asked it twenty times in the last half-hour. That old Mrs Matherson in the red shawl buttonholed me on the subject to such an extent that I thought I should never get away again. Wonderful thirst for information that old party has! And she appears to think that because I'm captain I must have a complete knowledge of geography, geology, history, etymology, mythology, *and* navigation. Well, for the twenty-first time, then, we are passing the isles off the coast of Greece, and that one straight ahead is Zante.'

'So that is Greece, is it?' I mused aloud. 'Well, from here at least it looks old enough and romantic enough to be the home of all those ancient heroes we read about – Alexander and Hercules and – and – Gorgons and those sorts of things.' I felt I had introduced the subject somewhat lamely, after all, and the captain looked me full in the face as if suspecting a plot. But if I am not very adroit in conversation, I can at least look innocent upon occasions, and he merely said, 'And what do you know about Gorgons, pray?'

'Oh, as much as most people, I expect!' I answered. 'They are only a sort of fairy tale, you know.'

'I am not so sure of that,' said Captain Brander. 'Those fairy tales, as you call them, often have truth at the bottom of them. And as to Gorgons, why, I could tell you a little incident that happened to me once – but it's rather a long story.'

Then I urged my best persuasions – not that he needed much pressing – and pushing his old cap off his bald forehead, and speaking slowly and with that almost American accent peculiar to him, he unfolded his tale of wonder as follows:

'It's nearly thirty years ago, Miss Baker – that's long before *you* were ever born or thought of – that I was fourth officer of the *Haslar*, 2,000-ton vessel of this same company I serve to this day. How times have altered, to be sure! The *Haslar* was reckoned a fine ship in those days, and if you had told me that I should presently command an 8,000-tonner, such as I do this day, with 11,000 horse-power engines, and more men for the crew alone than the *Haslar* could hold when she was packed her tightest, I very probably wouldn't have believed you. However, that is neither here nor there. But thirty years ago in the spring time – now I come to think of it, it was in the month of April – we were cruising in this very neighbourhood, and one thick foggy night our skipper lost his bearings a bit, got too near the coast, and ran us ashore off the south point of Zante.

'Of course there was a great fuss, and everybody came up on deck with lifebelts, and all the girls screamed, and all the young fellows swore to save them or die in the attempt; and the skipper turned as white as paper – not that he was afraid, for he was no coward – none of our officers are that – but because he knew his prospects were ruined, and he would be turned out of the company and perhaps lose his certificate, and he'd got a wife and a big family, poor chap! Of course that consideration didn't affect *me*, for I was in my bunk and asleep at the time, but it was certainly unfortunate for him.

'Well, it was very soon discovered that the ship wasn't going down in a hurry, and nobody got into the boats, though they were lowered ready. And when daylight came we saw we were fast on the rocks, with half the stern under water, and the saloon and a lot of the cabins flooded. But more than that the *Haslar* couldn't sink, and at low water you might almost walk dryshod on to the shore. There was no getting her off, however, and so all the passengers were landed and sent home as best they could across country, and a rough time they had of it, for Zante is not an over-hospitable sort of a place; while we officers had to stick to the shop till we could get help, and then till she was repaired sufficiently to work her into dock somewhere.

'It was a tedious job, for help was slow in coming; and then all her boilers had to be taken out before she would float, and we fellows got jolly sick of it, I can tell you, for we were hard worked, and Zante is a wretched hole to spend more than half an hour in. Our one amusement, when we were off duty, was to go ashore on foot or row round the island in a boat, shooting wild fowl and exploring the country. There was precious little to see and not much to shoot, and it was slow fun altogether till, one day, the second officer came back from a tramp ashore and told us he had found his way to some very remote village on the eastern coast, where there was a cave among the hills which the villagers warned him not to enter. He could not gather for what reason, because he didn't understand enough of their outlandish tongue, but as it was then growing late he was obliged to return to the ship without further investigation.

'I was always one for adventure when I was a lad, and directly the second officer told his tale I made up my mind to go and explore that cave before any of the rest had a chance. It so happened that next day was my turn for going ashore, and I went and looked up one of the assistant engineers and persuaded him to come with me. I wanted him because he was a chum of mine, and also he was the only one of us who could talk the language a bit. He had been in those parts before, and generally acted as interpreter in our dealings with the natives. His name was Travers, a queer little dark chap, with black eyes and a hot temper, but a pleasant enough fellow if you did not rub him up the wrong way, and game for anything under the sun. He readily agreed to come with me, and we started as soon as we could get away, telling no one of our destination, for we had no wish to be forestalled.

'It was a long tramp, right across the island, to the village which Jenkins, the second officer, had indicated. But at last after climbing a weary hill, we looked down on some clustering huts standing amid vineyards in the valley beneath, while another and much sheerer cliff rose on the opposite side, whose rugged scarp was all rent and riven as by an earthquake, and intersected by a deep ravine. Here and there among the rocks were dark shadows and black patches which might be the entrances to caverns in the crag. "This must be the place," I said, "and one of those is the forbidden cave. How are we to find out which?"

'As if in answer to my question, at this moment there came along the hill-top towards us a burly countryman with a sunburned face and tattered garments. He regarded us with astonishment, as well he might, for they get few strangers in those parts, and he made some remark to us in his queer language, which, of course, I didn't understand, but Travers did and replied to it. Finding he was understood, the countryman stopped and talked.

' "Ah!" he said, or so Travers interpreted. "So you have reached the valley of the Haunted Cavern! It is far to seek and hard to find, but it lies spread beneath you."

' "But which is the Haunted Cavern, and why is it so called?" asked Travers.

' "It lies in yonder cleft of the hills," answered the man, pointing to the opposite ravine, "and it is called the Haunted Cavern because none who venture there return alive. Nay, they return not either alive or dead. They are seen no more!"

' "Tell that to the Marines!" said Travers, only he translated it into Greek, of course, or what the Zante people think is Greek. "You don't expect me to believe such a yarn as that! Why, what is there up in that place?"

' "That is what none can tell," replied the peasant; "for none come back to say. And, indeed, it is the truth I speak. Many men have attempted to find the secret. In bygone days, I have heard, a whole party of soldiers were sent there to search for brigands supposed to be in hiding, but not one was seen again. The cavern has an evil name, and now is shunned by one and all, but every now and again there arises a youth venturesome beyond the rest; and he heeds not the warnings of the old, but hopes to break the spell and find the treasure that some say is hidden there, and he starts in high hope and courage, but never again do we behold his face!"

' "But what is the reason?" persisted Travers, the incredulous.

' "Nay, that we cannot say," reiterated the man. "A short distance can one go up the ravine that leads to the cavern. I have been there myself, and truly there is nothing that can be seen except a barren valley, scattered all over with big black stones. Nothing more, and farther than the entrance none must venture."

' "Oh, I say!" exclaimed Travers, in delight, "did you ever hear such an old liar? This beats anything I could have believed possible in the nineteenth century. Come on, Brander! We are in luck this time!" and the impetuous fellow dashed off down the hill, I at his heels, leaving the countryman dumb with amazement behind us.

'At the foot of the hill we entered the little village. An old, white-haired man of rather superior appearance was crossing the road before us. Travers accosted him and asked him the way to the Haunted Cavern. The old man turned quite pale with astonishment and apprehension.

'"The Haunted Cavern, my son!" he said, in quavering tones; "surely you are not going thither?"

'"Yes, we are, though," said Travers, his eyes dancing with excitement. It is wonderful what enterprise that boy – he was little more – had in him. "And if you won't tell us, we'll find the way out for ourselves!" and he pushed past the old man, who held out his skinny hands as if to detain him.

'Before we had got clear of the hamlet the news had somehow got circulated that we were about to explore the ravine, and the whole of the inhabitants turned out in the wildest excitement. Some were for staying us forcibly, till Travers began to get quite nasty, drew his revolver, and talked of firing. Many reiterated and emphasized alarming warnings and assurances that we should never return. All watched us with the most intense interest, and followed close on our footsteps until we began to near the fatal spot, when they fell off singly or in parties, till finally at the very entrance of the ravine we had left even the boldest spirits behind us.

'In truth, it was a strange spot to which we had penetrated. The narrow path had led us suddenly round the spur of the mountain, and now, look which way we might, the giant rocks towered up sheer above us, hundreds of feet high, in inaccessible grey walls. The sinking sun was now too low to shine within this well-like space, which his rays could only reach at midday, and the very air struck damp and chill. We were in an open valley, thus shut in by the cliffs, of considerable extent, but not to be reached by any path except that we had traversed. The ground was firm and smooth, but littered all over with the strangest black stones of all sorts of shapes, and in all positions, though of a fairly uniform size, and alike in material. There was something uncanny and weird about these queer black boulders, which strewed the valley the thicker the farther we advanced, till at the far end of the space, where a huge black hole yawned ominous in the cliff, they almost entirely blocked the way.

'The dark cavern looked terribly grim and forbidding in the fading light. A little stream issued from its mouth and trickled among the stones. It did not gurgle and glisten as most mountain streams, but flowed noiselessly, sluggish, and dull, and gathered in stagnant pools on its rocky bed. No birds sang in that dismal nook; no sound from without penetrated to its recesses. All was silent, dim, and chill as the tomb itself.

'Despite my utmost efforts, I felt the spell of the weird, wild spot stealing over me, and a cold shudder crept down my backbone. There was but room for one at a time in the ever-narrowing track, and I was at first leading. My steps became slower and slower, and finally I paused altogether and turned to look back on Travers to see if he too was feeling the oppressive sense of evil that seemed to hang heavy in the very air. But in his face was only visible an ecstasy almost of eagerness and delight. His dark eyes sparkled again, his cheeks were flushed, his breath came quick, and his whole body was quivering with excitement.

' "Go on, Brander!" he cried. "What are you stopping for, man? This is grand! This is luck, indeed! Did you ever see such a place? Come on, I want to get to that cave!"

'I felt utterly ashamed to confess my weakness, but it was that cave that I had begun to dread more and more. Whatever else I may be, Miss Baker, it is not boasting to say I am no coward. I have seen danger, aye, and courted it all my life, and until that moment I doubt if I had known what fear was. But I knew then: the blind, unreasoning fear that saps the strength of mind and limb and melts the heart and paralyzes all thought save that one overpowering instinct to fly – somewhere. Yet, in face of Travers's eagerness, I could not bear to show the white feather. I turned my back therefore on the dark cavern, now just ahead of us, and endeavoured to temporize.

' "Travers," I said, "did you ever see such queer stones? How do you suppose they have got here? They are quite a different nature from these cliffs, so they could not have fallen from the sides."

' "Oh, bother the stones!" said Travers. "I can't look at them now, I want to get into the cave. Quick, before it gets dark!" and as I still hesitated, he pushed past me into a more open space beyond, almost at the cavern's mouth. I did not dare to leave him, and was scrambling after him as best I might, when I suddenly heard him cry out in a voice such as I had never heard before, and hope never to again.

A shrill, high-pitched cry in which there were surprise, wonder, disgust, alarm, and awful horror all combined in one: a cry of astonishment, a shriek of agony, a shout of dismay. "Look, Brander! look! look!"

'I could have sworn that when he spoke my companion was in full view, close beside me, touching me almost, though at the exact moment my eyes were looking from him; but when I turned my head in answer to his cry he was gone.

'For one second only had my gaze been averted, but in that time he had utterly vanished from sight, disappeared in a flash, gone – whither? A large black stone stood close beside me, similar to the rest in that ghostly valley; yet it struck me somehow that I had not noticed it there before. I placed my hand upon it as I peered round behind to see if Travers were there and a shudder I could not explain ran up my arm, for the stone felt warm to the touch. I had not time then to analyze my unreasonable horror at this trivial circumstance; I was too eager to find my friend. I rushed madly among the stones, I yelled his name again and again, but the weird echoes of my cry, returned in countless reflections from cliff and cavern, alone answered me.

'In a frenzy of despair I continued my search, for certain was I that by no natural means could Travers have disappeared so utterly in so brief a space. Blind panic seized me, and I knew not what I did, till my eye suddenly fell on a shallow pool of water collected in a rocky hollow at my very feet. It was not more than a couple of inches deep, and scarce a yard across, but on its placid face were reflected the overhanging rock and opening of the cavern just behind it, and also something else that glued my eyes to it in horror and rooted my flying feet to the ground.

'Just above the cavern's mouth was a narrow ledge of rock, running horizontally, and of a few inches in width. On this natural shelf, reflected in the water, I saw, hanging downwards, a decayed fragment of goat-skin, rotten with age, but which might have been bound round something, long years before. Upon this, as if escaped from its folds, rested a Head.

'It was a human head, severed at the neck, but fresh and unfaded as if but newly dead. It bore the features of a woman – of a woman of more perfect loveliness than was ever told of in tale, or sculptured in marble, or painted on canvas. Every feature, every line was of the truest beauty, cast in the noblest mould – the face of a goddess.

But upon that perfect countenance was the mark of eternal pain, of deathless agony and suffering past words. The forehead was lined and knit, the death-white lips were tightly pressed in speechless torment; in the wide eyes seemed yet to lurk the flame of an unquenchable fire; while around the fair brows, in place of hair, curled and coiled the stark bodies of venomous serpents, stiff in death, but their loathsome forms still erect, their evil heads yet thrust forward as if to strike.

'My heart ceased beating, and the chill of death crept over my limbs, as with eyes starting from their sockets I stared at that awful head, reflected in the pool. For hours it seemed to me I gazed fascinated, as the bird by the eye of the snake that has charmed it. I was as incapable of thought as movement, till suddenly forgotten school-room learning began to cross my brain, and I knew that I looked at the reflection of Medusa, the Gorgon, fairest and foulest of living things, the unclean creature, half woman, half eagle, slain by the hero Perseus, and one glimpse of whose tortured face turned the luckless beholder into stone with the horror of it.

'If I once raised my eyes from the reflection to the actual head above I knew that I too should freeze in a moment into another black block, even as poor Travers, and every other who had entered the accursed valley had done before. And as this thought occurred to me, the longing to lift my eyes and look upon the real object became so overpowering that, in sheer self-preservation, I inclined my face closer and closer to the water till I seemed almost to touch it, when my senses fled and I knew no more.

'When I woke at last it was far on in the night, and a bright moon, riding high, shone full down upon the valley, revealing the ragged rocks and scattered stones with a cold brilliance that almost equalled the day. I was lying chilled and stiff beside the pool, and I started up in amazement, unable to recall to my mind, for a moment, where I was or what I was doing there. I had my back to the cavern, fortunately, and as I gazed over the ghostly and deserted scene the events of the day suddenly returned to my mind in a single flash of terror.

'To escape from this ghastly place was now my only thought, and in order to do this I resolved to look no more at the pool at my feet in case the terrible fascination should again take possession of me. What it cost me to adhere to this resolution I cannot tell you, but with the courage of despair I pressed blindly forward to the mouth of the ravine, only pausing a second to lay my hand upon the now ice-cold stone that once was Travers.

'Poor Travers! gay, light-hearted fellow! Ever in the forefront of mischief, of danger, of adventure. How eager he had been to solve the secret of the haunted valley, which now must be his tomb for ever. How full of health and spirits he had scrambled a few hours before among those very boulders, one of which now, standing stiffly erect among its forest of brethren, was at once the monument and sole relic of a fearless lad, a cheery friend, and a gallant seaman. Dear old Travers! Brave, foolish boy! My heart was heavy, indeed, for his awful fate, as I reverently touched the stone and murmured to the night breeze, stealing around the rocks, "Good-bye, old fellow; sleep sound!"

'It seemed to me, in my loneliness and terror, that my fearsome journey would never be ended: that, lost in a labyrinth, I should tread that valley for ever. But at last, after endless ages, I reached the mouth of the ravine, and once on open ground I stretched my cramped limbs and ran, without ceasing, till I once more reached the ship.'

Here the captain paused, more from want of breath than anything else, I think.

'Go on, Captain Brander,' I cried. 'You haven't half finished yet. What did they say when you returned, and how did you explain about poor Travers?'

'Young lady,' said Captain Brander, 'don't ask any more questions. I think I have told you enough for one afternoon,' and here, an officer coming up and summoning him, he left me.

THE MAN WHO COLLECTED POE
Robert Bloch

As was mentioned in the Introduction I have appeared in a number of anthology films consisting of three or four linked stories. Several of these have been scripted by the famous American writer, Robert Bloch, often based on his own work. For this reason there are quite a number of tales by Mr Bloch which I might have used here, but in the end I decided on the one which featured the great master of the horror story, Edgar Allan Poe, without whose pioneer work in this genre, we might not today enjoy such a wide range of terror tales. The story, The Man Who Collected Poe *was a segment in the film* Torture Garden *(1967) – and I played the obsessed bibliophile, Canning. It was also one of several films I have made with director Freddie Francis whom I have always found a joy to work with.*

During the whole of a dull, dark and soundless day in the autumn of the year, when the clouds hung oppressively low in the heavens, I had been passing alone, by automobile, through a singularly dreary tract of country; and at length found myself, as the shades of the evening drew on, within view of my destination.

I looked upon the scene before me – upon the mere house and the simple landscape features of the domain, upon the bleak walls, upon the vacant eyelike windows, upon a few rank sedges, and upon a few white trunks of decayed trees – with a feeling of utter confusion commingled with dismay. For it seemed to me as though I had visited this scene once before, or read of it, perhaps, in some frequently rescanned tale. And yet assuredly it could not be, for only three days had passed since I had made the acquaintance of Launcelot Canning and received an invitation to visit him at his Maryland residence.

The circumstances under which I met Canning were simple; I happened to attend a bibliophilic meeting in Washington and was introduced to him by a mutual friend. Casual conversation gave place to absorbed and interested discussion when he discovered my preoccupation with works of fantasy. Upon learning that I was travelling upon a vacation with no set itinerary, Canning urged me to become his guest for a day and to examine, at my leisure, his unusual display of *memorabilia*.

'I feel, from our conversation, that we have much in common,' he told me. 'For you see, sir, in my love of fantasy I bow to no man. It is a taste I have perhaps inherited from my father and from his father before him, together with their considerable acquisitions in the genre. No doubt you would be gratified with what I am prepared to show you, for in all due modesty I beg to style myself the world's leading collector of the works of Edgar Allan Poe.'

I confess that his invitation as such did not enthrall me, for I hold no brief for the literary hero-worshipper or the scholarly collector as a type. I own to a more than passing interest in the tales of Poe, but my interest does not extend to the point of ferreting out the exact date upon which Mr Poe first decided to raise a moustache, nor would I be unduly intrigued by the opportunity to examine several hairs preserved from that hirsute appendage.

So it was rather the person and personality of Launcelot Canning himself which caused me to accept his proffered hospitality. For the man who proposed to become my host might have himself stepped from the pages of a Poe tale. His speech, as I have endeavoured to indicate, was characterized by a courtly rodomontade so often exemplified in Poe's heroes – and beyond certainty, his appearance bore out the resemblance.

Launcelot Canning had the cadaverousness of complexion, the large, liquid, luminous eyes, the thin, curved lips, the delicately modelled nose, finely moulded chin, and dark, weblike hair of a typical Poe protagonist.

It was this phenomenon which prompted my acceptance and led me to journey to his Maryland estate which, as I now perceived, in itself manifested a Poe-etic quality of its own, intrinsic in the images of the grey sedge, the ghastly tree stems, and the vacant and eyelike windows of the mansions of gloom. All that was lacking was a tarn and a moat – and as I prepared to enter the dwelling I half-expected to encounter therein the carved ceilings, the sombre tapestries, the ebon floors and the phantasmagoric armorial trophies so vividly described by the author of *Tales of the Grotesque and Arabesque*.

Nor, upon entering Launcelot Canning's home, was I too greatly disappointed in my expectations. True to both the atmospheric quality of the decrepit mansion and to my own fanciful presentiments, the door was opened in response to my knock by a valet who conducted me, in silence, through dark and intricate passages to the study of his master.

The room in which I found myself was very large and lofty. The windows were long, narrow and pointed, and at so vast a distance from the black oaken floor as to be altogether inaccessible from within. Feeble gleams of encrimsoned light made their way through the trellised panes and served to render sufficiently distinct the more prominent objects around; the eye, however, struggled in vain to reach the remoter angles of the chamber or the recesses of the vaulted and fretted ceiling. Dark draperies hung upon the walls. The general furniture was profuse, comfortless, antique and tattered. Many books and musical instruments lay scattered about, but they failed to give any vitality to the scene.

Instead, they rendered more distinct that peculiar quality of quasi-recollection; it was as though I found myself once again, after a protracted absence, in a familiar setting. I had read, I had imagined, I had dreamed, or I had actually beheld this setting before.

Upon my entrance, Launcelot Canning arose from a sofa on which he had been lying at full length and greeted me with a vivacious warmth which had much in it, I at first thought, of an overdone cordiality.

Yet his tone, as he spoke of the object of my visit, of his earnest desire to see me, of the solace he expected me to afford him in a mutual discussion of our interests, soon alleviated my initial misapprehension.

Launcelot Canning welcomed me with the rapt enthusiasm of the born collector – and I came to realize that he was indeed just that. For the Poe collection he shortly proposed to unveil before me was actually his birthright.

The nucleus of the present accumulation, he disclosed, had begun with his grandfather, Christopher Canning, a respected merchant of Baltimore. Almost eighty years ago he had been one of the leading patrons of the arts in his community and as such was partially instrumental in arranging for the removal of Poe's body to the south-eastern corner of the Presbyterian Cemetery at Fayette and Green Streets, where a suitable monument might be erected. This event occurred in the year 1875, and it was a few years prior to that time that Canning laid the foundation of the Poe collection.

'Thanks to his zeal,' his grandson informed me, 'I am today the fortunate possessor of a copy of virtually every existing specimen of Poe's published works. If you will step over here,' – and he led me to a remote corner of the vaulted study, past the dark draperies, to a bookshelf which rose remotely to the shadowy ceiling – 'I shall be pleased to corroborate that claim. Here is a copy of *Al Aaraaf, Tamerlane and other Poems* in the 1829 edition, and here is the still earlier *Tamerlane and other Poems* of 1827. The Boston edition, which, as you doubtless know, is valued today at $15,000. I can assure you that Grandfather Canning parted with no such sum in order to gain possession of this rarity.'

He displayed the volumes with an air of commingled pride and cupidity which is oft-times characteristic of the collector and is by no means to be confused with either literary snobbery or ordinary greed. Realizing this, I remained patient as he exhibited further treasures – copies of the *Philadelphia Saturday Courier* containing early tales, bound volumes of *The Messenger* during the period of Poe's editorship, *Graham's Magazine*, editions of the *New York Sun* and the *New York Mirror* boasting, respectively, of *The Balloon Hoax* and *The Raven*, and files of *The Gentleman's Magazine*. Ascending a short library ladder, he handed down to me the Lea and Blanchard edition of *Tales of the Grotesque and Arabesque*, the *Conchologist's First Book*, the Putnam *Eureka*, and, finally, the little paper booklet, published in 1843 and sold for 12½ cents, entitled *The Prose Romances of Edgar A. Poe* – an insignificant trifle containing two tales which is valued by present-day collectors at $50,000.

Canning informed me of this last fact and, indeed, kept up a running commentary upon each item he presented. There was no doubt but that he was a Poe scholar as well as a Poe collector, and his words informed tattered specimens of the *Broadway Journal* and *Godey's Lady's Book* with a singular fascination not necessarily inherent in the flimsy sheets or their contents.

'I owe a great debt to Grandfather Canning's obsession,' he observed, descending the ladder and joining me before the bookshelves. 'It is not altogether a breach of confidence to admit that his interest in Poe did reach the point of an obsession, and perhaps eventually of an absolute mania. The knowledge, alas, is public property, I fear.

'In the early seventies he built this house, and I am quite sure that you have been observant enough to note that it in itself is almost a replica of a typical Poe-esque mansion. This was his study, and it was here that he was wont to pore over the books, the letters and the numerous mementos of Poe's life.

'What prompted a retired merchant to devote himself so fanatically to the pursuit of a hobby, I cannot say. Let it suffice that he virtually withdrew from the world and from all other normal interests. He conducted a voluminous and lengthy correspondence with ageing men and women who had known Poe in their lifetime – made pilgrimages to Fordham, sent his agents to West Point, to England and Scotland, to virtually every locale in which Poe had set foot during his lifetime. He acquired letters and souvenirs as gifts, he bought them and – I fear – stole them, if no other means of acquisition proved feasible.'

Launcelot Canning smiled and nodded. 'Does all this sound strange to you? I confess that once I too found it almost incredible, a fragment of romance. Now, after years spent amidst these surroundings, I have lost my own objectivity.'

'Yes, it is strange,' I replied. 'But are you quite sure that there was not some obscure personal reason for your grandfather's interest? Had he met Poe as a boy, or been closely associated with one of his friends? Was there, perhaps, a distant, undisclosed relationship?'

At the mention of the last word, Canning started visibly, and a tremor of agitation overspread his countenance.

'Ah!' he exclaimed. 'There you voice my own inmost conviction. A relationship – assuredly there must have been – I am morally, instinctively certain that Grandfather Canning felt or knew himself to be linked to Edgar Poe by ties of blood. Nothing else could account for his strong initial interest, his continuing defence of Poe in the literary controversies of the day, his final melancholy lapse into a world of delusion and illusion.

'Yet he never voiced a statement or put an allegation upon paper – and I have searched the collection of letters in vain for the slightest clue.

'It is curious that you so promptly divine a suspicion held not only by myself but by my father. He was only a child at the time of my Grandfather Canning's death, but the attendant circumstances left a profound impression upon his sensitive nature. Although he was immediately removed from this house to the home of his mother's people in Baltimore, he lost no time in returning upon assuming his inheritance in early manhood.

'Fortunately being in possession of a considerable income, he was able to devote his entire lifetime to further research. The name of Arthur Canning is still well known in the world of literary criticism, but for some reason he preferred to pursue his scholarly examination of Poe's career in privacy. I believe this preference was dictated by an inner sensibility; that he was endeavouring to unearth some information which would prove his father's, his, and for that matter, my own, kinship to Edgar Poe.'

'You say your father was also a collector?' I prompted.

'A statement I am prepared to substantiate,' replied my host, as he led me to yet another corner of the shadow-shrouded study. 'But first, if you would accept a glass of wine?'

He filled, not glasses, but veritable beakers from a large carafe, and we toasted one another in silent appreciation. It is perhaps unnecessary for me to observe that the wine was a fine old Amontillado.

'Now, then,' said Launcelot Canning. 'My father's special province in Poe research consisted of the accumulation and study of letters.'

Opening a series of large trays or drawers beneath the bookshelves, he drew out file after file of glassined folios, and for the space of the next half hour I examined Edgar Poe's correspondence – letters to Henry Herring, to Doctor Snodgrass, Sarah Shelton, James P. Moss, Elizabeth Poe; missives to Mrs Rockwood, Helen Whitman, Anne Lynch, John Pendleton Kennedy; notes to Mrs Richmond, to John Allan, to Annie, to his brother, Henry – a profusion of documents, a veritable epistolatory cornucopia.

During the course of my perusal my host took occasion to refill our beakers with wine, and the heady draught began to take effect –

for we had not eaten, and I own I gave no thought to food, so absorbed was I in the yellowed pages illumining Poe's past.

Here was wit, erudition, literary criticism; here were the muddled, maudlin outpourings of a mind gone in drink and despair; here was the draft of a projected story, the fragments of a poem; here was a pitiful cry for deliverance and a paean to living beauty; here was dignified response to a dunning letter and an auctorial pronunciamento to an admirer; here was love, hate, pride, anger, celestial serenity, abject penitence, authority, wonder, resolution, indecision, joy, and soul-sickening melancholia.

Here was the gifted elocutionist, the stammering drunkard, the adoring husband, the frantic lover, the proud editor, the indigent pauper, the grandiose dreamer, the shabby realist, the scientific inquirer, the gullible metaphysician, the dependent stepson, the free and untrammelled spirit, the hack, the poet, the enigma that was Edgar Allan Poe.

Again the beakers were filled and emptied. I drank deeply with my lips, and with my eyes more deeply still.

For the first time the true enthusiasm of Launcelot Canning was communicated to my own sensibilities – I divined the eternal fascination found in a consideration of Poe the writer and Poe the man; he who wrote Tragedy, lived Tragedy, was Tragedy; he who penned Mystery, lived and died in Mystery, and who today looms on the literary scene as Mystery incarnate.

And Mystery Poe remained, despite Arthur Canning's careful study of the letters. 'My father learned nothing,' my host confided, 'even though he assembled, as you see here, a collection to delight the heart of a Mabbott or a Quinn. So his search ranged further. By this time I was old enough to share both his interest and his inquiries. Come,' and he led me to an ornate chest which rested beneath the windows against the west wall of the study.

Kneeling, he unlocked the repository, and then drew forth, in rapid and marvellous succession, a series of objects, each of which boasted of intimate connection with Poe's life.

There were souvenirs of his youth and his schooling abroad; a book he had used during his sojourn at West Point; mementoes of his days as a theatrical critic in the form of playbills; a pen used during his editorial period; a fan once owned by his girl-wife, Virginia; a brooch of Mrs Clemm's – a profusion of objects including such diverse articles as a cravat and, curiously enough, Poe's battered and tarnished flute.

Again we drank, and I own the wine was potent. Canning's countenance remained cadaverously wan but, moreover, there was a species of mad hilarity in his eyes – an evident restrained hysteria in his whole demeanour. At length, from the scattered heap of *curiosa*, I happened to draw forth and examine a little box of no remarkable character, whereupon I was constrained to inquire its history and what part it had played in the life of Poe.

'In the *life* of Poe?' A visible tremor convulsed the features of my host, then rapidly passed in transformation to a grimace, a rictus of amusement. 'This little box – and you will note how, by some fateful design or contrived coincidence it bears a resemblance to the box he himself conceived of and described in his tale, *Berenice* – this little box is concerned with his death rather than his life. It is, in fact, the selfsame box my grandfather Christopher Canning clutched to his bosom when they found him down there.'

Again the tremor, again the grimace. 'But stay, I have not yet told you of the details. Perhaps you would be interested in seeing the spot where Christopher Canning was striken; I have already told you of his madness, but I did no more than hint at the character of his delusions. You have been patient with me, and more than patient. Your understanding shall be rewarded, for I perceive you can be fully entrusted with the facts.'

What further revelations Canning was prepared to make I could not say, but his manner was such as to inspire a vague disquiet and trepidation in my breast.

Upon perceiving my unease he laughed shortly and laid a hand upon my shoulder. 'Come, this should interest you as an *aficionado* of fantasy,' he said. 'But first, another drink to speed our journey.'

He poured, we drank, and then he led the way from that vaulted chamber, down the silent halls, down the staircase, and into the lowest recesses of the building until we reached what resembled a dungeon, its floor and the interior of a long archway carefully sheathed in copper. We paused before a door of massive iron. Again I felt in the aspect of this scene an element evocative of recognition or recollection.

Canning's intoxication was such that he misinterpreted or chose to misinterpret, my reaction.

'You need not be afraid,' he assured me. 'Nothing has happened down here since that day, almost seventy years ago, when his servants discovered him stretched out before this door, the little box clutched to his bosom; collapsed, and in a state of delirium from which he never emerged. For six months he lingered, a hopeless maniac – raving as wildly from the very moment of his discovery as at the moment he died – babbling his visions of the giant horse, the fissured house collapsing into the tarn, the black cat, the pit, the pendulum, the raven on the pallid bust, the beating heart, the pearly teeth, and the nearly liquid mass of loathsome – of detestable putridity from which a voice emanated.

'Nor was that all he babbled,' Canning confided, and here his voice sank to a whisper that reverberated through the copper-sheathed hall and against the iron door. 'He hinted other things far worse than fantasy – of a ghastly reality surpassing the phantasms of Poe.

'For the first time my father and the servants learned the purpose of the room he had built beyond this iron door, and learned too what Christopher Canning had done to establish his title as the world's foremost collector of Poe.

'For he babbled again of Poe's death, thirty years earlier, in 1849 – of the burial in the Presbyterian Cemetery and of the removal of the coffin in 1875 to the corner where the monument was raised. As I told you, and as was known then, my grandfather had played a public part in instigating that removal. But now we learned of the private part – learned that there was a monument and a grave, but no coffin in the earth beneath Poe's alleged resting place. The coffin now rested in the secret room at the end of this passage. That is why the room, the house itself, had been built.

'I tell you, he had stolen the body of Edgar Allan Poe – and as he shrieked aloud in his final madness, did not this indeed make him the greatest collector of Poe?

'His ultimate intent was never divined, but my father made one significant discovery – the little box clutched to Christopher Canning's bosom contained a portion of the crumbled bones, the veritable dust that was all that remained of Poe's corpse.'

My host shuddered and turned away. He led me back along that hall of horror, up the stairs, into the study. Silently, he filled our beakers, and I drank as hastily, as deeply, as desperately as he.

'What could my father do? To own the truth was to create a public scandal. He chose instead to keep silence, to devote his own life to study in retirement.

'Naturally, the shock affected him profoundly; to my knowledge he never entered the room beyond the iron door and, indeed, I did not know of the room or its contents until the hour of his death – and it was not until some years later that I myself found the key amongst his effects.

'But find the key I did, and the story was immediately and completely corroborated. Today I am the greatest collector of Poe – for he lies in the keep below, my eternal trophy!'

This time I poured the wine. As I did so, I noted for the first time the imminence of a storm – the impetuous fury of its gusts shaking the casements and the echoes of its thunder rolling and rumbling down the time-corroded corridors of the old house.

The wild, overstrained vivacity with which my host hearkened, or apparently hearkened, to these sounds did nothing to reassure me – for his recent revelation led me to suspect his sanity.

That the body of Edgar Allan Poe had been stolen; that this mansion had been built to house it; that it was indeed enshrined in a crypt below; that grandsire, son and grandson had dwelt here alone, apart, enslaved to a sepulchral secret – was beyond sane belief or tolerance.

And yet, surrounded now by the night and the storm, in a setting torn from Poe's own frezied fancies, I could not be sure. Here the past was still alive, the very spirit of Poe's tales breathed forth its corruption upon the scene.

As thunder boomed, Launcelot Canning took up Poe's flute, and, whether in defiance of the storm without or as a mocking accompaniment, he played; blowing upon it with drunken persistence, with eerie atonality, with nerve-shattering shrillness. To the shrieking of that infernal instrument the thunder added a braying counterpoint.

Uneasy, uncertain and unnerved, I retreated into the shadows of the bookshelves at the further end of the room and idly scanned the titles of a row of ancient tomes. Here was the *Chiromancy* of Robert Flud; the *Directorium Inquisitorum*, a rare and curious book in quarto Gothic that was the manual of a forgotten church; and betwixt and between the volumes of pseudo-scientific inquiry, theological speculation and sundry *incunabula* I found titles that arrested and appalled me. *De Vermis Mysteriis* and the *Liber Eibon*, treatises on demonology, or witchcraft, on sorcery, mouldered in crumbling bindings. The books were old, the books were tattered and torn, but the books were not dusty. They had been read –

'Read them?' It was as though Canning divined my inmost thoughts. He had put aside his flute and now approached me, tittering as though in continued drunken defiance of the storm. Odd echoes and boomings now sounded through the long halls of the house, and curious grating sounds threatened to drown out his words and his laughter.

'Read them?' said Canning. 'I study them. Yes, I have gone beyond Grandfather, and Father, too. It was I who procured the books that held the key, and it was I who found the key. A key more difficult to discover, and more important, than the key to the vaults below. I often wonder if Poe himself had access to these selfsame tomes, knew the selfsame secrets. The secrets of the grave and what lies beyond, and what can be summoned forth if one but holds the key.'

He stumbled away and returned with wine. 'Drink,' he said. 'Drink to the night and the storm.'

I brushed the proffered glass aside. 'Enough,' I said. 'I must be on my way.'

Was it fancy, or did I find fear frozen on his features? Canning clutched my arm and cried, 'No, stay with me! This is no night on which to be alone; I swear I cannot abide the thought of being alone. You must not, cannot leave me here alone; I can bear to be alone no more!'

His incoherent babble mingled with the thunder and the echoes; I drew back and confronted him. 'Control yourself,' I counselled. 'Confess that this is a hoax, an elaborate imposture arranged to please your fancy.'

'Hoax? Imposture? Stay, and I shall prove to you beyond all doubt – ' And so saying, Launcelot Canning stooped and opened a small drawer set in the wall beneath and beside the bookshelves. 'This should repay you for your interest in my story, and in Poe,' he murmured. 'Know that you are the first other than myself to glimpse these treasures.'

He handed me a sheaf of manuscripts on plain white paper – documents written in ink curiously similar to that I had noted while perusing Poe's letters. Pages were clipped together in groups, and for a moment I scanned titles alone.

'*The Worm of Midnight*, by Edgar Poe,' I read, aloud. '*The Crypt*,' I breathed. And here, '*The Further Adventures of Arthur*

Gordon Pym.' In my agitation I came close to dropping the precious pages. 'Are these what they appear to be – the unpublished tales of Poe?'

My host bowed. 'Unpublished, undiscovered, unknown, save to me – and to you.'

'But this cannot be,' I protested. 'Surely there would have been a mention of them somewhere, in Poe's own letters or those of his contemporaries. There would have been a clue, an indication – somewhere, someplace, somehow.'

Thunder mingled with my words, and thunder echoed in Canning's shouted reply.

'You dare to presume an imposture? Then compare!' He stooped again and brought out a glassined folio of letters. 'Here – is this not the veritable script of Edgar Poe? Look at the calligraphy of the letters, then at the manuscripts. Can you say they are not penned by the selfsame hand?'

I looked at the handwriting, wondered at the possibilities of a monomaniac's forgery. Could Launcelot Canning, a victim of mental disorder, thus painstakingly simulate Poe's hand?

'Read, then!' Canning screamed through the thunder. 'Read, and dare to say that these tales were written by any other than Edgar Poe, whose genius defies the corruption of Time and the Conquerer Worm!'

I read but a line or two, holding the topmost manuscript close to eyes that strained beneath wavering candlelight; but even in the flickering illumination I noted that which told me the only, the incontestable truth. For the paper, the curiously *unyellowed* paper, bore a visible watermark; the name of a firm of modern stationers and the date – 1949.

Putting the sheaf aside, I endeavoured to compose myself as I moved away from Launcelot Canning. For now I knew the truth; knew that, one hundred years after Poe's death, a semblance of his spirit still lived in the distorted and disordered soul of Canning. Incarnation, reincarnation, call it what you will; Canning was, in his own irrational mind, Edgar Allan Poe.

Stifled and dull echoes of thunder from a remote portion of the mansion now commingled with the soundless seething of my own inner turmoil, as I turned and rashly addressed my host.

'Confess!' I cried. 'Is it not true that you have written these tales, fancying yourself the embodiment of Poe? Is it not true that you suffer from a singular delusion born of solitude and everlasting brooding upon the past; that you have reached a stage characterized by the conviction that Poe still lives on in your own person?'

A strong shudder came over him, and a sickly smile quivered about his lips as he replied. 'Fool! I say to you that I have spoken the truth. Can you doubt the evidence of your senses? This house is real, the Poe collection exists, and the stories exist – exist, I swear, as truly as the body in the crypt below!'

I took up the little box from the table and removed the lid. 'Not so,' I answered. 'You said your grandfather was found with this box clutched to his breast, before the door of the vault, and that it contained Poe's dust. Yet you cannot escape the fact that the box is empty.' I faced him furiously. 'Admit it, the story is a fabrication, a romance. Poe's body does not lie beneath this house, nor are these his unpublished works, written during his lifetime and concealed.'

'True enough.' Canning's smile was ghastly beyond belief. 'The dust is gone because I took it and used it – because in the works of wizardry I found the formulae, the arcana whereby I could raise the flesh, recreate the body from the essential salts of the grave. Poe does not *lie* beneath this house – he *lives!* And the tales are his *posthumous works!*'

Accented by thunder, his words crashed against my consciousness. 'That was the be-all and end-all of my planning; of my studies, of my work, of my life! To raise, by sorcery, the veritable spirit of Edgar Poe from the grave – reclothed and animate in flesh – and set him to dwell and dream and do his work again in the private chambers I built in the vaults below – and this I have done! To steal a corpse is but a ghoulish prank; mine is the achievement of true genius!'

The distinct, hollow, metallic and clangorous, yet apparently muffled, reverberation accompanying his words caused him to turn in his seat and face the door of the study, so that I could not see the working of his countenance – nor could he read my reaction to his ravings.

His words came but faintly to my ears through the thunder that now shook the house in a relentless grip; the wind rattling the casements and flickering the candle flame from the great silver candelabra sent a soaring sighing in anguished accompaniment to his speech.

'I would show him to you, but I dare not; for he hates me as he hates life. I have locked him in the vault, alone, for the resurrected have no need of food nor drink. And he sits there, pen moving over paper, endlessly moving, endlessly pouring out the evil essence of all he guessed and hinted at in life and which he learned in death.

'Do you not see the tragic pity of my plight? I sought to raise his spirit from the dead, to give the world anew of his genius – and yet these tales, these works, are filled and fraught with a terror not to be endured. They cannot be shown to the world, he cannot be shown to the world; in bringing back the dead I have brought back the fruits of death!'

Echoes sounded anew as I moved toward the door – moved, I confess, to flee this accursed house and its accursed owner.

Canning clutched my hand, my arm, my shoulder. 'You cannot go!' he shouted above the storm. 'I spoke of his escaping, but did you not guess? Did you not hear it through the thunder – the grating of the door?'

I pushed him aside and he blundered backward, upsetting the candelabra, so that flames licked now across the carpeting.

'Wait!' he cried. 'Have you not heard his footstep on the stair? MADMAN, I TELL YOU THAT HE NOW STANDS WITHOUT THE DOOR!'

A rush of wind, a roar of flame, a shroud of smoke rose all about us. Throwing open the huge antique panels to which Canning pointed, I staggered into the hall.

I speak of wind, of flame, of smoke – enough to obscure all vision. I speak of Canning's screams, and of thunder loud enough to drown all sound. I speak of terror born of loathing and of desperation enough to shatter all sanity.

Despite these things, I can never erase from my consciousness that which I beheld as I fled past the doorway and down the hall.

There without the doors there *did* stand a lofty and enshrouded figure; a figure all too familiar, with pallid features, high, domed forehead, moustache set above a mouth. My glimpse lasted but an instant, an instant during which the man – the corpse, the apparition, the hallucination, call it what you will – moved forward into the chamber and clasped Canning to its breast in an unbreakable embrace. Together, the two figures tottered toward the flames, which now rose to blot out vision for evermore.

From that chamber, and from that mansion, I fled aghast. The storm was still abroad in all its wrath, and now fire came to claim the house of Canning for its own.

Suddenly there shot along the path before me a wild light, and I turned to see whence a gleam so unusual could have issued – but it was only the flames, rising in supernatural splendour to consume the mansion, and the secrets, of the man who collected Poe.

THE GHOUL OF GOLDERS GREEN

Michael Arlen

> The Ghoul *which I made in 1974 was one of several films I have appeared in based on an original screenplay by John Elder, who is a very talented writer in this field. He took the dictionary definition of the word ghoul, 'a person who lives on human flesh' and made a really quite moving story around this gruesome subject. I played a clergyman, Dr Lawrence, who made a pledge to his dying wife that he would take care of their son despite the fact that the boy had been turned into a cannibal by a weird Indian sect. Returned to England, the unfortunate man hides the boy in his attic and has to make secret forays to get human flesh to feed him. So, you can gather, the man was not driven by ghoulish intent but out of adoration for his dead wife. In this story by Michael Arlen we are introduced to another ghoul – but a rather surprising one . . .*

It is fortunate that the affair should have happened to Mr Ralph Wyndham Trevor and be told by him, for Mr Trevor is a scholar of some authority. It is in a spirit of almost ominous premonition that he begins the tale, telling how he was walking slowly up Davies Street one night when he caught a cab. It need scarcely be said that Davies Street owes its name to that Mary Davies, the heiress, who married into the noble house of Grosvenor. That was years and years ago, of course, and is of no importance whatsoever now, but it may be of interest to students.

It was very late on a winter's night, and Mr Trevor was depressed, for he had that evening lost a great deal more than he could afford at the card-game of auction-bridge. Davies Street was deserted; and the moon and Mr Trevor walked alone towards Berkeley Square. It was not the sort of moon that Mr Trevor remembered having seen before. It was, indeed, the sort of moon one usually meets only in books or wine. Mr Trevor was sober.

Nothing happened, Mr Trevor affirms, for quite a while; he just walked, and, at that corner where Davies Street and Mount Street join together the better to become Berkeley Square, stayed his walking, with the idea that he would soothe his depression with the fumes of a cigarette. His cigarette-case, however, was empty. All London, says Mr Trevor, appeared to be empty that night. Berkeley Square lay pallid and desolate: looking clear, not as though with moonlight, but with dead daylight; and never a voice to put life into the still streets, never a breeze to play with the bits of paper in the gutters or to sing among the dry boughs of the trees. Berkeley Square looked like nothing so much as an old stage-property that no one had any use for. Mr Trevor had no use at all for it; and became definitely antagonistic to it when a taxi-cab crawled wretchedly across the waste white expanse, and the driver, a man in a Homburg hat of green plush, looked into his face with a beseeching look.

'Taxi, sir?' he said.

Mr Trevor says that, not wanting to hurt the man's feelings, he just looked another way.

'Nice night, sir,' said the driver miserably, 'for a drive in an 'ackney-carriage.'

'I live,' said Mr Trevor with restraint, 'only a few doors off. So hackney-carriage to you.'

'No luck!' sighed the driver and accelerated madly away even as Mr Trevor changed his mind, for would it not be an idea to drive to the nearest coffee-stall and buy some cigarettes? This, however, he was not to do, for there was no other reply to his repeated calls of 'Taxi!' but certain heavy blows on the silence of Davies Street behind him.

'Wanting a taxi, sir?' said a voice which could only belong to a policeman.

'Certainly not,' said Mr Trevor bitterly. 'I never want a taxi. But now and then a taxi-driver thrusts himself on me and pays me to be seen in his cab, just to give it a tone. Next question.'

'Ho!' said the policeman thoughtfully.

'I beg your pardon?' said Mr Trevor.

'Ho!' said the policeman thoughtfully.

'The extent of your vocabulary,' said Mr Trevor gloomily, 'leads me to conclude that you must have been born a gentleman. Have you, in that case, a cigarette you could spare?'

'Gaspers,' said the policeman.

'Thank you,' said Mr Trevor, rejecting them. 'I am no stranger to ptomaine-poisoning.'

'That's funny,' said the policeman, 'your saying that. I was just thinking of death.'

'Death?' said Mr Trevor.

'You've said it,' said the policeman.

'I've said what?' said Mr Trevor.

'Death,' said the policeman.

'Oh, death!' said Mr Trevor. 'I always say "death", constable. It's my favourite word.'

'Ghoulish, I calls it, sir. Ghoulish, no less.'

'That entirely depends,' said Mr Trevor, 'on what you are talking about. In some things, ghoulish is as ghoulish does. In others, no.'

'You've said it,' said the policeman. 'But ghoulish goes, in this 'ere affair. One after the other lying in their own blood, and not a sign as to who's done it, not a sign!'

'Oh, come, constable! Tut-tut! Not even a thumbmark in the blood?'

'I'm telling you,' said the policeman severely. 'Corpses slit to ribbons all the way from 'Ampstead 'Eath to this 'ere Burkley Square. And why? That's what I asks myself. And why?'

'Of course,' said Mr Trevor gaily, 'there certainly have been a lot of murders lately. Ha-ha! But not, surely, as many as all that!'

'I'm coming to that,' said the policeman severely. 'We don't allow of the Press reporting more'n a quarter of them. No sir. That's wot it 'as come to, these larst few days. A more painful situation 'as rarely arisen in the hannals of British crime. The un'eard-of bestiality of the criminal may well baffle ordinary minds like yours and mine.'

'I don't believe a word of it!' snapped Mr Trevor.

'Ho, *you* don't!' said the policeman. '*You* don't!'

'That's right,' said Mr Trevor, 'I don't. Do you mean to stand there and tell me that I wouldn't 'ave 'eard – I mean, have heard of this criminal if he had really existed?'

'You're a gent,' said the policeman.

'You've said it,' said Mr Trevor.

'And gents,' said the policeman, 'know nothing. And what they do know is mouldy. Ever 'eard of Jack the Ripper?'

'Yes, I 'ave,' said Mr Trevor bitterly.

'Have is right, sir, if you'll excuse me. Well, Jack's death was never rightly proved, not it! So it might well be 'im at 'is old tricks again, even though 'e has been retired, in a manner of speaking, these forty years. Remorseless and hindiscriminate murder, swift and sure, was Jack's line, if you remember, sir.'

'Before my time,' said Mr Trevor gloomily.

'Well, Jack's method was just to slit 'em up with a razor, front-wise and from south to north, and not a blessed word spoken. No one's touched 'im yet, not for efficiency, but this new chap, 'e looks like catching Jack up. *And* at Jack's own game, razor and all. Makes a man fair sick, sir, to see the completed work. Just slits 'em up as clean as you or me might slit up a vealanam-pie. We was laying bets on 'im over at Vine Street only tonight, curious like to see whether 'e'd beat Jack's record. But it'll take some beating, I give you my word. Up to date this chap 'as only done in twelve in three weeks – not that that's 'alf bad, seeing as how 'e's new to the game, more or less.'

'Oh rather, more or less!' said Mr Trevor faintly. 'Twelve! Good God – only twelve! But why – why don't you catch the ghastly man?'

'Ho, why don't we!' said the policeman. 'Becos we don't know 'ow, that's why. Not us! It's the little one-corpse men we're good for, not these 'ere big artists. Look at Jack the Ripper – did we catch 'im? Did we? And look at Julian Raphael – did we catch 'im? I'm asking you.'

'I know you are,' said Mr Trevor gratefully. 'Thank you.'

'I don't want your thanks,' said the policeman. 'I'm just warning you.'

Mr Trevor gasped: 'Warning *me*!'

'You've said it,' said the policeman. 'You don't ought to be out alone at this time of night, an 'earty young chap like you. These twelve 'e's already done in were all 'earty young chaps. 'E's partial to 'em 'earty, I do believe. And social gents some of 'em was, too, with top 'ats to hand, just like you might be now, sir, coming 'ome from a smoking-concert. Jack the Ripper all over again, that's wot I say. Except that this 'ere new corpse-fancier, 'e don't seem to fancy women at all.'

'A chaps' murderer, what!' said Mr Trevor faintly. 'Ha-ha! What!'

'You've said it,' said the policeman. 'But you never know your luck, sir. And maybe as 'ow thirteen's your lucky number.'

Mr Trevor lays emphasis on the fact that throughout he treated the constable with the courtesy due from a gentleman to the law. He merely said: 'Constable, I am now going home. I do not like you very much. You are an alarmist. And I hope that when you go to sleep tonight your ears swell so that when you wake up in the morning you will be able to fly straight to Heaven and never be seen or heard of again. You and your razors and your thirteens!'

'Ho, they ain't mine, far from it!' said the policeman, and even as he spoke a voice crashed upon the silence from the direction of Mount Street. The voice belonged to a tall figure in black and white, and on his head was a top hat that shone under the pallid moon like a monstrous black jewel.

'That there,' said the policeman, 'is a Noise.'

'He's singing,' said Mr. Trevor.

'I'll teach 'im singing!' said the policeman.

Sang the voice:

> With an host of furious fancies,
> Whereof I am commander,
> With a burning spear
> And a horse of air
> To the wilderness I wander.

'You will,' said the policeman. 'Oh, you will!'

> By a knight of ghosts and shadows
> I summoned am to tourney
> Ten leagues beyond
> The wide world's end –
> Methinks it is no journey!'

'Not to Vine Street, it isn't,' said the policeman.

'Ho there!' cried the approaching voice. 'Who dares interrupt my song!'

'Beau Maturin!' cried Mr Trevor gladly. 'It's not you! Bravo, Beau Maturin! Sing, bless you, sing! For I am depressed.'

> From Heaven's Gate to Hampstead Heath
> Young Bacchus and his crew
> Came tumbling down, and o'er the town
> Their bursting trumpets blew.

'Fine big gent, your friend,' said the policeman thoughtfully.

> And when they heard that happy word
> Policemen leapt and ambled:
> The busmen pranced, the maidens danced,
> The men in bowlers gambolled.

'Big!' said Mr Trevor. 'Big? Let me tell you, constable, that the last time Mr Maturin hit Jack Dempsey, Dempsey bounced back from the floor so quick that he knocked Mr Maturin out on the rebound.'

Mr Trevor says that Beau Maturin came on through the night like an avenger through a wilderness, so little did he reck of cruel moons and rude policemen. Said he: 'Good evening, Ralph. Good evening, constable. Lo, I am in wine!'

'You've said it,' said the policeman.

'Gently, my dear! Or,' said Mr Maturin cordially, 'I will dot you one, and look at it which way you like it is a far far better thing to be in wine than in a hospital. Now, are there any good murders going tonight?'

'Going?' said the constable. 'I'm 'ere to see there ain't any coming. But I've just been telling this gent about some recent crises. Corpses slit to ribbons just as you or me might slit up a vealanam ...'

'Don't say that again!' snapped Mr Trevor.

'By Heaven, what's that?' sighed Mr Maturin; and, following his intent eyes, they saw, a yard or so behind them on the pavement, a something that glittered in the moonlight. Mr Trevor says that, without a thought for his own safety, he instantly took a step towards the thing, but that the policeman restrained him. It was Mr Maturin who picked the thing up. The policeman whistled thoughtfully.

'A razor, let's face it!' whispered Beau Maturin.

'*And* sharp!' said the policeman, thoughtfully testing the glittering blade with the ball of his thumb.

Mr Trevor says that he was never in his life less conscious of any feeling of excitement. He merely pointed out that he could swear there had been no razor there when he had come round the corner, and that, while he had stood there, no one had passed behind him.

'The chap that owns this razor,' said the policeman, emphasizing each word with a gesture of the blade, 'must 'ave slunk behind you and me as we stood 'ere talking and dropped it, maybe not finding it sharp enough for 'is purpose. What do you think, Mr Maturin?'

But Mr Maturin begged to be excused from thinking, protesting that men are in the hands of God, and God is in the hands of women and so what the devil is there to think about?

Mr Trevor says that the motive behind his remark at that moment, which was to the effect that he simply must have a drink, was merely that he was thirsty. A clock struck two.

'After hours,' said the policeman; and he seemed, Mr Trevor thought, to grin evilly.

'What do they know of hours,' sighed Mr Maturin, 'who only Ciro's know? Come, Ralph. My love, she jilted me but the other night. Therefore I will swim in wine, and thrice will I call upon her name when I am drowning. Constable, good-night to you.'

'Now I've warned you!' the policeman called after them. 'Don't go into any alleys or passages like Lansdowne Passage, else you'll be finding yourselves slit up like vealanam-pies.'

Maybe it was only the treacherous light of the moon, but Mr Trevor fancied as he looked back that the policeman, where he stood thoughtfully fingering the shining blade, seemed to be grinning evilly at them.

They walked in silence, their steps ringing sharp on the bitter-chill air. The night in the sky was pale at the white disdain of the moon. It was Mr Maturin who spoke at last, saying: 'There's too much talk of murder tonight. A man cannot go to bed on such crude talk. You know me, kid. Shall we go to "The Garden of My Grandmother"?'

At that moment a taxi-cab crawled across the moonlight; and the driver, a man in a Homburg hat of green plush, did not attempt to hide his pleasure at being able to satisfy the gentlemen's request to take them to 'The Garden of My Grandmother'.

Mr Trevor says that he has rarely chanced upon a more unsatisfactory taxi-cab than that driven by the man in the Homburg hat of green plush. By closing one's eyes one might perhaps have created an illusion of movement by reason of certain internal shrieks and commotions, but when one saw the slow procession of shops by the windows and the lampposts loitering by the curb, one was, as Beau Maturin pointed out, justified in believing that the hackney-cab in question was not going fast enough to outstrip a retired Czechoslovakian admiral in an egg-and-spoon race. Nor were they altogether surprised when the taxi-cab died on them in Conduit Street. The man in the Homburg hat of green plush jumped out and tried to re-start the engine. He failed. The gentlemen within waited the issue in silence. The silence, says Mr Trevor, grew terrible. But the taxi-cab moved not, and the man in the Homburg hat of green plush began, in his agitation, thumping the carburettor with his clenched fist.

'No petrol,' he pleaded. 'No petrol.'

Said Mr Trevor to Mr Maturin: 'Let us go. Let us leave this man.'

' 'Ere, my fare!' said the fellow.

'Your fare?' said Mr Maturin, with contracted brows. 'What do you mean, "your fare"?'

'Bob on the meter,' said the wretch.

'My friend will pay,' said Mr Maturin, and stalked away. Mr Trevor says that, while retaining throughout the course of that miserable night his undoubted flair for generosity, he could not but hold Beau Maturin's high-handed disavowal of his responsibilities against him; and he was hurrying after him up Conduit Street, turning over such phrases as might best point the occasion and make Mr Maturin ashamed of himself when that pretty gentleman swung round sharply and said: 'Ssh!'

But Mr Trevor was disinclined to Ssh, maintaining that Mr Maturin owed him ninepence.

'Ssh, you fool!' snapped Mr Maturin; and Mr Trevor had not obliged him for long before he discerned in the quietness of Conduit Street a small discordant noise, or rather, says Mr Trevor, a series of small discordant noises.

'She's crying, let's face it,' whispered Mr Maturin.

'She? Who?'

'Ssh!' snapped Mr Maturin.

They were at that point in Conduit Street where a turn to the right will bring one into a fat little street which looks blind but isn't, insomuch as close by the entrance to the Alpine Club Galleries there is a narrow passage or alley leading into Savile Row. Mr Trevor says that the repugnance with which he at that moment looked towards the darkness of that passage or alley had less than nothing to do with the bloodthirsty policeman's last words, but was due merely to an antipathy he had entertained towards all passages or alleys ever since George Tarlyon had seen a ghost in one. Mr Maturin and he stood for some minutes in the full light of the moon while, as though from the very heart of the opposite darkness, the lacerating tremors of weeping echoed about their ears.

'I can't bear it!' said Beau Maturin. 'Come along.' And he advanced towards the darkness, but Mr Trevor said he would not, pleading foot-trouble.

'Come,' said Beau Maturin, but Mr Trevor said: 'Tomorrow, yes. But not tonight.'

Then did Beau Maturin advance alone into the darkness towards the passage or alley, and with one pounce the darkness stole his top hat from the moon. Beau Maturin was invisible. The noise of weeping abated.

'Oi!' called Mr Trevor. 'Come back, you fool!'

'Ssh!' whispered the voice of Mr Maturin.

Mr Trevor said bitterly: 'You're swanking, that's all!'

'It's a girl!' whispered the voice of Mr Maturin, whereupon Mr Trevor, who yielded to no man in the chivalry of his address towards women, at once advanced, caught up Mr Maturin, and, without a thought for his own safety, was about to pass ahead of him, when Beau Maturin had the bad taste to whisper, ''Ware razors!' and thus again held the lead.

She who wept, now almost inaudibly, was a dark shape just within the passage. Her face, says Mr Trevor, was not visible, yet her shadow had not those rather surprising contours which one generally associates with women who weep in the night.

'Madam,' began Mr Maturin.

'Oh!' sobbed the gentle voice. 'He is insulting me!'

Mr Trevor lays some emphasis on the fact that throughout the course of that miserable night his manners were a pattern of courtliness. Thinking, however, that a young lady in a situation so lachrymose would react more favourably to a fatherly tone, he said:

'My child, we hope ...'

'Ah,' sobbed the gentle voice. 'Please go away, please! I am *not* that sort!'

'Come, come!' said Mr Maturin. 'It is us whom you insult with a suspicion so disagreeable. My friend and I are not of the sort to commit ourselves to so low a process as that which is called, I believe, "picking up".'

'We have, as a matter of fact, friends of our own,' said Mr Trevor haughtily.

'Speaking generally,' said Mr Maturin, 'women like us. Time over again I have had to sacrifice my friendship with a man in order to retain his wife's respect.'

'Ah, you are a man of honour!' sobbed the young lady.

'We are two men of honour,' said Mr Trevor.

'And far,' said Mr Maturin warmly, 'from intending you any mischief, we merely thought, on hearing you weeping . . .'

'You *heard* me, sir!'

'From Conduit Street,' said Mr Trevor severely, whereupon Mr Maturin lifted up his voice and sang:

> From Conduit Street, from Conduit Street,
>   The street of ties and tailors:
> From Conduit Street, from Conduit Street,
>   A shocking street for trousers.

'Oh!' sobbed the young lady. 'Is this chivalry?'

'Trousers,' said Mr Maturin, 'are closely connected with chivalry, insomuch as he who commits chivalry without them is to be considered a rude fellow. But, child,' Mr Maturin protested sincerely, 'we addressed you only in the hope that we might be of some service in the extremity of your grief. I assure you that you can trust us, for since we are no longer soldiers, rape and crime have ceased to attract us. However, you do not need us. We were wrong. We will go.'

'It was I who was wrong!' came the low voice; and Mr Trevor says that only then did the young lady raise her face, when it was instantly as though the beauty of that small face sent the surrounding darkness scurrying away. Not, however, that Mr Trevor was impressed altogether in the young lady's favour. Her eyes, which were large, dark, and charming, appeared to rest on handsome Beau Maturin with an intentness which Mr Trevor can only describe as bold; while her disregard of his own presence might have hurt him had he, says Mr Trevor, cared two pins for that kind of thing.

'You see, I have not eaten today,' the young lady told Beau Maturin, who cried: 'But, then, we *can* help you!'

'Ah, how do I know! Please,' the young lady began weeping again, and Mr Trevor says that had he not hardened his heart he could not say what he might not have done. 'Please, sirs, I simply do not know what to do! I am so unhappy, so alone – oh, but you cannot imagine! You are gentlemen?'

'Speaking for my friend,' said Mr Maturin warmly, 'he has been asked to resign from Buck's Club only after repeated bankruptcies.'

'Mr Maturin,' said Mr Trevor, 'has in his time been cashiered from no less a regiment than the Coldstream Guards.'

The young lady did not, however, favour Mr Trevor with so much as a glance, never once taking her beautiful eyes from the handsome face of Beau Maturin. Indeed, throughout the course of that miserable night she admirably controlled any interest Mr Trevor might have aroused in her, which Mr Trevor can only account for by the supposition that she must have been warned against him. Beau Maturin, meanwhile, had taken the young lady's arm, a familiarity with which Mr Trevor cannot too strongly dissociate himself, and was saying:

'Child, you may come with us, if not with honour, at least with safety. And while you refresh yourself with food and drink you can tell us, if you please, the tale of your troubles. Can't she, Ralph?'

'I don't see,' said Mr Trevor, 'what good we can do.'

'Your friend,' said the young lady sadly to Beau Maturin, 'does not like me. Perhaps you had better leave me alone to my misery.'

'My friend,' said Beau Maturin, guiding her steps down the fat little street towards Conduit Street, 'likes you only too well, but is restraining himself for fear of your displeasure. Moreover, he cannot quickly adapt himself to the company of ingenuous young ladies, for he goes a good deal into society, where somewhat cruder methods obtain.'

'But oh, where are you taking me to?' suddenly cried the young lady.

'To "The Garden of My Grandmother",' said Mr Trevor bitterly, and presently they found a taxi-cab on Regent Street which quickly delivered them at the place in Leicester Square. Mr Trevor cannot help priding himself on the agility with which he leapt out of that taxi-cab, saying to the driver: 'My friend will pay.'

But Mr Maturin, engrossed in paying those little attentions to the young lady which really attractive men, says Mr Trevor, can afford to neglect, told the driver to wait, and when the driver said he did not want to wait, to go and boil his head.

Mr Trevor describes 'The Garden of My Grandmother' in some detail, but that would be of interest only to the specialist. The place was lately raided, and is now closed; and remained open so long as it did only with the help of such devices as commend themselves to those aliens who know the laws of the land only to circumvent them. For some time, indeed, the police did not even know of its existence as a night-club, for the entrance to the place was through two mean-looking doors several yards apart, on one of which was boldly inscribed the word 'Gentlemen' and on the other 'Ladies'.

Within, all was gaiety and chic. From the respectable night-clubs and restaurants, all closed by this hour, would come the *jeunesse* of England; and an appetizing smell of kippers brought new life to the jaded senses of young ladies, while young gentlemen cleverly contrived to give the appearance of drinking ginger-ale by taking their champagne through straws. Mr Trevor says, however, that there was not the smallest chance of the place being raided on the night in question, for among the company was a Prince of the Blood; and it is an unwritten law in the Metropolitan Police Force that no night-club shall be raided while a Prince of the Blood is pulling a party therein.

The young lady and our two gentlemen were presently refreshing themselves at a table in a secluded corner; and when at last only the wine was left before them Mr Maturin assumed his courtliest manner to beg the young lady to tell her tale, and in detail, if she thought its relation would relieve her at all. She thought, with all the pensive beauty of her dark eyes, that it would, and immediately began on the following tale:

'I am (she said) twenty-three years old, and although I once spent two years in England at a boarding-school in Croydon, my life hitherto has been lived entirely in Bulgaria. My father was a Bulgar of the name of Samson Samsonovitch Samsonoff, my mother an Englishwoman of the Lancashire branch of the race of Jones, and for her tragic death in a railway accident just over a year ago I shall grieve all my life: which, I cannot help praying, may be a short one, for I weary of the insensate cruelties that every new day opens out for me.

'I must tell you that my mother was an unusual woman, of rigid principles, lofty ideals, and a profound feeling for the grace and dignity of the English tongue, in which, in spite of my father's opposition, for the Samsonoffs are a bitter proud race, she made me proficient at an early age. Never had this admirable woman a thought in her life that was not directed towards furthering her husband's welfare and to obtaining the happiness of her only child; and I am convinced that my father had not met his cruel death two months ago had she been spared to counsel him.

'My father came of an ancient Macedonian house. For hundreds of years a bearer of the name of Samson Samsonovitch Samsonoff has trod the stark hillsides of the Balkans and raided the sweet, rich valleys about Philippopolis. As brigands, the Samsonoffs had never a rival; as *comitadjis,* in war or peace, their name was a name for heroism and of terror; while as assassins – for the domestic economy of Bulgaria has ever demanded the occasional services of a hawk's eye and a ruthless hand – a Samsonoff has been honourably associated with some of the most memorable coups in Balkan history. I am well aware that pride of family has exercised a base dominion over the minds of many good men and women; yet I do not hesitate to confess that it is with almost unbearable regret that I look upon the fact that I, a wretched girl, am the last and only remnant of our once proud house.

'Such a man it was with whom my mother, while accompanying her father, a civil engineer, through Bulgaria, married. Nor did it need anything less than the ardour of her love and the strength of her character to seduce a Samson Samsonovitch from the dour dominion of the hills to the conventional life of the valleys. I loved my father, but cannot be blind to the grave flaws in his character. A tall, hairy man, with a beard such as would have appalled your English description of Beaver, he was subject to ungovernable tempers and, occasionally, to regrettable lapses from that moral code which is such an attractive feature of English domestic life. Ah, you who live in the content and plenty of so civilized a land, how can you even imagine the horrors of lawlessness that obtain among primitive peoples! Had not that good woman my mother always willed him to loving-kindness, Samsonovitch Samsonoff had more than once spilled the blood of his dearest friends in the heat of some petty tavern brawl.

'We lived in a farmhouse in what is surely the loveliest valley in the world, that which is called the Valley of the Roses, and whence is given to the world that exquisite essence known as attar of roses. Our little household in that valley was a happy and united one; more and more infrequent became my father's demoniac tempers;

and, but for his intolerance of fools and cravens, you had taken the last of the Samsonoffs to be a part of the life of the valley-men, of whose industry, the cultivation of roses, he rapidly became a master.

'Thus we come to the time which I now think of as two months before my mother's death. My father had attained to a certain degree of wealth, and was ever enticing my mother with dreams of a prolonged visit to her beloved birthplace, Southport, which is, I believe, a pretty town on the seaboard of Lancashire, and which I look forward with delight to visiting. While enticing her, however, with such visions, he did not hesitate to warn her that she must wait on the issue of his fanciful hobby, which daily grew on him; for the last of the Samsonoffs had become an inventor of flowers!

'You may well look bewildered. But had you known my father you would in some measure have understood how a man, of an extreme audacity of temperament, might be driven into any fanciful pursuit that might lend a spice to a life of intolerable gentility. Nor was that pursuit so fanciful as might at first appear to those of conventionally studious minds: my father had a profound knowledge of the anatomy of flowers; and was in the habit of saying that he could not but think that the mind of man had hitherto neglected the invention and cultivation of the most agreeable variations. In fine, the tempestuous but simple mind of Samsonovitch Samsonoff had been captivated by the possibility of growing green carnations.

'My mother and I were, naturally enough, not at all averse from his practising so gentle a hobby as the invention and cultivation of improbable flowers. And it was long before we even dreamt of the evil consequences that might attend so inoffensive an ambition. But my poor mother was soon to be rid of the anxieties of this life.

'One day she and I were sitting in the garden discussing the English fashion-journals, when, silently as a cloud, my father came out of the house and looked towards us in the half-frowning, half-smiling way of his best mood. Tall and patriarchal, he came towards us – and in his hand we saw a flower with a long slender stem, and we stared at it as though we could not believe our eyes, for it was a green carnation!

' "You have painted it!" we cried, my mother and I, for his success had seemed to us as remote as the stars.

' "I have *made* it!" said my father, and he smiled into his beard, which was ever his one confidential friend. "Women, I have made it in my laboratory. And as I have made this I can make thousands, millions, and thousands of millions!"

'He waved a closely-covered piece of paper towards me. "My daughter," he said, "here is your dower, your heritage. I am too old to burden myself with the cares of great riches, but by the help of this paper, you, my beloved child, will become an heiress who may condescend to an emperor or an American. We will not lose a minute before going to England, the land of honest men, to put the matter of the patent in train. For on this paper is written the formula by which green carnations, as well as all previously known varieties of carnations, can be *made* instead of grown. *Made*, I say, instead of grown! Women, do you understand what it is that I have achieved? I have stolen something of the secret of the sun!"

' "Samson, boast not!" cried my mother, but he laughed at her and fondled me, while I stared in great wonder at the slip of paper that fluttered in his hand, and dreamed the fair dreams of wealth and happiness in a civilized country. Ah, me, ah me, the ill-fated excellence of dreams! For here I am in the most civilized country in the world, a pauper, and more wretched than a pauper!

'Our preparations for removal to England were not far advanced before that happened which brought the first cruel turn to our fortunes. On an evil day my mother set out to Vienna to buy some trivial thing, and – but I cannot speak of that, how she was returned to us a mangled corpse, her dear features mutilated beyond recognition by the fury of the railway accident.

'My father took his sudden loss strangely: it was as though he was deprived at one blow of all the balance, the restraint, with which so many years of my mother's influence had softened the dangerous temper of the Samsonoff; and the brooding silence he put upon his surroundings clamoured with black thoughts. Worst of all, he began again to frequent the taverns in the valley, wherein he seemed to find solace in goading to fury the craven-hearted lowlanders among whom he had lived in peace for so long. The Samsonoff, in short, seemed rapidly to be reverting to type; and I, his daughter, must stand by and do nothing, for my influence over him was never but of the pettiest sort.

'The weeks passed, and our preparations for departure to England proceeded at the soberest pace. In England we were going to stay with my mother's brother, a saintly man of some little property who lived a retired life in London, and whose heir I would in due course be, since he was himself without wife or children.

'My father, never notable for the agreeable qualities of discretion and reticence, soon spread about the report of his discovery of the green carnation. He could not resist boasting of it in his cups, of the formula with which he could always make them, of the fortune he must inevitably make. Nor did he hesitate to taunt the men of the valley, they who came of generations of flower-growers, with his own success in an occupation which, he said, he had never undertaken but at a woman's persuasion, since it could be regarded as manly only by those who would describe as manly the painted face of a Circassian eunuch. Thus he would taunt them, laughing me to scorn when I ventured to point out that even worms will turn and cravens conspire. Woe and woe to the dour and high-handed in a world of polity, for their fate shall surely find them out!

'One day, having been to the village to procure some yeast for the making of a *yaourt* or *yawort*, which is that same Bulgarian "sour milk" so strongly recommended to Anglo-Saxon digestions, I was startled, as I walked up the path to the door, by the bruit of loud, rough voices. Only too soon was my fear turned to horror. One of the voices was my father's, arrogant and harsh as only his could be, with a sneer like a snake running through it. The other I could not recognize, but could hear only too well that it had not the soft accents of the men of the valley; and when, afraid to enter, I peered in through the window, I saw my father in violent altercation with a man his equal in stature and demeanour – another bearded giant, as fair as my father was dark, and with the livid eyes of a wolf.

'What was my horror on recognizing him as Michaelis the *comitadji*, the notorious and brutal Michaelis of the hills. The Michaelis and the Samsonovitch Samsonoffs had always been the equal kings of the *banditti*, and, in many a fight between Christian and Turk, the equal champions of the Cross against the Crescent. And now, as I could hear through the window, the last of the Michaelis was asking of the last of the Samsonoffs some of his great wealth, that he might arm and munition his troop to the latest mode.

'My father threw back his head and laughed. But his laugh had cost him dear had I not screamed a warning, for the Michaelis with the wolfish eyes had raised a broad knife. My father leapt to one side, and taking up the first thing that came to hand, a heavy bottle of mastic, crashed it down like an axe on the fair giant's head; and then, without so much as a glance at the unconscious man, and massive though the Michaelis was, slung him over his shoulder, strode out of the house and garden, and flung him into the middle of the roadway, where he lay for long moaning savagely with the pain of his broken head. I had gone to the aid of the wretch, but my father would not let me, saying that no Michaelis ever yet died of a slap on the crown and that a little blood-letting would clear the mans' mind of his boyish fancies. Ah, if it had!

'It was at a late hour of the very next night – for since my mother's death my father would loiter in the taverns until all hours – that his hoarse voice roused me from my sleep; and on descending I found him raging about the kitchen like a wounded tiger, his clothes in disorder and showing grim dark stains that, as I clung to him foully wetted my hands. I prayed him, in an access of terror, to tell me he was not hurt, for what other protection than him had I in that murderous land?

' "I am not hurt, child," he growled impatiently. "But I have been driven to hurt some so that they can never again feel pain."

'They had ambushed him; the cowards, as he came home through the wood – as though a hundred of those maggots of the valley could slay a Samsonovitch Samsonoff! My father had caught the last of them by the throat, and the trembling coward had saved himself by confessing the plot. It appeared that it was they who had persuaded the Michaelis to visit us the day before, inflaming his fancy with tales of the discovery of the carnation and of the great riches the Samsonoff had concealed about the house. And the Michaelis had come to our house not for part of my father's wealth but for all he could find, as also for the secret of the carnation, which he might sell at a great price to some Jew in Sofia – he had come to kill my father!

' "And I, like a fool," cried my father, "only broke the skin of his wolfish head! Girl, we must be off at once! I have not lived in unwilling peace all these years to die like a rat; and now that these weak idiots have failed to kill me Michaelis and his troop will surround the house, and who shall escape the wolves of the hills? Now linger not for your clothes and fineries. Grigory Eshekovitch has horses for us at the edge of the wood, and we can make Philippopolis by the morning. Here is all our money in notes. Take them, so that you will be provided for should these scum get me. And the formula – take care of the formula, child, for that is your fortune! Should I have to stay behind, your mother's brother in England is a good man and will probably not rob you of more than half the profits of it."

'And so we came to leave our beloved home, stealing like thieves through the darkness of a moonless night. How shall I ever forget those desperate moments! Our farm lay far from any other habitation, and a long sloping lane joined our pastures to the extensive Karaloff Wood, a wood always evoked by Bulgarian poets of past centuries as the home of vampires and the kennel of the hounds of hell.

'There, at its borders, Grigory Eshekovitch, a homely man devoted to our interests, awaited us with two horses; and, although I could not see his face in the darkness, I could imagine by the tremor of his never very assured voice how pallid, indeed green, it must have been; for poor Grigory Eshekovitch suffered from some internal affection, which had the effect of establishing his complexion very uncertainly.

' "Have you seen any one in the wood?" my father asked him.

' "No, but I have heard noises," Grigory Eshekovitch trembled.

' "Bah!" growled my father. "That was the chattering of your own miserable teeth."

'I wonder what has happened to poor Grigory Eshekovitch, whether he survived that hideous night. We left him there, a trembling figure on the borders of the wood, while we put our horses into the heart of that darkness; and I tried to find solace in our desperate situation by looking forward to the safety and comfort of our approaching life in England. Little I knew that I was to suffer such agonies of fear in this huge city that I would wish myself back in the land of wolves!

'My dreams were shattered by a low growl from my father, and we pulled up our horses, listening intently. By this time we were about half-way through the wood; and had we not known the place by heart we had long since lost our way, for the curtain of leaves between us and the faint light of the stars made the place so black that we could not even see the faintest glimmer of each other. At last my father whispered that it was all right, and we were in the act of spurring our tired horses for the last dash through the wood when torches flamed on all sides, and we stood as in the tortured light of a crypt in moonlight.

' "Samson Samsonovitch," cried a hoarse voice, and like a stab at my heart I knew it for the voice of the Michaelis, "we hope your sins are not too heavy, for your time has come."

'It ill becomes a girl to boast of her parent; but shall I neglect to mention the stern fortitude, the patriarchal resignation, the monumental bravery of my father, how he sat his horse still as a rock in a tempest and only his lips moved in a gentle whisper to me. "Child, save yourself," said he, and that was his farewell. "I command you to go – to save yourself and my secret from these hounds. Maybe I too will get through. God is as good to us as we deserve. Head right through them. Their aim, between you and me, will be so unsure that we might both escape. Go, and God go with you!"

'Can you ask me to remember the details of the awful moment? The darkness, the flaming torches, the hoarse cries of the bandits as they rode in on us, my father's great courage – all these combined to produce in me a state for which the word "terror" seems altogether too homely. Perhaps I should not have left my father. Perhaps I should have died with him. I did not know what I was doing. Blindly as in a nightmare I spurred my horse midway between two moving torches. The horse, startled already, flew madly as the wind. Cries, curses, shots seemed to sweep about me, envelop me, but terror lent wings to my horse, and the shots and shouts faded behind me as phantoms might fade in a furious wind. Last of all came a fearful fusillade of shots, then a silence broken only by the harsh rustle of the bracken under my horse, which with the livid intelligence of fear, did not stop before we reached Philippopolis in the dawn.

'I was never to see my father again. Until noon of the next day I sat anxiously in the only decent inn of the ancient town, praying that some act of Providence had come to his aid and that he might at any moment appear; when, from a loquacious person, who did not know my name, I heard that the last of the Samsonoffs had that morning been found in Karaloff Wood nailed to a tree-trunk with eighteen bullet wounds in his body.

'I will spare you my reflections on the pass in which I then found myself. No young girl was ever so completely alone as she who sat the day through in the parlour of the Bulgarian inn, trying to summon the energy with which to arrange for her long journey on the Orient Express to England.

'Arrived in London, I at once set out to my uncle's house in Golgotha Road, Golders Green. I was a little surprised that he had not met me at the station, for I had warned him of my arrival by telegram; but, knowing he was a gentleman of particular though agreeable habits, it was with a sufficiently good heart that I rang the bell of his tall, gloomy house, which stood at the end of a genteel street of exactly similar houses.

'Allow me, if you please, to hurry over the relation of my further misfortunes. My uncle had died of a clot of blood on the heart a week before my arrival. His property he had, of course, left to me; and I could instantly take possession of his house in Golgotha Road. I was utterly alone.

'That was four weeks ago. Though entirely without friends or acquaintance – for my uncle's lawyer, Mr Tarbold, was a man who bore his own lack of easy conversation and human sympathy with a resigned fortitude worthy of more wretched sorrows – I passed the first two weeks pleasantly enough in arranging the house to my taste, in engaging a housekeeper and training her to my ways, and in wondering how I must proceed as regards the patenting and exploiting of the carnation, the formula for which I kept locked in a secret drawer of my toilet-table.

'At the end of three weeks – one week ago – my housekeeper gave me notice of her instant departure, saying that no consideration would persuade her to spend another night in the house. She was, it seemed, psychic, and the atmosphere of the house, which was certainly oppressive, weighed heavily on her mind. She had heard noises in the night, she affirmed, and also spoke indignantly of an unpleasant smell in the basement of the house, a musty smell which she for one made no bones of recognizing as of a graveyard consistency; and if she did not know a graveyard smell, she asked, from one of decent origins, who did, for she had buried three husbands?

'Of course I laughed at her tremors, for I am not naturally of a nervous temper, and when she insisted on leaving that very day I was not at all disturbed. Nor did I instantly make inquiries for another woman, for I could very well manage by myself, and the work of the house, I thought, must help to fill in the awful spaces made by the utter lack of companionship. As to any nervousness at being left entirely alone in a house, surrounded as it was by the amenities of Golders Green, I never gave a thought to it, for I had been inured to a reasonable solitude all my life. And, putting up a notice of "Apartments to Let" in one of the ground-floor windows,

I set about the business of the house in something of a spirit of adventure natural, if I may say so, to one of my years.

'That, as I have said, was one week ago; and the very next day but one after my housekeeper had left me was to see my hardly-won peace shattered at one blow. I do not know if you gentlemen are aware of the mode of life that obtains in Golders Green; but I must tell you that the natives of that quarter do not discourage the activities of barrel-organs – a somewhat surprising exercise of restraint to one who has been accustomed to the dolorous and beautiful songs of the Balkan *cziganes*. It is true, however, that these barrel-organs are played mostly by foreigners, and I have been given to understand that foreigners are one of the most sacred institutions of this great country.

'The very next morning after my housekeeper had left me I was distracted from my work by a particularly disagreeable combination of sounds, which, I had no doubt, could come only from a barrel-organ not of the first order and the untrained voice of its owner. A little amused, I looked out of the window – and with a heart how still leapt back into the room, for the face of the organ-grinder was the face of the Michaelis!

'I spent an hour of agony in wondering if he had seen me, for how could I doubt but that he had followed me to England in quest of the formula of the carnation? At last, however, I decided that he could not have seen me, and I was in some degree calmed by the decreasing noise of the barrel-organ as it inflicted itself on more distant streets. London, I told myself, was a very large city; it was not possible that the Michaelis could have the faintest idea in what part of it I lodged; and it could only have been by the most unfortunate combination of chances that he had brought his wretched organ into Golgotha Road. Nevertheless I took the precaution to withdraw the notice of Apartments to Let from the window, lest yet another unfortunate combination of chances should lead him or his minions to search for lodging in my house.

'The next day passed quietly enough. I went out shopping with a veil over my face, for reasons you can well understand. And little did I dream that the approaching terror was to come from a quarter which would only be known to the Michaelis when he was dead.

'That evening in my bedroom, in a curious moment of forgetfulness, I chanced to pull the bell-rope. I wanted some hot water, had for the moment forgotten that the silly woman had left me, and only remembered it with a smile when, far down in the basement, I heard the thin clatter of the bell. The bathroom was some way down the passage, and I had reached the door, empty jug in hand, when I was arrested by the sound of approaching steps! They were very faint, they seemed to be coming up from the basement, as though in answer to the bell! I pressed my hand to my forehead in a frantic attempt to collect my wits, and I have no hesitation in saying that for those few moments I was near insane. The accumulation of terrors in my recent life had, I thought, unhinged my mind; and I must that day have engaged a servant and forgotten it.

'Meantime the steps ascended, slowly, steadily, exactly as an elderly servant might ascend in answer to the bell; and as they ascended I was driven, I cannot tell you how, somehow past fear. Maybe it was the blood of the Samsonoffs at last raging in me. I was not afraid, and, without locking the door, I withdrew to a far corner of the room, awaiting the moment when the steps must reach the door. I must not forget to add that the empty jug was still in my hand.

'Steadily, but with a shuffling as of carpet-slippers, the steps came up the passage: slowly the door was opened, and a gaunt, grey-haired woman in musty black stood there, eyeing me with strange contempt. Fear returned, enveloped me, shook me, and I sobbed, I screamed. The woman did not move, did not speak, but stood there, gaunt and grey and dry, eyeing me with a strange contempt; and on her lined face there was such an undreamt-of expression of evil. Yet I recognized her.

'I must tell you that my mother had often, in telling me of her brother, spoken of his confidential housekeeper. My mother was a plain-spoken woman, and I had gathered from her that the woman had exercised some vulgar art to enthral my poor uncle and had dominated him, to his hurt, in all things. At the news of this woman's death just before my mother's tragic end, she had been unable to resist an expression of relief; and I, on having taken possession of the house a few weeks before, had examined with great interest, as girls will, the various photographs of her that stood about the rooms.

'It was from these that I recognized the woman who stood in the doorway. But she was dead, surely she had died more than a year ago! Yet there she now stood, eyeing me with that strange contempt – with such contempt, indeed, that I, reacting from fear to anger, sternly demanded of her what she did there and what she wanted.

'She was silent. That was perhaps the most awful moment of all – but no, no, there was worse to come! For, sobbing with terror, I hurled the empty jug at her vile face with a precision of aim which now astonishes me: but she did not waver so much as the fraction of an inch as the jug came straight at her – and, passing through her head, smashed into pieces against the wall of the passage outside. I must have swooned where I stood, for when I was again conscious of my surroundings she was gone: I was alone; but, far down in the house, I could hear the shuffling steps, retreating, descending, to the foul shades whence she had come.

'Now I am one who cannot bear any imposition; and unable, despite the witness of my own eyes, to believe in the psychic character of the intruder, I ran out of the room and in hot pursuit down the stairs. The gaunt woman must have descended with a swiftness surprising in one of her years, for I could only see her shadow far below, on the last flight of stairs that would take her to the basement. Into that lower darkness, I must confess, I had not the courage to follow her; and still less so when, on peering down the pitch-dark stairs into the kitchen, I was assailed by that musty smell which my housekeeper had spoken of with such indignant conviction as of a graveyard consistency.

'I locked the door of my room and slept, I need scarcely say, but ill that night. However, in the cheerful light of the following morning, I was inclined, as who would not, to pooh-pooh the incredible events of the previous night; and again pulled the bell-rope, just to see the event, if any. There was; and, unable to await the ascent of the shuffling steps, I crammed on a hat and ran down the stairs.

'The woman was coming upstairs, steadily, inevitably. As she heard me descending she stopped and looked up, and I cannot describe the effect that the diabolical wickedness of her face had on me in the clear daylight. I stopped, was rooted there, could not move. To get to the front door I must pass the foul thing, and that I could not summon the courage to do. And then she raised an arm, as though to show me something, and I saw the blade of a razor shining in her hand. You may well shudder, gentlemen!

'When I came to, it was to find myself lying at the foot of the stairs, whither I must have fallen, and the foul thing gone. Why she did not kill me, I do not know. God will pardon me for saying that maybe it had been better if she had, for what miseries are not still in store for me! Trembling and weak, I reached the door and impelled myself into the clear air of morning. Nor could the fact that I had forgotten my veil, and the consequent fear of the Michaelis, persuade me to re-enter that house until I had regained some degree of calmness.

'All day long I wandered about, knowing neither what to do nor where to go. I am not without some worldly sense, and I knew what little assistance the police could give me in such a dilemma, even had they believed me; while, as for the lawyer, Mr Tarbold, how could I face a man of so little sympathy in ordinary things with such an extraordinary tale?

'Towards ten o'clock that night, I determined to return and risk another night in that house; I was desperate with weariness and hunger; and could not buy food nor lodging for the night, for in my flight I had forgotten my purse; while I argued to myself that if, after all, she had intended to murder me, she could without any difficulty have done so that morning when I lay unconscious on the stairs.

'My bravery, however, did not help me to ascend the stairs to my bedroom with any resolution. I stole upstairs, myself verily like a phantom. But, hearing no sound in the house, I plucked up the courage to switch on the light on my bedroom landing. My bedroom-door stood open, but I could not remember whether or not I had left it so that morning. It was probable, in my hasty descent. I tiptoed to it and peered in – and I take the liberty to wonder whether any man, was he never such a lion-heart, had been less disturbed than I at the sight which the light of the moon revealed to my eyes.

'The Michaelis lay full length on the floor, his great fair beard darkened with his blood, which came, I saw, from a great gash behind his ear. Across him, with her back to me, sat straddled the gaunt, foul thing, as silent as the grave. Yet even my terror could not overcome my curiosity as to her actions, for she kept on lowering and raising her left hand to and from the Michaelis's beard, while with her right, in which shone the bloody razor, she sawed the air from side to side. I could not realize what that vile shape was doing – I could, and could not admit the realization. For with her left hand she was plucking out one by one the long hairs of the Michaelis's beard, while with the razor in her right she was slicing them to the floor!

'I must have gasped, made some noise, for she heard me; and, turning on me and brandishing the dripping razor, she snarled like an animal and leapt towards me. But I am young and quick, and managed just in time to reach the street door and slam it against her enraged pursuit.

'That was last night. Since then, gentlemen, I have wandered about the streets of London, resting a little among the poor people in the parks. I have had no food, for what money I have is in that house, together with the formula for the green carnation; but nothing, not death by exposure nor death by starvation, would induce me to return to the house in Golders Green while it is haunted by that foul presence. Is she a homicidal lunatic or a phantom from hell? I do not know, I am too tired to care. I have told you two gentlemen my story because you seem kind and capable, and I can only pray that I have not wearied you overmuch. But I do beg you to believe that nothing is farther from my mind than to ask, and indeed nothing would induce me to accept, anything from you but the generous sympathy of your understanding and the advice of your chivalrous intelligence. My tale is finished, gentlemen. And, alas, am not I?'

Mr Trevor is somewhat confused in his relation of the course of events immediately subsequent to Miss Samsonoff's narrative. During its course he had time, he says, to study the young lady's beauty, which, though of a very superior order, was a little too innocent and insipid for his taste. His judgment, however, cannot be entirely fair, for such was the direction of the young lady's eyes that Mr Trevor could judge her by her features only. As to the story itself, Mr Trevor says that, while yielding to no one in his liking for a good story, he could not see his way to considering Miss Samsonoff's notable either for interest, entertainment, or that human note of stark realism which makes for conviction; and while, in the ordinary way, a murderer was to him like a magnet, he could not rouse himself to feel irresistibly attracted towards the ghoul of Golders Green. It was therefore with surprise not unmixed with pain that he heard Mr Maturin saying:

'Ralph, we are in luck!'

'To what,' Mr Trevor could not entirely cleanse his voice from the impurity of sarcasm, 'to what do you refer?' But it was not without some compunction that he heard the young lady sigh miserably to Beau Maturin:

'I am afraid I have wearied your friend. Forgive me.'

'My friend,' said Beau Maturin gently, 'is an ass. In point of fact, Miss Samsonoff, far from wearying us, you have put us under a great obligation ...'

'Ah, you are kind!' the young lady was moved to sob.

'On the contrary,' Mr Maturin warmly protested, 'I am selfish. I gather you have not been reading the newspapers lately? Had you done so, you would have read of a murderer who has recently been loose in London and has so far evaded not only capture but even identification. So far as the public know through the newspapers, this criminal has been responsible for only two or three murders; but this very night my friend and I have had private information to the effect that within the last few weeks twelve mutilated corpses have been found in various parts of London; to which we must now, no doubt, add a thirteenth, the remains of your late enemy, Mr Michaelis. But where *your* information,' said Mr Maturin gallantly, 'is especially valuable is that the police do not dream that the criminal is of your sex. To my friend and me it is this original point that invests the pursuit ...'

'Pursuit?' Mr Trevor could not help starting.

'... with,' said Mr Maturin coldly, 'an added charm. And now with your permission, Miss Samsonoff, we will not only return to you your formula, as to the financial worth of which I cannot entirely share your late parent's optimism, but also ...'

'Also,' Mr Trevor said with restraint, 'we will first of all call at Vine Street and borrow a few policemen.'

'Oh yes!' the young lady said eagerly. 'We will be sure to need some policemen. Please get some policemen. They will listen to you.'

'I do not find an audience so difficult to find as all that,' said Mr Maturin coldly. 'The London police, Miss Samsonoff, are delightful, but rather on the dull side. They are much given to standing in the middle of crowded roads and dreaming, and in even your short stay in London you must have observed what a serious, nay intolerable, obstruction they are to the traffic. No, no, my friend and I will get this murderer ourselves. Come, Miss Samsonoff.'

'But I dare not come with you!' cried the young lady. 'I simply dare not approach that house again! May I not await your return here?'

'The attacks of ten murderers,' said Mr Maturin indignantly, 'cannot disfigure your person more violently than being left alone in a night-club will disfigure your reputation. Bulgarians may be violent, Miss Samsonoff. But lounge-lizards are low dogs.'

Mr Trevor says that he was so plunged in thought that he did not arise from the table with his usual agility; and the first notice he had that Mr Maturin had risen and was nearly at the door was on hearing him waive aside a pursuing waiter with the damnable words: 'My friend will pay.'

Without, the taxi-cab was still waiting. Its driver, says Mr Trevor, was one of those stout men of little speech and impatient demeanour: on which at this moment was plainly written the fact that he had been disagreeably affected by waiting in the cold for nearly two hours; and on Mr Maturin's sternly giving him a Golders Green direction he just looked at our two gentlemen and appeared to struggle with an impediment in his throat.

Golgotha Road was, as the young lady had described it, a genteel street of tall, gloomy houses. Mr Trevor says that he cannot remember when he liked the look of a street less. The taxi-cab had not penetrated far therein when Miss Samsonoff timidly begged Mr Maturin to stop its farther progress, pointing out that she could not bear to wait immediately opposite the house, and would, indeed, have preferred to await her brave cavaliers in an altogether different part of London. Mr Maturin, however, soothed her fears; and, gay as a schoolboy, took the key of the house from her reluctant fingers and was jumping from the cab when Miss Samsonoff cried:

'But surely you have weapons!'

Mr Trevor says that, while yielding to no one in deploring the use of weapons in daily life, in this particular instance the young lady's words struck him as full of a practical grasp of the situation.

'Of course,' said Mr Trevor nonchalantly, 'we must have weapons. How stupid of us to have forgotten! I will go back to my flat and get some. I won't be gone a moment.'

'That's right,' Mr Maturin agreed, 'because you won't be gone at all. My dear Miss Samsonoff, my friend and I do not need weapons. We put our trust in God and St George. Come along, Ralph. Miss Samsonoff, we will be back in a few moments.'

'And wot do I do?' asked the taxi-driver.

'Nothing,' cried Mr Maturin gaily. 'Nothing at all. Aren't you lucky!'

The house which the young lady had pointed out to them had an air of even gloomier gentility than the others, and Mr Trevor says he cannot remember when he liked the look of a house less, particularly when the ancient brown door gave to Beau Maturin's hand before he had put the key into the lock. Mr Trevor could not resist a natural exclamation of surprise. Mr Maturin begged him not to shout. Mr Trevor said that he was not shouting, and, without a thought for his own safety, was rushing headlong into the house to meet the terror singlehanded when he found that his shoe-lace was untied.

He found Beau Maturin in what, he supposed, would be called a hall when it was not a pit of darkness. A stealthily lit match revealed that it was a hall, a narrow one, and it also revealed by Mr Trevor's elbow a closed door to the right, which he removed. The match went out.

'Quietly,' said Mr Maturin quite unnecessarily, for Mr Trevor says he cannot remember when he felt less noisy. He heard the door to his right open, softly, softly.

'Is it you opening that door?' he asked, merely from curiosity.

'Ssh!' snapped Beau Maturin. 'Hang on to my shoulder-blades.'

Mr Trevor thought it better to calm Beau Maturin's fears by acceding to his whim, and clung close behind him as they entered the room. The moon, which Mr Trevor already had reason to dislike, was hanging at a moderate elevation over Golders Green as though on purpose to reveal the darkness of that room. Mr Trevor's foot then struck a shape on the floor. The shape was soft and long. Mr Trevor was surprised. Mr Maturin whispered:

'Found anything?'

Mr Trevor said briefly that his foot had.

'So's mine,' said Beau Maturin. 'What's your's like? Mine's rather soft to the touch.'

'And mine,' said Mr Trevor.

'They're corpses, let's face it,' sighed Mr Maturin. 'Making fifteen in all. With us, seventeen. Just give yours a kick, Ralph, to see if it's alive. I've kicked mine.'

'I don't kick corpses,' Mr Trevor was muttering when he felt a hard round thing shoved into the small of his back.

'Ow!' said Mr Trevor.

'Found anything?' said Mr Maturin.

Mr Trevor said briefly that there was something against his back.

'And mine,' sighed Mr Maturin. 'What's yours like? Mine's rather hard on the back.'

'So is mine,' said Mr Trevor.

'They're revolvers, let's face it,' sighed Beau Maturin.

'They are,' said a harsh voice behind them. 'So don't move.'

'I've got some sense, thank you,' snapped Beau Maturin.

'Sir,' said the harsh voice, and it was a woman's voice, 'I want none of your lip. I have you each covered with a revolver . . .'

'Waste,' said Beau Maturin. 'One revolver would have been quite enough. Besides, my friend and I were distinctly given to understand that you were partial to a razor. Or do you use that for shaving?'

'I use a razor,' said the harsh voice, 'only when I want to kill. But I have a use for you two.'

The light was suddenly switched on, a light so venomous, says Mr Trevor, that they had to blink furiously. And that must have been a very large room, for they could not see into its far corners. The light came from what must have been a very high-powered lamp directly above a table in the middle of the room; and it was concentrated by a shade in such a way as to fall, like a searchlight, exactly on the two helpless gentlemen. Mr Trevor says that Beau Maturin's handsome face looked white and ghastly, so the Lord knows what Mr Trevor's must have looked like. Meanwhile their captor leapt from her station behind them, and they were privileged to see her for the first time. She was, says Mr Trevor, exactly as Miss Samsonoff had described her, grey and gaunt and dry, and her expression was strangely contemptuous and evil as sin. And never for a moment did she change the direction of her revolvers, which was towards our gentlemen's hearts. Mr Trevor says he cannot remember when he saw a woman look less afraid that a revolver might go off in her hand.

'Look down,' she commanded.

'It's all right,' said Beau Maturin peaceably; 'we've already guessed what they are. Corpses. Nice cold night for them, too. Keep for days in weather like this.'

Mr Trevor could not resist looking down to his feet. The corpses were of two youngish men in dress-clothes.

'They're cut badly,' said Mr Maturin.

'They're not cut at all,' said the woman harshly. 'I shot these two for a change.'

'I meant their clothes,' Mr Maturin explained. 'Death was too good for them with dress-clothes like that.'

'Well, I can't stop here all night talking about clothes,' snapped the woman. 'Now then, to business. These bodies have to buried in the back-garden. You will each take one. There are spades just behind you. I shall not have the slightest hesitation in killing you as I have killed these two, but it will be more convenient if you do as you are told. I may kill you later, and I may not. Now be quick!'

'Lord, what's that!' cried Mr Trevor sharply. He had that moment realized a strange muffled, ticking noise which must, he thought, come either from somewhere in the room or from a room nearby. And, while he was never in his life less conscious of feeling fear, he could not help but be startled by that ticking noise, for he had heard it before when timing a dynamite-bomb.

'That is why,' the woman explained with what, Mr Trevor supposed, was meant to be a smile, 'you will be safer in the garden. Women are but weak creatures, and so I take the precaution of having a rather large size in dynamite-bombs so timed that I have but to press a button to send us all to blazes. It will not be comfortable for the police when, if ever, they catch me. But pick up those spades and get busy.'

'Now don't be rude,' begged Beau Maturin. 'I can stand anything from plain women but discourtesy. Ralph, you take the bigger corpse, as you are smaller than I am, while I take this little fellow on my shoulder – which will probably be the nearest he will ever get to Heaven, with clothes cut as badly as that.'

'You can come back for the bodies when you've dug the graves,' snapped the woman. 'Take the spades and go along that passage. No tricks! I am just behind you.'

There was a lot of rubbish in that garden. It had never been treated as a garden, it did not look like a garden, it looked even less like a garden than did 'The Garden of My Grandmother'. High walls enclosed it. And over it that deplorable moon threw a sheet of dead daylight.

'Dig,' said the woman with the revolvers, and they dug.

'Do you mind if we take our coats off?' asked Beau Maturin. Mr Trevor says that he was being sarcastic.

'I don't mind what you take off,' snapped the woman.

'Now don't say naughty things!' said Mr Maturin. 'Nothing is more revolting than the naughtiness of plain women.'

'Dig,' said the woman with the revolvers, and they dug.

They dug, says Mr Trevor, for a long time, for a very long time. Not, however, that it was difficult digging once one had got into the swing of it, for that garden was mostly dug-up soil. Suddenly Beau Maturin said:

'Bet you a fiver I dig a grave for my fellow before you.'

'Right!' said Mr Trevor.

'Dig,' said the woman with the revolvers, and they dug.

'*And,*' said the woman, 'I don't allow any betting in this house. So call that bet off.'

'What?' said Mr Maturin.

'Dig,' said the woman with the revolvers.

Mr Maturin threw down his spade.

'Dig,' said the woman with the revolvers.

Mr Trevor dug.

Mr Maturin said: 'Dig yourself!'

'Dig,' said the woman with the revolvers.

Mr Trevor brandished his spade from a distance. He noticed for the first time that they had been digging in the light of the dawn and not of the moon.

'And who the deuce,' said Mr Maturin dangerously, 'do you think you are, not to allow any betting? I have stood a lot from you, but I won't stand that.'

'Dig,' said the woman with the revolvers, but Mr Maturin advanced upon the revolvers like a punitive expedition. Mr Trevor brandished his spade.

'Another step, and I fire!' cried the woman harshly.

'Go ahead,' said Mr Maturin. 'I'll teach you to stop me betting! And I hate your face.'

'Oh dear, oh dear!' the woman suddenly cried with a face of fear, and, lowering her revolvers, fled into the house.

Mr Trevor was so surprised that he could scarcely speak. Mr Maturin laughed so much that he could not speak.

'What's there to laugh about?' Mr Trevor asked at last.

'It's funny. They've had us, let's face it. Come on, let's follow her in.'

'She may shoot,' Mr Trevor cautioned.

'Shoot my eye!' sighed Beau Maturin.

Once in the house, Mr Trevor stopped spellbound. There were voices, there was laughter – from the room of the two corpses!

'They're laughing at us!' said Mr Trevor.

'Who wouldn't!' laughed Beau Maturin, and, opening the door, said: 'Good morning.'

'You've said it,' said the policeman. 'Haw-haw!'
'You'll have some breakfast?' asked the woman with the revolvers.
'Please do!' said Miss Samsonoff.
'You *ought* to be hungry,' said the taxi-driver with the Homburg hat of green plush.
'Look here!' gasped Mr Trevor. 'What the blazes . . .'
'Haw-haw!' laughed the policeman. ' 'Ave a bit of vealanam-pie?'
'Now, Ted, don't be rude to the gentlemen!' said the woman with the revolvers.
'Quite right, mother,' said Miss Samsonoff. 'We owe these gentlemen an explanation and an apology . . .'
'And if they don't take it we *are* in the soup!' miserably said the man in the Homburg hat of green plush.
'Now, you two, go and get cups and plates for the two gentlemen,' said the woman with the revolvers to the two corpses in dress-clothes.
'Listen, please,' Miss Samsonoff gravely addressed Mr Maturin, 'my name isn't Samsonoff at all but Kettlewell, and that's my mother and these are my four brothers . . .'
'How do you do?' said Mr Maturin, absently drinking the policeman's coffee, but Mr Trevor is glad that no one heard what he said.
'You see,' said Miss Kettlewell, and she was shy and beautiful, 'we are The Kettlewell Film Company, just us, but of course we haven't got a lot of money . . .'
'A "lot" is good!' said the policeman.
'My brother there,' and Miss Kettlewell pointed to the wretched man with the Homburg hat of green plush, 'was the director of an American company in Los Angeles, but he got the sack lately, and so we thought we would make some films on our own. You see, we are such a large family! And the recent murders gave us a really brilliant idea for a film called *The Ghoul of Golders Green*, which, thanks to you two gentlemen, we have completed tonight.* Oh, I do hope it will be a success, especially as you have been kind enough to help us in our predicament, for we hadn't any money to engage actors – and we did so need two gentlemen, just like you, who really looked the part, didn't we, mother?'

---

* When the film was released by the Kettlewell Film Corporation, evidences of public favour were so notably lacking that it was offered to the Society for Presenting Nature Films to the Blind.
Surely, after the above exposure of the methods adopted, no further reasons should be sought for the so much deplored inferiority of British films.

'But, my dear child,' cried Beau Maturin, 'I'm afraid your film can't have come out very well. Trevor and I will look perfectly ghastly, as we neither of us had any make-up on.'

'But it's that kind of film!' smiled Miss Kettlewell. 'You see, you and your friend are supposed to be corpses who, by some powerful psychic agency, are digging your own graves – Heavens, what's that?'

There, at the open door, stood an apparition with a dreadful face. He appeared, says Mr Trevor, to have some difficulty in choosing among the words that his state of mind was suggesting to him.

'And me?' gasped the taxi-driver hoarsely. 'Wot abaht me? 'Angingabahtallnight! 'Oo's going to pay me, that's wot I want to know? There's four quid and more on that clock ...'

Mr Maturin swept his empty coffee-cup round to indicate the family Kettlewell.

'My friends will pay,' sighed Mr Maturin.

THERE SHALL BE NO DARKNESS

James Blish

The only other famous monster that I have been called upon to hunt on the screen and which has not so far been featured in these stories is the werewolf, and as two of my most recent pictures have been about this creature I think it would make a most suitable finale. I have to admit that werewolves as such are a group of beings that I have never been quite able to accept in films. Somehow the idea of a wolf's head on a man's body always seems phoney and rather obviously a make-up job, however brilliantly done. In my first werewolf picture, The Beast Must Die *(1973) I played Dr Christopher Lundgren and the film was based on an excellent short story,* There Shall Be No Darkness *which is reprinted here. In the second,* Legend of the Werewolf *(1975), I played what today would be called a police pathologist, with quite a sense of humour. A man doing this kind of job dealing with murder and death would probably need a little light relief now and then, and I was very gratified when I got so many letters from people saying how they enjoyed seeing me play comedy. As a professional actor, of course, I am prepared to play any role, and I think it is as important to approach each part with the same dedication and concentration, whether it be the latest Frankenstein film or Osric in* Hamlet. *I believe I owe that to all those who have given me such success and pleasure in my chosen career.*

It was about 10.00 p.m. when Paul Foote decided that there was a monster at Newcliffe's house party.

Foote was tight at the time – tighter than he liked to be ever. He sprawled in a too-easy chair in the front room, slanted on the end of his spine, his forearms resting on the high arms of the chair. A half-empty glass depended laxly from his right hand. A darker spot on one grey trouser-leg showed where some of the drink had gone. Through half-shut eyes he watched Jarmoskowski at the piano.

The pianist was playing, finally, his transcription of the Wolf's-Glen scene from von Weber's *Der Freischuetz*. Though it was a tremendous technical showpiece, Jarmoskowski never used it in concert, but only at social gatherings. He played it with an odd, detached amusement which only made more astounding the way the notes came swarming out of Newcliffe's big Baldwin; the rest of the gathering had been waiting for it all evening.

For Foote, who was a painter with a tin ear, it wasn't music at all. It was an enormous, ominous noise, muted occasionally to allow the repetition of a cantrap whose implications were secret.

The room was stuffy and was only half as large as it had been during the afternoon, and Foote was afraid that he was the only living man in it except for Jan Jarmoskowski. The rest of the party were wax figures, pretending to be humans in an aesthetic trance.

Of Jarmoskowski's vitality there could be no question. He was not handsome, but there was in him a pure brute force that had its own beauty – that and the beauty of precision with which the force was controlled. When his big hairy hands came down it seemed that the piano should fall into flinders. But the impact of fingers upon keys was calculated to the single dyne.

It was odd to see such delicacy behind such a face. Jarmoskowski's hair grew too long on his rounded head, despite the fact that he had avoided carefully any suggestion of Musician's Haircut. His brows were straight, rectangular, so shaggy that they seemed to meet over his high-bridged nose.

From where Foote sat he noticed for the first time the odd way the Pole's ears were placed – tilted forward as if in animal attention, so that the vestigial 'point' really was in the uppermost position. They were cocked directly toward the keyboard, reminding Foote irresistibly of the dog on the His Master's Voice trademark.

Where had he seen that head before? In Matthias Gruenewald, perhaps – in that panel on the Isenheim Altar that showed the

Temptation of St Anthony. Or had it been in one of the illustrations in the *Red Grimoire*, those dingy, primitive woodcuts which Chris Lundgren called 'Rorschak tests of the medieval mind?'

On a side-table next to the chair the painter's cigarette burned in an onyx ashtray which bore also a tiny dancer frozen in twisted metal. From the unlit end of the cigarette a small tendril of white smoke flowed downward and oozed out into a clinging pool, an amoeboid blur against the dark mahogany. The river of sound subsided suddenly and the cantrap was spoken, the three even, stony syllables and the answering wail. The pool of smoke leapt up in the middle exactly as if something had been dropped into it. Then the piano was howling again under Jarmoskowski's fingers, and the tiny smoke-spout twisted in the corner of Foote's vision, becoming more and more something like the metal dancer. His mouth dry, Foote shifted to the outer edge of the chair.

The transcription ended with three sharp chords, a 'concert ending' contrived to suggest the three plucked notes of the cantrap. The smoke-figurine toppled and slumped as if stabbed; it poured over the edge of the table and disintegrated swiftly on the air. Jarmoskowski paused, touched his fingertips together reflectively, and then began a work more purely his own: the *Galliard Fantasque*.

The wax figures did not stir, but a soft eerie sigh of recognition came from their frozen lips. Through the window behind the pianist a newly risen moon showed another petrified vista, the snowy expanse of Newcliffe's Scottish estate.

There was another person in the room, but Foote could not tell who it was. When he turned his unfocused eyes to count, his mind went back on him and he never managed to reach a total; but somehow there was the impression of another presence that had not been of the party before. Someone Tom and Caroline hadn't invited was sitting in. Not Doris, nor the Labourite Palmer, either; they were too simple. By the same token, Bennington, the American critic, was much too tubbily comfortable to have standing as a menace. The visiting psychiatrist, Lundgren, Foote had known well in Sweden, and Hermann Ehrenberg was only another refugee novelist and didn't count; for that matter, no novelist was worth a snap in a painter's universe, so that crossed out Alec James, too.

His glance moved of itself back to the composer. Jarmoskowski was not the presence. He had been there before. But he had something to do with it. There was an eleventh presence now, and it had something to do with Jarmoskowski.

What was it?

For it was there – there was no doubt about that. The energy which the rest of Foote's senses ordinarily would have consumed was flowing into his instincts now, because his senses were numbed. Acutely, poignantly, his instincts told him of the monster. It hovered around the piano, sat next to Jarmoskowski as he caressed the musical beast's teeth, blended with the long body and the serpentine fingers.

Foote had never had the horrors from drinking before, and he knew he did not have them now. A part of his mind which was not drunk and could never be drunk had recognized real horror somewhere in the room; and the whole of his mind, its barriers of scepticism tumbled, believed and trembled within itself.

The bat-like circling of the frantic notes was stilled abruptly. Foote blinked, startled.

'Already?' he said stupidly.

'Already?' Jarmoskowski echoed. 'But that's a long piece, Paul. Your fascination speaks well for my writing.'

His eyes turned directly upon the painter; they were almost completely suffused, though Jarmoskowski never drank. Foote tried frantically to remember whether or not his eyes had been red during the afternoon, and whether it was possible for any man's eyes to be as red at any time as this man's were now.

'The writing?' he said, condensing the far-flung diffusion of his brain. Newcliffe's highballs were damn strong. 'Hardly the writing, Jan. Such fingers as those could put fascination into *Three Blind Mice.*'

He snickered inside at the parade of emotions which marched across Jarmoskowski's face: startlement at a compliment from Foote – for the painter had a reputation for a savage tongue, and the inexplicable antagonism which had arisen between the two since the pianist had first arrived had given Foote plenty of opportunity to justify it – then puzzled reflection – and then at last veiled anger as the hidden slur bared its fangs in his mind. Nevertheless the man could laugh at it.

'They are long, aren't they?' he said to the rest of the group, unrolling the fingers like the party noisemakers which turn from snail to snake when blown through. 'But it's a mistake to suppose that they assist my playing, I assure you. Mostly they stumble over each other. Especially over this one.'

He held up his hands for inspection. On both, the index fingers and the middle fingers were exactly the same length.

'I suppose Lundgren would call me a mutation,' Jarmoskowski said. 'It's a nuisance at the piano. I have to work out my own fingerings for everything, even the simplest pieces.'

Doris Gilmore, once a student of Jarmoskowski's in Prague, and still obviously, painfully in love with him, shook coppery hair back from her shoulders and held up her own hands.

'My fingers are so stubby,' she said ruefully. 'Hardly pianist's hands at all.'

'On the contrary – the hands of a master pianist,' Jarmoskowski said. He smiled, scratching his palms abstractedly, and Foote found himself in a universe of brilliant, perfectly even teeth. No, not perfectly even. The polished rows were bounded almost mathematically by slightly longer canines. They reminded him of that idiotic Poe story – was it *Berenice*? Obviously Jarmoskowski would not die a natural death. He would be killed by a dentist for possession of those teeth.

'Three fourths of the greatest pianists I know have hands like truck drivers,' Jarmoskowski was saying, 'Surgeons too, as Lundgren will tell you. Long fingers tend to be clumsy.'

'You seem to manage to make tremendous music, all the same,' Newcliffe said, getting up.

'Thank you, Tom.' Jarmoskowski seemed to take his host's rising as a signal that he was not going to be required to play any more. He lifted his feet from the pedals and swung them around to the end of the bench. Several of the others rose also. Foote struggled up onto numb feet from the infernal depths of the armchair. Setting his glass on the side-table a good distance away from the onyx ashtray, he picked his way cautiously over to Christian Lundgren.

'Chris, I'm a fan of yours,' he said, controlling his tongue with difficulty. 'Now I'm sorry. I read your paper, the one you read to the Stockholm Endo-crin-ological Congress. Aren't Jarmoskowski's hands . . .'

'Yes, they are,' the psychiatrist said, looking at Foote with sharp, troubled eyes. Suddenly Foote was aware of Lundgren's chain of thought; he knew the scientist very well. The grey, craggy man was assessing Foote's drunkenness, and wondering whether or not he would have forgotten the whole affair in the morning.

Lundgren made a gesture of dismissal. 'I saw them too,' he said, his tone flat. 'A mutation, probably, as he himself suggested. Not every woman with a white streak through her hair is a witch; I give Jan the same reservation.'

'That's not all, Chris.'

'It is all I need to consider, since I live in the twentieth century. I am going to bed and forget all about it. Which you may take for advice as well as for information, Paul, if you will.'

He stalked out of the room, leaving Foote standing alone, wondering whether to be reassured or more alarmed than before. Lundgren should know, and certainly the platinum path which parted Doris Gilmore's absurdly red hair indicated nothing about Doris but that her coiffure was too chic for her young, placid face. But Jarmoskowski was not so simple; if he was despite Lundgren just what he seemed ...'

The party appeared to be surviving quite nicely without Foote, or Lundgren either. Conversations were starting up about the big room. Jarmoskowski and Doris shared the piano bench and were talking in low tones, punctuated now and then by brilliant bits of passage work; evidently the Pole was showing her better ways of handling the Hindemith sonata she had played before dinner. James and Ehrenberg were dissecting each other's most recent books with civilized savagery before a fascinated Newcliffe. Blandly innocent Caroline Newcliffe was talking animatedly to Bennington and Palmer about nothing at all. Nobody missed Lundgren, and it seemed even less likely that Foote would be missed.

He walked with wobbly nonchalance into the dining room, where the butler was still clearing the table.

' 'Scuse me,' he said. 'Little experiment, if y'don't mind. Return it in the morning.' He snatched a knife from the table, looked for the door which led directly from the dining room into the foyer, propelled himself through it. The hallway was dim, but intelligible; so was the talk in the next room.

As he passed the French door, he saw Bennington's figure through the ninon marquisette, now standing by the piano watching the progress of the lesson. The critic's voice stopped him dead as he was sliding the knife into his jacket. Foote was an incurable eavesdropper.

'Hoofy's taken his head to bed,' Bennington was remarking. 'I'm rather relieved. I thought he was going to be more unpleasant than he was.'

'What was the point of that fuss about the silverware, at dinner?' the girl said. 'Is he noted for that sort of thing?'

'Somewhat. He's really quite a brilliant artist, but being years ahead of one's time is frequently hard on the temper.'

'He had me worried,' Jarmoskowski confessed. 'He kept looking at me as if I had forgotten to play the repeats.'

Bennington chuckled. 'In the presence of another inarguable artist he seems to become very malignant. You were being flattered, Jan.'

Foote's attention was attracted by a prodigious yawn from Palmer. The Labourite was showing his preliminary signals of boredom, and at any moment now would break unceremoniously for his bed. Reluctantly Foote resumed his arrested departure; still the conversations babbled on indifferently behind him. The corners of his mouth pulled down, he passed the stairway and on down the hall.

As he swung closed the door of his bedroom, he paused a moment to listen to Jarmoskowski's technical exhibition on the keys, the only sound from the living room which was still audible at this distance. Then he shut the door all the way with a convulsive shrug. Let them say about Foote what they liked, even if it sometimes had to be the truth; but nevertheless it might be that at midnight Jarmoskowski would give another sort of exhibition.

If he did, Foote would be glad to have the knife.

At 11.30, Jarmoskowski stood alone on the terrace of Newcliffe's country house. Although there was no wind, the night was frozen with a piercing cold – but he did not seem to notice it. He stood motionless, like a black statue, with only the long streamers of his breathing, like twin jets of steam from the nostrils of a dragon, to show that he was alive.

Through the haze of watered silk which curtained Foote's window, Jarmoskowski was an heroic pillar of black stone – a pillar above a fumarole.

The front of the house was evidently entirely dark: there was no light on the pianist's back or shoulders. He was silhouetted against the snow, which gleamed dully in the moonlight. The shadow of the heavy tower which was the house's axis looked like a donjon keep. Thin slits of embrasures, Foote remembered, watched the landscape with a dark vacuity, and each of the crowning merlons wore a helmet of snow.

He could feel the house huddling against the malice of the white Scottish night. A sense of age invested it. The curtains smelled of dust and spices. It seemed impossible that anyone but Foote and Jarmoskowski could be alive in it.

After a long moment, Foote moved the curtain very slightly and drew it back. His face was drenched in reflected moonlight and he stepped back into the dark again, leaving the curtains parted.

If Jarmoskowski saw the furtive movement he gave no sign. He remained engrossed in the acerb beauty of the night. Almost the whole of Newcliffe's estate was visible from where he stood. Even the black border of the forest, beyond the golf course to the right could be seen through the dry frigid air. A few isolated trees stood nearer the house, casting sharply-etched shadows on the snow, shadows that flowed and changed shape with the slow movement of the moon.

Jarmoskowski sighed and scratched his left palm. His lips moved soundlessly.

A cloud floated across the moon, its shadow preceding it, gliding in a rush of ink athwart the house. The gentle ripples of the snow-field reared ahead of the wave, like breakers, falling back, engulfed, then surging again much closer. A thin singing of wind rose briefly, whirling crystalline showers of snow from the terrace flagstones.

The wind died as the umbra engulfed the house. For a long instant, the darkness and silence persisted. Then, from somewhere near the stables and greenhouses behind the house, a dog raised his voice in a faint sustained throbbing howl. Others joined in.

Jarmoskowski's teeth gleamed in the occluded moonlight. He stood a moment longer; then his head turned with a quick jerk and his eyes flashed a feral scarlet at the dark window where Foote hovered. Foote released the curtains hastily. Even through them he could see the pianist's phosphorescent smile.

The dog keened again. Jarmoskowski went back into the house. Foote scurried to his door and cocked one eye around the jamb.

Some men, as has somewhere been remarked, cannot pass a bar; some cannot pass a woman; some cannot pass a rare stamp or a good fire. Foote could not help spying, but in this one case he knew that one thing could be said for him: *this* time he wanted to be in the wrong.

There was a single small light burning in the corridor. Jarmoskowski's room was at the end of the hall, next to Foote's. As the pianist walked reflectively toward it, the door of the room directly across from Foote's swung open and Doris Gilmore came out, clad in a quilted sapphire housecoat with a high Russian collar. The effect was marred a little by the towel over her arm and the toothbrush in her hand, but nevertheless she looked startlingly pretty.

'Oh!' she said. Jarmoskowski turned toward her, and then neither of them said anything for a while.

Foote ground his teeth. Was the girl, too, to be a witness to the thing he expected from Jarmoskowski? That would be beyond all decency. And it must be nearly midnight now.

The two still had not moved. Trembling, Foote edged out into the hall and slid behind Jarmoskowski's back along the wall to Jarmoskowski's room. By the grace of God, the door was open.

In a quieter voice, Doris said, 'Oh, it's you, Jan. You startled me.'

'So I see. I'm most sorry,' Jarmoskowski's voice said. Foote again canted his head until he could see them both. 'It appears that we are the night-owls of the party.'

'I think the rest are tight. Especially that horrible painter. I've been reading the magazines Tom left by my bed, and I finally decided I'd better try to sleep too. What have you been up to?'

'I was out on the terrace, getting a breath. I like the winter night – it bites.'

'The dogs are restless, too,' she said. 'Did you hear them? I suppose Brucey started them off.'

Jarmoskowski smiled. 'Very likely. Why does a full moon make a dog feel so sorry for himself?'

'Maybe there's a banshee about.'

'I doubt it,' Jarmoskowski said. 'This house isn't old enough to have any family psychopomps; it's massive, but largely imitation. And as far as I know, none of Tom's or Caroline's relatives have had the privilege of dying in it.'

'Don't. You talk as if you believed it.' She wrapped the housecoat tighter about her waist; Foote guessed that she was repressing a shiver.

'I came from a country where belief in such things is common. In Poland most sceptics are imported.'

'I wish you'd pretend to be an exception,' she said. 'You're giving me the creeps, Jan.'

He nodded seriously. 'That's – fair enough,' he said gently.

There was another silence, while they looked at each other anew in the same dim light. Then Jarmoskowski stepped forward and took her hands in his.

Foote felt a long-belated flicker of embarrassment. Nothing could be more normal than this, and nothing interested him less. He was an eavesdropper, not a voyeur. If he were wrong after all, he'd speedily find himself in a position for which no apology would be possible.

The girl was looking up at Jarmoskowski, smiling uncertainly. Her smile was so touching as to make Foote writhe inside his skin. 'Jan,' she said.

'No ... Doris, wait,' Jarmoskowski said indistinctly. 'Wait just a moment. It has been a long time since Prague.'

'I see,' she said. She tried to release her hands.

Jarmoskowski said sharply: 'You don't see. I was eighteen then. You were – what was it? – eleven, I think. In those days I was proud of your school-girl crush, but of course infinitely too old for you. I am not so old any more, and when I saw this afternoon how lovely you have become the years went away like dandelion-fluff – no, no, hear me out, please! There is much more. I love you now, Doris, as I can see you love me; but ...'

In the brief pause Foote could hear the sharp indrawn breaths that Doris was trying to control. He felt like crawling. He had no business ...

'But we must wait a little, Doris. I know something that concerns you that you do not know yourself. And I must warn you of something in Jan Jarmoskowski that neither of us could even have dreamed in the old days.'

'Warn – me?'

'Yes.' Jarmoskowski paused again. Then he said: 'You will find it hard to believe. But if you can, we may be happy. Doris, I cannot be a sceptic. I am ...'

He stopped. He had looked down abstractedly at her hands, as if searching for precisely the right English words. Then, slowly, he turned her hands over until they rested palms up on his. An expression of absolute shock transformed his face, and Foote saw his grip tighten spasmodically.

In that tetanic silence Foote heard his judgment of Jarmoskowski confirmed. It gave him no pleasure. He was frightened.

For an instant Jarmoskowski shut his eyes. The muscles along his jaw stood out with the violence with which he was clenching his teeth. Then, deliberately, he folded Doris's hands together, and his curious fingers made a fist about them. When his eyes opened again they were as red as flame in the weak light.

Doris jerked her hands free and crossed them over her breasts. 'Jan – Jan, what is it? What's the matter?'

His face, that should have been flying into flinders under the force of the knowledge behind it, came under control muscle by muscle.

'Nothing,' he said. 'There's really no point in what I was going to say. I have been foolish; please pardon me. Nice to have seen you again, Doris. Goodnight.'

He brushed past her and stalked on down the corridor. Doris turned to look after him, her cheeks beginning to glisten, one freed hand clutching her toothbrush.

Jarmoskowski wrenched the unresisting doorknob of his room and threw the door shut behind him. Foote only barely managed to dodge out of his way.

Behind the house, a dog howled and went silent again.

In Jarmoskowski's room the moonlight played in through the open window upon a carefully turned-down bed. The cold air had penetrated every cranny. He ran both hands through his hair and went directly across the carpet to the table beside his bed. As he crossed the path of colourless light his shadow was oddly foreshortened, so that it looked as if he were walking on all fours. There was a lamp on the side table and he reached for it.

Then he stopped dead still, his hand halfway to the switch. He seemed to be listening. Finally, he turned and looked back across the room, directly at the spot behind the door where Foote was standing.

It was the blackest spot of all, for it had its back to the moon; but Jarmoskowski said immediately, 'Hello, Paul. Aren't you up rather late?'

Foote did not reply for a while. His senses were still alcohol-numbed, and he was further poisoned by the sheer outrageous impossibility of the thing he knew to be true. He stood silently in the darkness, watching the Pole's barely-visible figure beside the fresh bed, and the sound of his own breathing was loud in his ears.

The broad flat streamer of moonlight lay between them like a metallic river.

'I'm going to bed shortly,' he said at last. His voice sounded flat and dead and faraway, as if it belonged to someone else entirely. 'I just came to issue a little warning.'

'Well, well,' said Jarmoskowski pleasantly. 'Warnings seem to be all the vogue this evening. Do you customarily pay your social calls with a knife in your hand?'

'That's the warning, Jarmoskowski. The knife. I'm sleeping with it. It's made of silver.'

'You must be drunker than usual,' said the composer. 'Why don't you just go to bed – with the knife, if you fancy it? We can talk again in the morning.'

'Don't give me that,' Foote snapped savagely. 'You can't fool me. I know you for what you are.'

'All right, you know me. Is it a riddle? I'll bite, as Bennington would say.'

'Yes, you'd bite,' Foote said, and his voice shook a little despite himself. 'Should I really give it a name, Jarmoskowski? Where you were born it was *vrolok*, wasn't it? And in France it was *loup-garou*. In the Carpathians it was *stregoica* or *strega*, or sometimes *vlkoslak*. In . . .'

'Your command of languages is greater than your common sense,' Jarmoskowski said. 'And *stregoica* and *strega* are different in sex, and neither of them is equivalent to *loup-garou*. But all the same you interest me. Isn't it a little out of season for all such things? Wolfbane does not bloom in the dead of winter. And perhaps the things you give so many fluent names are also out of season in 1952.'

'The dogs hate you,' Foote said softly. 'That was a fine display Brucey put on this afternoon, when Tom brought him in from his run and he found you here. I doubt that you've forgotten it. I think you've seen a dog behave like that before, walking sidewise through a room where you were, growling, watching you with every step until Tom or some other owner dragged him out. He's howling now.

'And that shock you got from the table silverware at dinner – and your excuse about rubber-soled shoes. I looked under the table, if you recall, and your shoes turned out to be leather-soled. But it was a pretty feeble excuse anyhow, for anybody knows that you can't get an electric shock from an ungrounded piece of tableware, no matter how long you've been scuffing rubber. Silver's deadly, isn't it, Jarmoskowski?

'And those fingers – the index fingers as long as the middle ones – you were clever about those. You were careful to call everybody's attention to them. It's supposed to be the obvious that everybody misses. But Jarmoskowski, that "Purloined Letter" mechanism has been ground through too often already in detective stories. It didn't fool Lundgren, it didn't fool me.'

'Ah, so,' Jarmoskowski said. 'Quite a catalogue.'

'There's more. How does it happen that your eyes were grey all afternoon, and turned red as soon as the moon rose? And the palms of your hands – there was some hair growing there, but you shaved it off, didn't you, Jarmoskowski? I've been watching you scratch them. Everything about you, the way you look, the way you talk, every move you make – it all screams out your nature in a dozen languages to anyone who knows the signs.'

After a long silence, Jarmoskowski said, 'I see. You've been most attentive, Paul – I see you are what people call the suspicious drunk. But I appreciate your warning, Paul. Let us suppose that what you say of me is true. What then? Are you prepared to broadcast it to the rest of the house? Would you like to be known until the day you die as "The Boy Who Cried . . ."'

'I don't intend to say anything unless you make it necessary. I want you to know that I know, in case you've seen a pentagram on anyone's palm tonight.'

Jarmoskowski smiled. 'Have you thought that, knowing that you know, I could have no further choice? That the first word you said to me about it all might brand *your* palm with the pentagram?'

Foote had not thought about it. He had spent far too much time convincing himself that it had all come out of the bottle. He heard the silver knife clatter against the floor before he was aware that he had dropped it; his eyes throbbed with the effort to see through the dimness the hands he was holding before them.

From the other side of his moonlit room, Jarmoskowski's voice drifted, dry, distant, and amused. 'So – you hadn't thought. That's too bad. *Better never* than late, Paul.'

The dim figure of Jarmoskowski began to sink down, rippling a little in the reflected moonlight. At first it seemed only as if he were sitting down upon the bed; but the foreshortening proceeded without any real movement, and the pianist's body was twisting, too, and his clothing with it, his shirt-bosom dimming to an indistinct blaze upon his broadening chest, his shoulders hunching, his pointed jaw already squared into a blunt muzzle, his curled pads ticking as they struck the bare floor and moved deliberately toward Foote. His tail was thrust straight out behind him, and the ruff of coarse hair along his back stirred gently. He sniffed.

Somehow Foote got his legs to move. He found the doorknob and threw himself out of Jarmoskowski's room into the corridor.

A bare second after he had slammed the door, something struck it a massive blow from inside. The panelling split sharply. He held it shut by the knob with all the strength in his body. He could see almost nothing; his eyes seemed to have rolled all the way back into his head.

A dim white shape drifted down upon him through the dark corridor, and a fresh spasm of fear sent rivers of sweat down his back, his sides, his cheeks. But it was only the girl.

'Paul! What on Earth! What's the *matter?*'

'Quick!' he said, choking. 'Get something silver – something heavy made out of silver – quick, *quick*!'

Despite her astonishment, the frantic urgency in his voice drove her away. She darted back into her room. Kalpas of eternity went by after that while he listened for sounds inside Jarmoskowski's room. Once he thought he heard a low rumble, but he was not sure. The sea-like hissing and sighing of his blood, rushing through the channels of the middle ear, seemed very loud to him. He couldn't imagine why it was not arousing the whole countryside. He clung to the doorknob and panted.

Then the girl was back, bearing a silver candlestick nearly three feet in length – a weapon that was almost too good, for his fright-weakened muscles had some difficulty in lifting it. He shifted his grip on the knob to the left hand alone, and hefted the candlestick awkwardly with his right.

'All right,' he said, in what he hoped was a grim voice. 'Now let him come.'

'What in heaven's name is this all about?' Doris said. 'You're waking everybody in the house with this racket. Look – even the dog's come in to see ...'

'*The dog!*'

He swung around, releasing the doorknob. Not ten paces from them, an enormous coal-black animal, nearly five feet in length, grinned at them with polished fangs. As soon as it saw Foote move it snarled. Its eyes gleamed red under the single bulb.

It sprang.

Foote heaved the candlestick high and brought it down – but the animal was not there. Somehow the leap was never completed. There was a brief flash of movement at the open end of the corridor, then darkness and silence.

'He saw the candlestick,' Foote panted. 'Must have jumped out the window and come around through the front door. Then he saw the silver and beat it.'

'Paul!' Doris cried. 'What – how did you know that thing would jump? It was so big! And what has silver ...'

He chuckled, surprising even himself. He had a mental picture of what the truth was going to sound like to Doris. 'That,' he said, 'was a wolf and a whopping one. Even the usual kind isn't very friendly and ...'

Footsteps sounded on the floor above, and the voice of Newcliffe, grumbling loudly, came down the stairs. Newcliffe liked his evenings noisy and his nights quiet. The whole house now seemed to have heard the commotion, for in a moment a number of half-clad figures were elbowing out into the corridor, wanting to know what was up or plaintively requesting less noise.

Abruptly the lights went on, revealing blinking faces and pyjama-clad forms struggling into robes. Newcliffe came down the stairs. Caroline was with him, impeccable even in disarray, her face openly and honestly ignorant and unashamedly beautiful. She was no lion-hunter but she loved parties. Evidently she was pleased that the party was starting again.

'What's all this?' Newcliffe demanded in a gravelly voice. 'Foote, are you the centre of this whirlpool? Why all the noise?'

'Werewolf,' Foote said, as painfully conscious as he had expected to be of how meaningless the word would sound. 'We've got a were-wolf here. And somebody's marked out for him.'

How else could you put it? Let it stand.

There was a chorus of 'What's' as the group jostled about him. 'Eh? What was it? ... Werewolf, I thought he said ... What's this all about? ... Somebody's been a wolf ... Is that new? ... What an uproar!'

'Paul,' Lundgren's voice cut through. 'Details, please.'

'Jarmoskowski's a werewolf,' Foote said grimly, making his tone as emotionless and factual as he could. 'I suspected it earlier tonight and went into his room and accused him of it. He changed shape, right on the spot while I was watching.'

The sweat started out afresh at the recollection of that half-seen mutation. 'He came around into the hall and went for us. I scared him off with a silver candlestick for a club.' He realized that he still held the candlestick and brandished it as proof. 'Doris saw the wolf – she'll vouch for that.'

'I saw a big dog-like thing, all right,' Doris admitted. 'And it did jump at us. It was black and had a lot of teeth. But – Paul, was that supposed to be Jan? Why, that's ridiculous.'

'It certainly is,' Newcliffe said feelingly. 'Getting us all up for a practical joke. Probably one of the dogs is loose.'

'Do you have any all-black dogs five feet long?' Foote demanded desperately. 'And where's Jarmoskowski now? Why isn't he here? Answer me that!'

Bennington gave a sceptical grunt from the background and opened Jarmoskowski's door. The party tried to jam itself as a unit into the room. Foote forced his way through the clot.

'See? He isn't here, either. And the bed's not been slept in. Doris . . .' He paused for an instant, realizing what he was about to admit, then plunged ahead. The stakes were now too big to hesitate over social conventions. 'Doris, you saw him go in here. Did you see him come out again?'

The girl looked startled. 'No, but I was in my room . . .'

'All right. Here. Look at this.' Foote led the way over to the window and pointed out. 'See?' The prints on the snow?'

One by one the others leaned out. There was no arguing it. A set of animal prints, like large dog-tracks, led away from a spot just beneath Jarmoskowski's window – a spot where the disturbed snow indicated the landing of some heavy body.

'Follow them around,' Foote said. 'They lead around to the front door, and away again – I hope.'

'Have you traced them?' James asked.

'I didn't have to. I saw the thing, James.'

'The tracks could be coincidence,' Caroline suggested. 'Maybe Jan just went for a walk.'

'Barefoot? There are his shoes.'

Bennington vaulted over the windowsill with an agility astonishing in so round a man, and ploughed away with slippered feet along the line of tracks. A little while later he entered the room behind their backs.

'Paul's right,' he said, above the hubbub of excited conversation. 'The tracks go around to the terrace to the front door, then away again and around the side of the house toward the golf-course.' He rolled up his wet pyjama-cuffs awkwardly. A little of the weight came off Foote's heart; at least the beast was not still in the house, then ...'

'This is crazy,' Newcliffe declared angrily. 'We're like a lot of little children, panicked by darkness. There's no such thing as a werewolf.'

'I wouldn't place any wagers on that,' Ehrenberg said. 'Millions of people have believed in the werewolf for hundreds of years. One multiplies the years by the people and the answer is a big figure, *nicht wahr?*'

Newcliffe turned sharply to Lundgren. 'Chris, I can depend upon you at least to have your wits about you.'

The psychiatrist smiled wanly. 'You didn't read my Stockholm paper, did you, Tom? I mean my paper on psychoses of Middle Age populations. Much of it dealt with lycanthropy – werewolfism.'

'You mean – you believe this idiot story?'

'I spotted Jarmoskowski early in the evening,' Lundgren said. 'He must have shaved the hair on his palms, but he has all the other signs – eyes bloodshot with moonrise, first and second fingers of equal length, pointed ears, merged eyebrows, domed prefrontal bones, elongated upper cuspids. In short, the typical hyperpineal type – a lycanthrope.'

'Why didn't you say something?'

'I have a natural horror of being laughed at,' Lundgren said drily. 'And *I didn't want to draw Jarmoskowski's attention to me.* These endocrine-imbalance cases have a way of making enemies very easily.'

Foote grinned ruefully. If he had thought of that part of it before he had confronted Jarmoskowski, he would have kept his big mouth shut. It was deflating to know how ignoble one's motives could be in the face of the most demanding situations.

'Lycanthropy is no longer common,' Lundgren droned, 'and so seldom mentioned except in out-of-the-way journals. It is the little-known aberration of a little-known ductless gland; beyond that we know only what we knew in 1400, and that is that it appears to enable the victim to control his shape.'

'I'm still leery of this whole business,' Bennington growled, from somewhere deep in his teddy-bear chest. 'I've known Jan for years. Nice fella – helped me out of a bad hole once, without owing me any favours at all. And I think there's enough discord in this house so that I won't add to it much if I say I wouldn't trust Paul Foote as far as I could throw him. By God, Paul, if this does turn out to be some practical joke of yours . . .'

'Ask Lundgren,' Foote said.

There was dead silence, disturbed only by heavy breathing. Lundgren was known to almost all of them as the world's ultimate authority on hormone-created insanity. Nobody seemed to want to ask him.

'Paul's right,' Lundgren said at last. 'You must take it or leave it. Jarmoskowski is a lycanthrope. A hyperpineal. No other gland could affect the blood-vessels of the eyes like that or make such a reorganization of the soma possible. Jarmoskowski is inarguably a werewolf.'

Bennington sagged, the light of righteous incredulity dying from his eyes. 'I'll be damned!' he muttered. 'It can't be. It can't be.'

'We've got to get him tonight,' Foote said. 'He's seen the pentagram on somebody's palm – somebody in the party.'

'What's that?' asked James.

'It's a five-pointed star inscribed in a circle, a very old magical symbol. You find it in all the old mystical books, right back to the so-called fourth and fifth Books of Moses. The werewolf sees it on the palm of his next victim.'

There was a gasping little scream from Doris. 'So that's it!' she cried. 'Dear God, I'm the one! He saw something on my hand tonight while we were talking in the hall. He was awfully startled and went away with hardly another word. He said he was going to warn me about something and then he . . .'

'Steady,' Bennington said, in a soft voice that had all the penetrating power of a thunderclap. 'There's safety in numbers. We're all here.' Nevertheless, he could not keep himself from glancing surreptitiously over his shoulder.

'It's a common illusion in lycanthropic seizures,' Lundgren agreed. 'Or hallucination, I should say. But Paul, you're wrong about its significance to the lycanthrope; I believe you must have gotten that idea from some movie. The pentagram means something quite different. Doris, let me ask you a question.'

'Why – certainly, Dr Lundgren. What is it?'

'*What were you doing with that piece of modelling clay this evening?*'

To Foote, and evidently to the rest of the party, the question was meaningless. Doris, however, looked down at the floor and scuffed one slippered toe back and forth over the carpet.

'Answer me, please,' Lundgren said patiently. 'I watched you manipulating it while Jan was playing, and it seemed to me to be an odd thing for a woman to have in her handbag. What were you doing with it?'

'I – was trying to scare Paul Foote,' she said, in so low a voice that she could scarcely be heard at all.

'How? Believe me, Doris, this is most important. How?'

'There was a little cloud of smoke coming out of his cigarette. I was ... trying to make it take ...'

'Yes. Go on.'

'... Take the shape of a statuette near it,' Foote said flatly. He could feel the droplets of ice on his forehead. The girl looked at him sideways; then she nodded and looked back at the floor. 'The music helped,' she murmured.

'Very good,' Lundgren said. 'Doris, I'm not trying to put you on the spot. Have you had much success at this sort of game?'

'Lately,' she said, not quite so reluctantly. 'It doesn't always work. But sometimes it does.'

'Chris, what does this mean?' Foote demanded.

'It means that we have an important ally here, if only we can find out how to make use of her,' Lundgren said. 'This girl is what the Middle Ages would have called a witch. Nowadays we'd probably say she's been given a liberal helping of extra-sensory powers, but I must confess that never seems to me to explain much that the old term didn't explain.

'That is the significance of the pentagram, and Jarmoskowski knows it very well. The werewolf hunts best and ranges most widely when he has a witch for an accomplice, as a mate when they are both in human form, as a marker or stalker when the werewolf is in the animal form. The appearance of the pentagram identifies to the lycanthrope the witch he believes appointed for him.'

'That's hardly good news,' Doris said faintly.

'But it is. In all these ancient psychopathic relationships there is a natural – or, if you like, a supernatural – balance. The werewolf adopts such a partner with the belief – for him of course it is a certain foreknowledge – that the witch inevitably will betray him. That is what so shocked Jarmoskowski; but his changing to the wolf form shows that he has taken the gambit. He knows as well as we do, probably better, that as a witch Doris is only a beginner, unaware of most of her own powers. He is gambling very coolly on our being unable to use her against him. It is my belief that he is most wrong.'

'So we still don't know who Jan's chosen as a victim,' James said in earnest, squeaky tones. 'That settles it. We've got to trail the – the beast and kill him. We must kill him before he kills one of us – if not Doris, then somebody else. Even if he misses us, it would be just as bad to have him roaming the countryside.'

'What are you going to kill him with?' Lundgren asked matter-of-factly.

'Eh?'

'I said, what are you going to kill him with? With that pineal hormone in his blood he can laugh at any ordinary bullet. And since there are no chapels dedicated to St Hubert around here, you won't be able to scare him to death with a church-blessed bullet.'

'Silver will do,' Foote said.

'Yes, silver will do. It poisons the pinearin-catalysis. But are you going to hunt a full-grown wolf armed with table silver and candlesticks? Or is somebody here metallurgist enough to cast a decent silver bullet?'

Foote sighed. With the burden of proof lifted from him, and completely sobered up by shock, he felt a little more like his old self, despite the pall which hung over him and the others.

'Like I always tell my friends,' he said, 'there's never a dull moment at a Newcliffe houseparty.'

The clock struck 1.30. Foote picked up one of Newcliffe's rifles and hefted it. It felt – useless. He said, 'How are you coming?'

The group by the kitchen range shook their heads in comical unison. One of the gas burners had been jury-rigged as a giant Bunsen burner, and they were trying to melt down over it some soft unalloyed silver articles, mostly of Mexican manufacture.

They were using a small earthenware bowl, also Mexican, for a crucible. It was lidded with the bottom of a flower pot, the hole in which had been plugged with shredded asbestos yanked forcibly out of the insulation of the garret; garden clay gave the stuff a dubious cohesiveness. The awkward flame leapt uncertainly and sent fantastic shadows flickering over their intent faces.

'We've got it melted, all right,' Bennington said, lifting the lid cautiously with a pair of kitchen tongs and peering under it. 'But what do we do with it now? Drop it from the top of the tower?'

'You can't kill a wolf with buckshot unless you're damned lucky,' Newcliffe pointed out. Now that the problem had been reduced temporarily from a hypernatural one to a matter of ordinary hunting, he was in his element. 'And I haven't got a decent shot-gun here anyhow. But we ought to be able to whack together a mould. The bullet should be soft enough so that it won't stick in the rifling of my guns.'

He opened the door to the cellar stairs and disappeared down them, carrying in one hand several ordinary rifle cartridges. Faintly, the dogs renewed their howling. Doris began to tremble. Foote put his arm around her.

'It's all right,' he said. 'We'll get him. You're safe enough.'

She swallowed. 'I know,' she agreed in a small voice. 'But every time I think of the way he looked at my hands, and how red his eyes were – You don't suppose he's prowling around the house? That that's what the dogs are howling about?'

'I don't know,' Foote said carefully. 'But dogs are funny that way. They can sense things at great distances. I suppose a man with pinearin in his blood would have a strong odour to them. But he probably knows that we're after his scalp, so he won't be hanging around if he's smart.'

She managed a tremulous smile. 'All right,' she said. 'I'll try not to be hysterical.' He gave her an awkward reassuring pat, feeling a little absurd.

'Do you suppose we can use the dogs?' Ehrenberg wanted to know.

'Certainly,' said Lundgren. 'Dogs have always been our greatest allies against the abnormal. You saw what a rage Jarmoskowski's very presence put Brucey in this afternoon. He must have smelled the incipient seizure. Ah, Tom – what did you manage?'

Newcliffe set a wooden transplanting box on the kitchen table. 'I pried the slug out of one shell for each gun,' he said, 'and used one of them to make impressions in the clay here. The cold has made the stuff pretty hard, so the impressions should be passable moulds. Bring the silver over here.'

Bennington lifted his improvised crucible from the burner, which immediately shot up a tall, ragged blue flame. James carefully turned it off.

'All right, pour,' Newcliffe said. 'Chris, you don't suppose it might help to chant a blessing or something?'

'Not unless Jarmoskowski overheard it – probably not even then, since we have no priest among us.'

'Very well. Pour, Bennington, before the goo hardens.'

Bennington decanted sluggishly molten silver into each depression in the clay, and Newcliffe cleaned away the oozy residue from the casts before it had time to thicken. At any other time the whole scene would have been funny – now it was grotesque, as if it had been composed by a Holbein. Newcliffe picked up the box and carried it back down to the cellar, where the emasculated cartridges awaited their new slugs.

'Who's going to carry these things, now?' Foote asked. 'There are six rifles. James, how about you?'

'I couldn't hit an elephant's rump at three paces. Tom's an expert shot. So is Bennington here, with a shot-gun anyhow; he holds skeet-shooting medals.'

'I can use a rifle,' Bennington said diffidently.

'So can I,' said Palmer curtly. 'Not that I've got much sympathy for this business. This is just the kind of thing you'd expect to happen in this place.'

'You had better shelve your politics for a while,' James said, turning an unexpectedly hard face to the Labourite. 'Lycanthropy as a disease isn't going to limit its activities to the House of Lords. Suppose a werewolf got loose in the Welsh coal fields?'

'I've done some shooting,' Foote said. 'During the show at Dunkirk I even hit something.'

'I,' Lundgren said, 'am an honorary member of the Swiss Militia.'

Nobody laughed. Even Palmer was aware that Lundgren in his own oblique way was bragging, and that he had something to brag about. Newcliffe appeared abruptly from the cellar.

'I pried 'em loose, cooled 'em with snow and rolled 'em smooth with a file. They're probably badly crystallized, but we needn't let that worry us. At worst it'll just make 'em go dum-dum on us – no one here prepared to argue that that would be inhumane, I hope?'

He put one cartridge into the chamber of each rifle in turn and shot the bolts home. 'There's no sense in loading these any more thoroughly – ordinary bullets are no good anyhow, Chris says. Just make your first shots count. Who's elected?'

Foote, Palmer, Lundgren and Bennington each took a rifle. Newcliffe took the fifth and handed the last one to his wife.

'I say, wait a minute,' James objected. 'Do you think that's wise, Tom? I mean, taking Caroline along?'

'Why, certainly,' Newcliffe said, looking surprised. 'She shoots like a fiend – she's snatched prizes away from me a couple of times. I thought *everybody* was going along.'

'That isn't right,' Foote said. 'Especially not Doris, since the wolf – that is, I don't think she ought to go.'

'Are you going to subtract a marksman from the hunting party to protect her? Or are you going to leave her here by herself?'

'Oh no!' Doris cried. 'Not here! I've got to go! I don't want to wait all alone in this house. He might come back, and there'd be nobody here. I couldn't stand it.'

'There is no telling what Jarmoskowski might learn from such an encounter,' Lundgren added 'or, worse, what he might teach Doris without her being aware of it. For the rest of us – forgive me, Doris, I must be brutal – it would go harder with us if he did not kill her than if he did. Let us keep our small store of magic with us, not leave it here for Jan.'

'That would seem to settle the matter,' Newcliffe said grimly. 'Let's get under way. It's after two now.'

He put on his heavy coat and went out with the heavy-eyed groom to rouse out the dogs. The rest of the company fetched their own heavy clothes. Doris and Caroline climbed into ski-suits. They assembled again, one by one, in the living room.

Lundgren's eyes swung on a vase of iris-like flowers on top of the closed piano. 'Hello, what are these?' he said.

'Monkshood,' Caroline informed him. 'We grow it in the greenhouse. It's pretty, isn't it? Though the gardener says it's poisonous.'

'Chris,' Foote said. 'That isn't – wolfbane, is it?'

The psychiatrist shook his head. 'I'm no botanist. I can't tell one aconite from another. But it doesn't matter; hyperpineals are allergic to the whole group. The pollen, you see. As in hay fever, your hyperpineal case breathes the pollen, anaphylaxis sets in, and . . .'

'The last twist of the knife,' James murmured.

A clamouring of dogs outside announced that Newcliffe was ready. With sombre faces the party filed out onto the terrace. For some reason all of them avoided stepping on the wolf's prints in the snow. Their mien was that of condemned prisoners on the way to the tumbrels. Lundgren took one of the sprigs of flowers from the vase.

The moon had long ago passed its zenith and was almost halfway down the sky, projecting the bastille-like shadow of the house a long way out onto the grounds; but there was still plenty of light, and the house itself was glowing from cellar to tower room. Lundgren located Brucey in the milling, yapping pack and abruptly thrust the sprig of flowers under his muzzle. The animal sniffed once, then crouched back and snarled softly.

'Wolfbane,' Lundgren said. 'Dogs don't dislike the other aconites – basis of the legend, no doubt. Better fire your gardener, Caroline. In the end he may be the one to blame for all this happening in the dead of winter. Lycanthropy normally is an autumn affliction.'

James said:

> Even a man who says his prayers
> Before he sleeps each night
> May turn to a wolf when the wolfbane blooms
> And the moon is high and bright.

'Stop it, you give me the horrors,' Foote snapped angrily.

'Well, the dog knows now,' said Newcliffe. 'Good. It would have been hard for them to pick up the trail from hard snow, but Brucey can lead them. Let's go.'

The tracks of the wolf were clear and sharp in the ridged drifts. The snow had formed a hard crust from which fine, powdery showers of tiny ice-crystals were whipped by a fitful wind. The tracks led around the side of the house, as Bennington had reported, and out across the golf course. The little group plodded grimly along beside them. The spoor was cold for the dogs, but every so often they would pick up a faint trace and go bounding ahead, yanking their master after them. For the most part, however, the party had to depend upon its eyes.

A heavy mass of clouds had gathered in the west over the Firth of Lorne. The moon dipped lower. Foote's shadow, knobby and attenuated, marched on before him and the crusted snow crunched and crackled beneath his feet. The night seemed unnaturally still and watchful, and the party moved in tense silence except for an occasional growl or subdued bark from the dogs.

Once the marks of the werewolf doubled back a short distance, then doubled again, as if the monster had turned for a moment to look back at the house before resuming his prowling. For the most part, however, the trail led directly toward the dark boundary of the woods.

As the brush began to rise around them they stopped by mutual consent and peered warily ahead, rifles lifted half-way, muzzles weaving nervously as the dogs' heads shifted this way and that. Far out across the countryside behind them, the great cloud-shadow continued its sailing. The brilliantly-lit house stood out against the gloom as if it were on fire.

'Should have turned those out,' Newcliffe muttered, looking back at it. 'Outlines us.'

The dogs strained at their leashes. In the black west there was a barely audible muttering, as of winter thunder. Brucey pointed a quivering nose at the woods and snarled.

'He's in there, all right.'

'We'd better step on it,' Bennington said, whispering. 'Going to be plenty dark in about five minutes. Looks like a storm.'

Still they hesitated, looking at the noncommittal darkness of the forest. Then Newcliffe waved his gun hand and his dog hand in the conventional deploy-as-skirmishers signal and ploughed forward. The rest spread out in a loosely-spaced line and followed him. Foote's finger trembled over his trigger.

The forest was shrouded and very still. Occasionally a branch groaned as someone pushed against it, or twigs snapped with sharp, tiny musical explosions. Foote could see almost nothing. The underbrush tangled his legs; his feet broke jarringly through the crust of snow, or were supported by it when he least expected support. Each time his shoulder struck an unseen trunk gouts of snow fell on him.

After a while the twisted, leafless trees began to remind him of something; after a brief mental search he found it. It was a Doré engraving of the woods of Hell, from an illustrated Dante which had frightened him green as a child: the woods where each tree was a sinner in which harpies nested, and where the branches bled when they were broken off. The concept still frightened him a little – it made the forest by Newcliffe's golf-course seem almost cosy.

The dogs strained and panted, weaving, no longer growling, silent with a vicious intentness. A hand touched Foote's arm and he jumped; but it was only Doris.

'They've picked up something, all right,' Bennington's whisper said. 'Turn 'em loose, Tom?'

Newcliffe pulled the animals to a taut halt and bent over them, snapping the leashes free. One by one, without a sound, they shot ahead and vanished

Over the forest the oncoming storm-clouds cruised across the moon. Total blackness engulfed them. The beam of a powerful flashlight splashed from Newcliffe's free hand, flooding a path of tracks on the brush-littered snow. The rest of the night drew in closer about the blue-white glare.

'Hate to do this,' Newcliffe said. 'It gives us away. But he knows we're ... Hello, it's snowing.'

'Let's go then,' Foote said. 'The tracks will be blotted out shortly.'

A many-voiced, clamorous baying, like tenor bugles, rang suddenly through the woods. It was a wild and beautiful sound! Foote, who had never heard it before, thought for an instant that his heart had stopped. Certainly he would never have associated so pure a choiring with anything as prosaic as dogs.

'That's it!' Newcliffe shouted. 'Listen to them! That's the view-halloo. Go get him, Brucey!'

They crashed ahead. The belling cry seemed to ring all around them.

'What a racket!' Bennington panted. 'They'll raise the whole countryside.'

They ploughed blindly through the snow-filled woods. Then, without any interval, they broke through into a small clearing. Snowflakes flocculated the air. Something dashed between Foote's legs, snapping savagely, and he tripped and fell into a drift.

A voice shouted something indistinguishable. Foote's mouth was full of snow. He jerked his head up – and looked straight into the red rage-glowing eyes of the wolf.

It was standing on the other side of the clearing, facing him, the dogs leaping about it, snapping furiously at its legs. It made no sound at all, but stood with its forefeet planted, its head lowered below its enormous shoulders, its lips drawn back in a travesty of Jarmoskowski's smile. A white streamer of breath trailed horizontally from its long muzzle, like the tail of a malign comet.

It was more powerful than all of them, and it knew it. For an instant it hardly moved, except to stir lazily the heavy brush of tail across its haunches. Then one of the dogs came too close.

The heavy head lashed sidewise. The dog yelped and danced back. The dogs already had learned caution: one of them already lay writhing on the ground, a black pool spreading from it, staining the snow.

'Shoot, in God's name!' James screamed.

Newcliffe clapped his rifle to his shoulder with one hand, then lowered it indecisively. 'I can't,' he said. 'The dogs are in the way...'

'To hell with the dogs – this is no fox-hunt! Shoot, Tom, you're the only one of us that's clear – '

It was Palmer who shot first. He had no reason to be chary of Newcliffe's expensive dogs. Almost at the same time the dogs gave Foote a small hole to shoot through and he took it.

The double flat crack of the two rifles echoed through the woods and snow puffed up in a little explosion behind the wolf's left hind pad. The other shot – whose had come closest could never be known – struck a frozen tree-trunk and went squealing away. The wolf settled deliberately into a crouch.

A concerted groan had gone up from the party; above it Newcliffe's voice thundered, ordering his dogs back. Bennington aimed with inexorable care.

The werewolf did not wait. With a screaming snarl it launched itself through the ring of dogs and charged.

Foote jumped in front of Doris, throwing one arm across his own throat. The world dissolved into rolling pandemonium, filled with shouts, screams, snarls, and the frantic hatred of dogs. The snow flew thick. Newcliffe's flashlight fell and tumbled away, coming to rest at last on the snow on its base, regarding the tree-tops with an idiot stare.

Then there was the sound of a heavy body moving swiftly away. The noise died gradually.

'Anybody hurt?' James' voice asked. There was a general chorus of 'no's.'

'That's not good enough,' Bennington puffed. 'How does a dead man answer No? Let's have a nose-count.'

Newcliffe retrieved his flashlight and played it about, but the snowstorm had reached blizzard proportions, and the light showed nothing but shadows and cold confetti. 'Caroline?' he said anxiously.

'Yes, dear. Soaked, but here.'

'Doris? Good. Paul, where are you – oh, I see you, I think. Ehrenberg? And Palmer? So; there you have it, Bennington. We didn't invite anybody else to this party – except...'

'He got away,' Bennington said ironically. 'Didn't like the entertainment. And the snow will cover his tracks this time. Better call your dogs back, Tom.'

'They're back,' Newcliffe said. He sounded a little tired, for the first time since the beginning of the trouble. 'When I call them off, they come off.'

He walked heavily forward to the body of the injured animal, which was still twitching feebly, as if trying to answer his summons. He squatted down on his hams and bent his shoulders, stroking the restlessly rolling head.

'So – so,' he said softly. 'So, Brucey. Easy – easy. So, Brucey – so.'

Still murmuring, he brought his rifle into position with one arm. The dog's tail beat once against the snow.

The rifle leapt noisily against Newcliffe's shoulder.

Newcliffe arose slowly, and looked away.

'It looks like we lose round one,' he said tonelessly.

It seemed to become daylight very quickly. The butler went phlegmatically around the house, snapping off the lights. If he knew what was going on he gave no sign of it.

Newcliffe was on the phone to London. 'Cappy? Tom here – listen and get this straight, it's damned important. Get Consolidated Warfare – no, no, not the Zurich office, they've offices in the City – and place an order for a case of .30 calibre rifle cartridges – listen to me, dammit, I'm not through yet – with *silver slugs*. Yes, that's right – silver – and it had better be the pure stuff, too. No, not sterling, that's too hard for my purposes. Tell them I want them flown up, and that they've got to arrive here tomorrow . . . I don't care if it is impossible. Make it worth their while; I'll cover it. And I want it direct to the house here. On Loch Rannoch 20 kilometres due west of Blair Atholl . . . Of course you know the house but how will cws' pilot unless you tell them? Now read it back to me.'

'Garlic,' Lundgren was saying to Caroline. She wrote it dutifully on her marketing list. 'How many windows does this house have? All right, buy one clove for each, and get a half dozen tins of ground rosemary, also.'

He turned to Foote. 'We must cover every possibility,' he said sombrely. 'As soon as Tom gets off the line I will try to raise the local priest and get him out here with a drayload of silver crucifixes.

Understand, Paul, there is a strong physiological basis beneath all that mediaeval mumbo-jumbo.

'The herbs, for example, are anti-spasmodics – they act rather as ephedrine does, in hay-fever, to reduce the violence of the seizure. It's possible that Jan may not be able to maintain the wolf shape if he gets a heavy enough sniff.

'As for the religious trappings, their effects are perhaps solely psychological – and perhaps not, I have no opinion in the matter. It's possible that they won't bother Jan if he happens to be a sceptic in such matters, but I suspect that he's . . .' Lundgren's usually excellent English abruptly gave out on him. The word he wanted obviously was not in his vocabulary. *'Aberglaeubig,'* he said. *'Criandre.'*

'Superstitious?' Foote suggested, smiling grimly.

'Is that it? Yes. Yes, certainly. Who has better reason, may I ask?'

'But how does he maintain the wolf shape at all, Chris?'

'Oh, that's the easiest part. You know how water takes the shape of the vessel it sits in? Well, protoplasm is a liquid. This pineal hormone lowers the surface-tension of the cells; and at the same time it short-circuits the sympathetic nervous system directly through to the cerebral cortex, by increasing the efficiency of the cerebrospinal fluid as an electrolyte beyond the limits in which it's supposed to function . . .'

'Whoa there, I'm lost already.'

'I'll go over it with you later, I have several books in my luggage which have bearing on the problem which I think you should see. In any event, the result is a plastic, malleable body, within limits. A wolf is the easiest form because the skeletons are so similar. Not much pinearin can do to bone, you see. An ape would be easier still, but lycanthropes don't assume shapes outside their own ecology. A were-ape would be logical in Africa, but not here. Also, of course, apes don't eat people; there is the really horrible part of this disease.'

'And vampires?'

'Vampires,' Lundgren said pontifically, 'are people we put in padded cells. It's impossible to change the bony structure *that* much. They just think they are bats. But yes, that too is advanced hyper-pinealism.

'In the last stages it is quite something to see. As the pinearin blood-level increases, the cellular surface tension is lowered so much that the cells literally begin to boil away. At the end there is just a – a mess. The process is arrested when the vascular systems no longer can circulate the hormone, but of course the victim dies long before that stage is reached.'

Foote swallowed. 'And there's no cure?'

'None yet. Palliatives only. Someday, perhaps, there will be a cure – but until then – Believe me, we will be doing Jan a favour.'

'Also,' Newcliffe was saying, 'drive over and pick me up six automatic rifles. No, not Brownings, they're too hard to handle. Get American T-47's. All right, they're secret – what else are we paying cws a retainer for? What? Well, you might call it a siege. All right, Cappy. No, I won't be in this week. Pay everybody off and send them home until further notice. No, that doesn't include you. All right. Yes, that sounds all right.'

'It's a good thing,' Foote said, 'that Newcliffe has money.'

'It's a good thing,' Lundgren said, 'that he has me – and you. We'll see how twentieth-century methods can cope with this Middle Ages madness.'

Newcliffe hung up, and Lundgren took immediate possession of the phone.

'As soon as my man gets back from the village,' Newcliffe said, 'I'm going to set out traps. Jan may be able to detect hidden metal – I've known dogs that could do it by smell in wet weather – but it's worth a try.'

'What's to prevent his just going away?' Doris asked hopefully. The shadows of exhaustion and fear around her eyes touched Foote obscurely; she looked totally unlike the blank-faced, eager youngster who had bounded into the party in ski-clothes so long ago.

'I'm afraid you are,' he said gently. 'As I understand it, he believes he's bound by the pentagram.' At the telephone, where Lundgren evidently was listening to a different speaker with each ear, there was an energetic nod. 'In the old books, the figure is supposed to be a sure trap for demons and such, if you can lure or conjure them into it. And once the werewolf has seen his appointed partner marked with it, he feels compelled to remain until he has made the alliance good.'

'Doesn't it – make you afraid of me?' Doris said, her voice trembling.

He touched her hand. 'Don't be foolish. There's no need for us to swallow all of a myth just because we've found that part of it is so. The pentagram we have to accept; but I for one reserve judgment on the witchcraft.'

Lundgren said 'Excuse me' and put one hand over the mouthpiece. 'Only lasts seven days,' he said.

'The compulsion? Then we'll have to get him before then.'

'Well, maybe we'll sleep tonight anyhow,' Doris said dubiously.

'We're not going to do much sleeping until we get him,' Newcliffe announced. 'I could boil him in molten lead just for killing Brucey.'

'Brucey!' Palmer snorted. 'Don't you think of anything but your damned prize dogs, even when all our lives are forfeit?' Newcliffe turned on him, but Bennington grasped his arm.

'That's enough,' the American said evenly. 'Both of you. We certainly don't dare quarrel among ourselves with this thing hanging over us. I know your nerves are shot. We're all in the same state. But dissension among us would make things just that much easier for Jan.'

'Bravo,' Lundgren said. He hung up the phone and rejoined them. 'I didn't have much difficulty in selling the good Father the idea,' he said. 'He was stunned, but not at all incredulous. Unfortunately, he has only crucifixes enough for our groundfloor windows, at least in silver; gold, he says, is much more popular. By the way, he wants a picture of Jan, in case he should turn up in the village.'

'There are no existing photographs of Jarmoskowski,' Newcliffe said positively. 'He never allowed any to be taken. It was a headache to his concert manager.'

'That's understandable,' Lundgren said. 'With his cell radiogens under constant stimulation, any picture of him would turn out over-exposed anyhow – probably a total blank. And that in turn would expose Jan.'

'Well, that's too bad, but it's not irreparable,' Foote said. He was glad to be of some use again. He opened Caroline's secretary and took out a sheet of stationery and a pencil. In ten minutes he had produced a head of Jarmoskowski in three-quarter profile, as he had seen him at the piano that last night so many centuries ago. Lundgren studied it.

'To the life,' he said. 'Tom can send this over by messenger. You draw well, Paul.'

Bennington laughed. 'You're not telling him anything he doesn't know,' he said. Nevertheless, Foote thought, there was considerably less animosity in the critic's manner.

'What now?' James asked.

'We wait,' Newcliffe said. 'Palmer's gun was ruined by that one hand-made slug, and Foote's isn't in much better shape. The one thing we can't afford is to have our weapons taken out of action. If I know Consolidated, they'll have the machine-made bullets here tomorrow, and then we'll have some hope of getting him. Right now we'll just have to lie doggo and hope that our defences are effective – he's shown that he's more than a match for us in open country.'

The rest looked at each other uneasily. Some little understanding of what it would be like to wait through helpless, inactive days and dog-haunted nights already showed on their faces. But before the concurrence of both master hunters – Newcliffe and Lundgren – they were forced to yield.

The conference broke up in silence.

When Foote came into the small study with one of the books Lundgren had given him, he was surprised and somewhat disappointed to find that both Caroline and Doris had preceded him. Doris was sitting on a hassock near the grate, with the fire warming her face, and a great sheaf of red-gold hair pouring down her back. Caroline, seated just behind her, was brushing it out with even strokes.

'I'm sorry,' he said. 'I didn't know you were in here. I had a little reading to do and this looked like the best place for it . . .'

'Why, of course, Paul,' Caroline said. 'Don't let us distract you in the least. We came in here for the fire.'

'Well, if you're sure it's all right . . .'

'Of course it's all right,' Doris said, 'If our talking won't annoy you . . .'

'No, no.' He found the desk with the gooseneck lamp on it, turned on the lamp, and put down the heavy book in the pool of light. Caroline's arm resumed its monotonous, rhythmic movement over Doris's bent head. Both of them made a wonderful study: Caroline no longer the long-faced hounds-and-horses Englishwoman in jodhpurs, but now the exactly opposite type, tall, clear-skinned, capable of carrying a bare-shouldered evening gown with enchanting naturalness, yet in both avatars clearly the wife of the same man; Doris transformed from the bouncing youngster to the preternaturally still virgin waiting beside the lake, her youth not so much emphasized as epiphanized by the maternal shape stroking her head.

But for once in his life he had something to do that he considered more pressing than making a sketch for an abstraction. He turned his back on them and sat down, paging through the book to the chapter Lundgren had mentioned. He would have preferred studying it with Lundgren at his side, but the psychiatrist, wiry though he was, felt his years as the hour grew late, and was now presumably asleep.

The book was hard going. It was essentially a summary of out-of-the-way psychoses associated with peasant populations, and it had been written by some American who assumed an intolerably patronizing attitude toward the beliefs he was discussing, and who was further handicapped by a lack of basic familiarity with the English language. Foote suspected that sooner or later someone like Lundgren was going to have to do the whole job over again from scratch.

Behind him the murmuring of the two women's voices blended with the sighing of the fire in the grate. It was a warm, musical sound, so soothing that Foote found himself nodding at the end of virtually every one of the book's badly-constructed paragraphs, and forced to reread nearly every other sentence.

'I do believe you've conquered Tom completely,' Caroline was saying. The brush went crackle ... crackle ... through the girl's hair. 'He hates women who talk. About anything. That's hard on him, for he loves artists of all sorts, and so many of them are women, aren't they?'

... Within a few years I was able to show to a startled world that between sympathetic magic and the sympatheticomimetic rituals of childhood there is a distinct relationship, directly connectable to the benighted fantasies of Balkan superstition of which I have just given so graphic a series of instances. Shortly thereafter, with the aid of Drs Egk and Bergenweiser, I was able to demonstrate ...

'So many of them are pianists, anyhow,' Doris said. 'Sometimes I wish I'd taken to the harp, or maybe the bassoon.'

'Well, now, I sometimes feel that way about being a woman. There really is a great deal of competition abroad in the world. Your hair is lovely. That white part is so fashionable now that it's a pleasure to see one that's natural.'

'Thank you, Caroline. You've been very brave and kind. I feel better already.'

'I've never known a woman,' Caroline said, 'who didn't feel better with the tangles out of her hair. Does this affair really disturb you greatly?'

... in order to make it clear that this total misconception of the real world can have no REAL consequences except in the mind of the ignorant. To explain the accounts of the deceived observers we must first of all assume ...

'Shouldn't it? I wouldn't have taken it seriously for a moment a few days ago, but – well, we did go out to hunt for Jan, and there really doesn't seem to be much doubt about it. It is frightening.'

'Of course it is,' Caroline said. 'Still I wouldn't dream of losing my sleep over it. I remember when Brucey had the colic when he was five weeks old; London was being bombed at the same time by those flying things. Tom carried on terribly, and the house was full of refugees, which simply made everything more difficult. And Jan is really very sweet and he's been most effective in the World Federation movement, really one of the best speakers we've ever had; I can't imagine that he would hurt anyone. I know what Tom would do if he discovered he could turn himself into a wolf. He'd turn himself in to the authorities; he's really very serious-minded, and fills every weekend with these artists until one wonders if anybody else in the world is sane. But Jan has a sense of humour. He'll be back tomorrow laughing at us.'

Foote turned a page in the book, but he had given up everything but the pretence of reading it.

'Chris takes it very seriously,' Doris said.

'Of course, he's a specialist. There now, that should feel better. And there's Paul, studying his eyes out; I'd forgotten you were there. What have you found?'

'Nothing much,' Foote said, turning to look at them. 'I really need Chris to understand what I'm reading. I haven't the training to extract meaning out of this kind of study. I'll tackle it with him tomorrow.'

Caroline sighed. 'Men are so single-minded. Isn't it wonderful how essential Chris turned out to be? I'd never have dreamed that he'd be the hero of the party.'

Doris got up. 'If you're through with me, Caroline, I'm very tired. Goodnight, and thank you. Goodnight, Paul.'

'Goodnight,' Foote said.

'Quite through,' Caroline said. 'Goodnight, dear.'

Then it was deep night again. The snowstorm had passed, leaving fresh drifts, and the moon was gradually being uncovered. The clouds blew across the house toward the North Sea on a heavy wind which hummed under the gutters, rattled windows, ground together the limbs of trees.

The sounds stirred the atmosphere of the house, which was hot and stuffy because of the closed windows and reeking with garlic. It was not difficult to hear in them other noises less welcome. In the empty room next to Foote's there was the imagined coming and going of thin ghosts to go with them, and the crouched expectancy of a turned-down bed which awaited a curiously-deformed guest – a guest who might depress its sheets regardless of the tiny glint of the crucifix upon the pillow.

The boundary between the real and the unreal had been let down in Foote's mind, and between the comings and goings of the cloud-shadows and the dark errands of the ghosts there was no longer any way of making a selection. He had entered the cobwebby borderland between the human and the animal, where nothing is ever more than half true, and only as much as half true for the one moment.

After a while he felt afloat on the stagnant air, ready to drift all the way across the threshold at the slightest motion. Above him, other sleepers turned restlessly, or groaned and started up with a creak of springs. Something was seeping through the darkness among them. The wind followed it, keeping a tally of the doors that it passed.

One.

Two.

Three. Closer now.

Four. The fourth sleeper struggled a little; Foote could hear a muffled squeaking of floorboards above his head.

Five.

Six. Who was six? Who's next? When?

Seven . . .

Oh my God, I'm next . . . I'm next . . .

He curled into a ball, trembling. The wind died away and there was silence, tremendous and unquiet. After a long while he uncurled, swearing at himself; but not aloud, for he was afraid to hear his own voice. Cut that out, now, Foote, you bloody fool. You're like a kid hiding from the trolls. You're perfectly safe. Lundgren says so.

Mamma says so.

How the hell does Lundgren know?

He's an expert. He wrote a paper. Go ahead, be a kid. Remember your childhood faith in the printed word? All right, then. Go to sleep, will you?

There goes that damned counting again.

But after a while his worn-down nerves would be excited no longer. He slept a little, but fitfully, falling in his dreams through such deep pits that he awoke fighting the covers and gasping for the vitiated, garlic-heavy air. There was a foulness in his mouth and his heart pounded. He threw off the blankets and sat up, lighting a cigarette with shaking hands and trying not to see the shadows the match-flame threw.

He was no longer waiting for the night to end. He had forgotten that there had ever been such a thing as daylight. He was waiting only to hear the low, inevitable snuffling that would tell him he had a visitor.

But when he looked out the window, he saw dawn brightening over the forest. After staring incredulously at it for a long while, he snubbed out his cigarette in the socket of the candlestick – which he had been carrying about the house as if it had grown to him – and fell straight back. With a sigh he was instantly in profound and dreamless sleep.

When he finally came to consciousness he was being shaken, and Bennington's voice was in his ears. 'Get up, man,' the critic was saying. 'No, you needn't reach for the candlestick – everything's okay thus far.'

Foote grinned and reached for his trousers. 'It's a pleasure to see a friendly expression on your face, Bennington,' he said.

Bennington looked a little abashed. 'I misjudged you,' he admitted. 'I guess it takes a crisis to bring out what's really in a man so that blunt brains like mine can see it. You don't mind if I continue to dislike your latest abstractions, I trust?'

'That's your function: to be a gadfly,' Foote said cheerfully. 'Now, what's happened?'

'Newcliffe got up early and made the rounds of the traps. We got a good-sized rabbit out of one of them and made Hassenpfeffer – very good – you'll see. The other one was empty, but there was blood on it and on the snow around it. Lundgren's still asleep, but we've saved scrapings for him; still there doesn't seem to be much doubt about it – there's a bit of flesh with coarse black hair on it – '

James poked his head around the doorjamb, then came in. 'Hope it cripples him,' he said, dexterously snaffling a cigarette from Foote's shirt pocket. 'Pardon me. All the servants have deserted us but the butler, and nobody will bring cigarettes up from the village.'

'My, my,' Foote said. 'You're a chipper pair of chaps. Nice sunrise, wasn't it?'

'Wasn't it, though.'

In the kitchen they were joined by Ehrenberg, his normally ruddy complexion pale and shrunken from sleeplessness.

'Greetings, Hermann. How you look! And how would you like your egg?'

'*Himmel, Asch und Zwirn*, how can you sound so cheerful? You must be part ghoul.'

'You must be part angel – nobody human could be so deadly serious so long, even at the foot of the scaffold.'

'Bennington, if you burn my breakfast I'll turn you out of doors without a shilling. Hello, Doris; can you cook?'

'I'll make some coffee for you.' Newcliffe entered as she spoke, a pipe between his teeth. 'How about you, Tom?'

'Very nice, I'm sure,' Newcliffe said: 'Look – what do you make of this?' He produced a wad of architect's oiled tracing cloth from his jacket pocket and carefully unwrapped it. In it were a few bloody fragments. Doris choked and backed away.

'I got these off the trap this morning – you saw me do it, Bennington – and they had hair on 'em then. Now look at 'em.'

Foote poked at the scraps with the point of his pencil. 'Human,' he said.

'That's what I thought.'

'Well, isn't that to be expected? It was light when you opened the trap, evidently, but the sun hadn't come up. The werewolf assumes human form in full daylight – these probably changed just a few moments after you wrapped them up. As for the hair – this piece here looks to me like a blood-stained sample of Jarmoskowski's shirt-cuff.'

'We've nipped him, all right,' Bennington agreed.

'By the way,' Newcliffe added, 'we've just had our first desertion. Palmer left this morning.'

'No loss,' James said. 'But I know how he feels. When this affair is over, I'm going to take a month off at Brighton and let the world go to hell.'

'What? In the winter?'

'I don't care. I'll watch the tides come in and out in the w.c.'

'Just be sure to live to get there,' Ehrenberg said gloomily.

'Hermann, you are a black cloud and a thunderclap of doom.'

There was a sound outside. It sounded like the world's biggest tea-kettle. Something flitted through the sky, wheeled and came back. Foote went to the nearest window.

'Look at that,' he said, shading his eyes. 'An Avro jet – and he's trying to land here. He must be out of his mind.'

The plane circled silently, engines cut. It lost flying speed and glided in over the golf course, struck, and rolled at breakneck speed directly for the forest. At the last minute the pilot groundlooped the ship expertly and the snow fountained under its wheels.

'By heaven, I'll bet that's Newcliffe's bullets!'

They pounded through the foyer and out onto the terrace. Newcliffe, without bothering to don coat or hat, ploughed away toward the plane. A few minutes later, he and the pilot came puffing into the front room, carrying a small wooden case between them. Then they went back and got another, larger but obviously not so heavy.

Newcliffe pried the first crate open. Then he sighed. 'Look at 'em,' he said. 'Shiny brass cartridges, and dull silver heads, machined for perfect accuracy – there's a study in beauty for you artist chaps. Where'd you leave from?'

'Croydon,' said the pilot. 'If you don't mind, Mr Newcliffe, the company said I was to collect from you. That's six hundred pounds for the weapons, two-fifty for the ammo and a hundred fifty for me, just a thousand in all.'

'Fair enough. Hold on, I'll write you a cheque.'

Foote whistled. It was obvious – not that there had ever been any doubt about it – that Tom Newcliffe did not paint for a living.

The pilot took the cheque, and shortly thereafter the tea-kettle began to whistle again. From the larger crate Newcliffe was handing out brand-new rifles, queer ungainly things with muzzle brakes and disproportionately large stocks.

'Now let him come,' he said grimly. 'Don't worry about wasting shots. There's a full case of clips. As soon as you see him, blaze away like mad. Use it like a hose if you have to. This is a high-velocity weapon: if you hit him square anywhere – even if it's only his hand – you'll kill him from shock. If you get him in the body, there won't be enough of that area left for him to reform, no matter what his powers.'

'Somebody go wake Chris,' Bennington said. 'He should have lessons too. Doris, go knock on his door like a good girl.'

Doris nodded and went upstairs. 'Now this stud here,' Newcliffe said, 'is the fire-control button. You put it in this position and the gun will fire one shot and reload itself, like the Garand. Put it here and you have to reload it yourself, like a bolt-action rifle. Put it here and it goes into automatic operation, firing every shell in the clip, one after the other and in a hurry.'

'Thunder!' James said admiringly. 'We could stand off an army.'

'Wait a minute – there seem to be two missing.'

'Those are all you unpacked,' Foote pointed out.

'Yes, but there were two older models of my own. I never used 'em because it didn't seem sporting to hunt with such cannon. But I got 'em out last night on account of this trouble.'

'Oh,' Bennington said with an air of sudden enlightenment. 'I thought that thing I had looked odd. I slept with one last night. I think Lundgren has the other.'

'Where is Lundgren? Doris should have had him up by now. Go see, Bennington, and fetch back that rifle while you're at it.'

'Isn't there a lot of recoil?' Foote asked.

'Not a great deal; that's what the muzzle brake is for. But it would be best to be careful when you have the stud on fully-automatic. Hold the machine at your hip, rather than at your shoulder – what's *that*!'

'Bennington's voice,' Foote said, his jaw muscles suddenly almost unmanageable. 'Something must be wrong with Doris.' The group stampeded for the stairs.

They found Doris at Bennington's feet in front of Lundgren's open door. She was perfectly safe; she had only fainted. The critic was in the process of being very sick. On Lundgren's bed something was lying.

The throat had been ripped out, and the face and all the soft parts of the body were gone. The right leg had been gnawed in one place all the way to the bone, which gleamed white and polished in the reassuring sunlight.

Foote stood in the living room by the piano in the full glare of all the electric lights. He hefted the T-47 and surveyed the remainder of the party, which was standing in a puzzled group before him.

'No,' he said, 'I don't like that. I don't want you all bunched together. String out in a line, please, against the far wall, so that I can see everybody.'

He grinned briefly. 'Got the drop on you, didn't I? Not a rifle in sight. Of course, there's the big candlestick behind you, Tom – aha, I saw you sneak your hopeful look at it – but I know from experience that it's too heavy to throw. I can shoot quicker than you can club me, too.' His voice grew ugly. '*And I will*, if you make it necessary. So I would advise everybody – including the women – not to make any sudden movements.'

'What's this all about, Paul?' Bennington demanded angrily. 'As if things weren't bad enough . . .'

'You'll see directly. Get into line with the rest, Bennington. *Quick!*' He moved the gun suggestively. 'And remember what I said about moving too suddenly. It may be dark outside, but I didn't turn on all the lights for nothing.'

Quietly the line formed. The eyes that looked at Foote were narrowed with suspicion of madness, or something worse.

'Good. Now we can talk comfortably. You see, after what happened to Chris I'm not taking any chances. That was partly his fault, and partly mine. But the gods allow no one to err twice in matters of this kind. He paid for his second error – a price I don't intend to pay, or to see anyone else here pay.'

'Would you honour us with an explanation of this error?' Newcliffe said icily.

'Yes. I don't blame you for being angry, Tom, since I'm your guest. But you see I'm forced to treat you all alike for the moment. I was fond of Lundgren.'

There was silence for a moment, then a thin indrawing of breath from Bennington. 'All alike?' he whispered raggedly. 'My God, Paul. Tell us what you mean.'

'You know already, I see, Bennington. I mean that Lundgren was not killed by Jarmoskowski. He was killed by someone else. Another werewolf – yes, we have two now. One of them is standing in this room at this moment.'

A concerted gasp went up.

'Surprised?' Foote said, coldly, and deliberately. 'But it's true. The error for which Chris paid so dearly, an error which I made too, was this: we forgot to examine everyone for injuries after the encounter with Jan. We forgot one of the cardinal laws of lycanthropy.

'A man who survives being bitten by a werewolf himself becomes a werewolf. That's how the disease is passed on. The pinearin in the wolf's saliva evidently gets into the bloodstream, stimulates the victim's own pineal gland, and ...'

'But nobody was bitten, Paul,' Doris said in a suspiciously reasonable voice.

'Somebody was, even if only lightly. None of you but Chris and myself could have known about the bite-infection. Evidently somebody got a few small scratches, didn't think them worth mentioning, put iodine on them and forgot about them – until it was too late.'

There were slow movements in the line – heads turning surreptitiously, eyes swinging to neighbours left and right.

'Paul, this is merely a hypothesis,' Ehrenberg said. 'There is no reason to suppose that it is so, just because it sounds likely.'

'But there is. Jarmoskowski can't get in here.'

'Unproven,' Ehrenberg said.

'I'll prove it. Once the seizure occurred, Chris was the logical first victim. The expert, hence the most dangerous enemy. I wish I had thought of this before lunch. I might have seen which one of you was uninterested in his lunch. In any event, if I'm right, Chris's safeguards against letting Jarmoskowski in also keep you from getting out. If you think you'll ever leave this room again, you're bloody wrong ...'

He gritted his teeth and brought himself back into control. 'All right,' he said. 'This is the end of the line. Everybody hold up both hands in plain view.'

Almost instantly there was a ravening wolf in the room.

Only Foote, who could see at one glance the order of the people in the staggered line, could know who it was. His drummed-up courage, based solely on terror, went flooding out of him on a tide of sick pity; he dropped the rifle and began to weep convulsively. The beast lunged for his throat like a reddish projectile.

Newcliffe's hand darted back and grasped the candlestick. He leapt forward with swift clumsy grace and brought it down, whistling, against the werewolf's side. Ribs burst with a sharp splintering sound. The wolf spun, its haunches hitting the floor. Newcliffe hit it again. It fell, screaming like a great dog run down by a car, its fangs slashing the air.

Three times, with scientific viciousness, Newcliffe heaved the candlestick back and struck at its head. Then it cried out in an almost-familiar voice, and died.

Slowly the cells of its body groped back toward their natural positions. Even its fur moved, becoming more matted, more regular – more fabric-like.

The crawling metamorphosis was never completed; but the hairy-haunched thing with the crushed skull which sprawled at Newcliffe's feet was recognizable.

It had been Caroline Newcliffe.

Tears coursed along Foote's palms, dropped from under them, fell to the carpet. After a while he dropped his hands. Blurrily he saw a frozen tableau of wax figures in the yellow lamplight. Bennington's face was grey with illness, but rigidly expressionless, like a granite statue. James' back was against the wall; he watched the anomalous corpse as if waiting for some new movement. Ehrenberg had turned away, his pudgy fists clenched.

As for Newcliffe, he had no expression at all. He merely stood where he was, the bloody candlestick hanging straight down from a limp hand.

His eyes were quite empty.

After a moment Doris walked over to Newcliffe and touched his shoulder compassionately. The contact seemed to let something out of him. He shrank visibly into himself, shoulders slumping, his whole body withering to a dry husk.

The candlestick thumped against the floor, rocked wildly on its base, toppled across the body. As it struck, Foote's cigarette butt, which had somehow remained in its socket all day, tumbled out and rolled crazily along the carpet.

'Tom,' Doris said softly. 'Come away now. There's nothing you can do.'

'It was the blood,' his empty voice said. 'She had a cut. On her hand. Handled the scrapings from the trap. My trap. I did it to her. Just a breadknife cut from making canapés. I did it.'

'No you didn't, Tom. You're not to blame. Let's get some rest.'

She took his hand. He followed her obediently, stumbling a little as his spattered shoes scuffed over the thick carpet, his breath expelling from his lungs with a soft whisper. The French doors closed behind them.

Bennington bolted for the kitchen sink.

Foote sat down on the piano bench, his worn face taut with dried tears. Like any non-musician he was drawn almost by reflex to pick at the dusty keys. Ehrenberg remained standing where he was, so motionless as to absent himself from the room altogether, but the lightly-struck notes aroused James. He crossed the room, skirting the body widely, and looked down at Foote.

'You did well,' the novelist said shakily. 'Don't condemn yourself, Paul. What you did was just and proper – and merciful in the long run.'

Foote nodded. He felt – nothing. Nothing at all.

'The body?' James said.

'Yes. I suppose so.' He got up from the bench. Together they lifted the ugly shape; it was awkward to handle. Ehrenberg remained dumb, blind and deaf. They manoeuvred their way through the house and on out to the greenhouse.

'We should leave her here,' Foote said, the inside of his mouth suddenly sharp and sour. 'Here's where the wolfbane bloomed that started the whole business.'

'Poetic justice of sorts, I suppose,' James said. 'But I don't think it's wise. Tom has a toolshed at the other end that isn't steam heated. It should be cold enough there.'

Gently they lowered the body to the cement floor, laid down gunnysacks and rolled it onto them. There seemed to be nothing available to cover it. 'In the morning,' Foote said, 'we can have someone come for her.'

'How about legal trouble?' James said, frowning. 'Here's a woman whose skull has been crushed with a blunt instrument . . .'

'I think we can get Lundgren's priest to help us there, and with Lundgren too,' Foote said sombrely. 'They have authority to make death certificates in Scotland. Besides, Alec – is that a woman? Inarguably it isn't Caroline.'

James looked sidewise at the felted, muscular haunches. 'No. It's – legally it's nothing. I see your point.'

Together they went back into the house. 'Jarmoskowski?' James said.

'Not tonight, I imagine. We're all too tired and sick. And we do seem to be safe enough in here. Chris saw to that.'

Ehrenberg had gone. James looked around the big empty room.

'Another night. What a damnable business. Well, goodnight, Paul.'

He went out. Foote remained in the empty room a few minutes

longer, looking thoughtfully at the splotch of blood on the priceless Persian carpet. Then he felt of his face and throat, looked at his hands, arms and legs, and explored his chest under his shirt.

Not a scratch. Tom had been very fast.

He was exhausted, but he could not bring himself to go to bed. With Lundgren dead, the problem was his; he knew exactly how little he knew about it still, but he knew as well how much less the rest of the party knew. Hegemony of the house was his now – and the next death would be his responsibility.

He went around the room, making sure that all the windows were tightly closed and the crucifixes in place, turning out the lights as he went. The garlic was getting rancid – it smelled like mercaptan – but as far as he knew it was still effective. He clicked out all but the last light, picked up his rifle and went out into the hall.

Doris's room door was open and there was no light coming out of it. Evidently she was still upstairs tending Newcliffe. He stood for a few moments battling with indecision, then toiled up the staircase.

He found her in Caroline's room, her head bowed upon her arm among the scattered, expensive vials and flasks which had been Caroline's armamentarium. The room was surprisingly froufrou; even the telephone had a doll over it. This, evidently, had been the one room in the house which Caroline had felt was completely hers, where her outdoorsy, estate-managing daytime personality had been ousted by her nocturnal femininity.

And what, in turn, had ousted that? Had the womanly Caroline been crowded, trying not to weep, into some remote and impotent corner of her brain as the monster grew in her? What did go on in the mind of a werewolf?

Last night, for instance, when she had brushed Doris's hair, she had seemed completely and only herself, the Caroline Newcliffe with the beautiful face and the empty noggin toward whom Foote had so long felt a deep affection mixed with no respect whatsoever. But she had already been taken. It made his throat ache to realize that in her matronly hovering over the girl there had already been some of the tenseness of the stalker.

Men are so single-minded. Isn't it wonderful how essential Chris turned out to be?

At that moment she had shifted her target from Doris to Chris, moved by nothing more than Foote's remark about being unable to progress very far without the psychiatrist. Earlier this evening he had said that Chris had been the most logical target because he was the expert – yet that had not really occurred to Caroline except as an afterthought. It was wolf-reasoning; Caroline's own mind had seen danger first in single-mindedness.

And it had been Caroline's mind, not the wolf's, which had dictated the original fix on Doris. The girl, after all, was the only other woman in the party, thanks to Tom's lion-hunting and his dislike of the Modern Girl; and Caroline had mentioned that Tom seemed drawn to Doris. Which was wolf, which human? Or had they become blended, like two innocuous substances combining to form a poison? Caroline had once been incapable of jealousy – but when the evil had begun to seethe in her bloodstream she had been no longer entirely Caroline ...

He sighed. Doris had seemed to be asleep on the vanity, but she stirred at the small sound, and the first step he took across the threshold brought her bolt upright. Her eyes were reddened and strange.

'I'm sorry,' he said. 'I was looking for you. I have to talk to you, Doris; I've been putting it off for quite a while, but I can't do that any longer. May I?'

'Yes, of course, Paul,' she said wearily. 'I've been very rude to you. It's a little late for an apology, but I am sorry.'

He smiled. 'Perhaps I had it coming. How is Tom?'

'He's – not well. He doesn't know where he is or what he's doing. He ate a little and went to sleep, but he breathes very strangely.' She began to knead her hands in her lap. 'What did you want?'

'Doris – what about this witchcraft business? Lundgren seemed to think it might help us. God knows we need help. Have you any idea why Chris thought it was important? Beyond what he told us, that is?'

She shook her head. 'Paul, it seemed a little silly to me then, and I still don't understand it. I can do a few small tricks, that's all, like the one I did to you with the smoke. I never thought much about them; they came more or less naturally, and I thought of them just as a sort of sleight-of-hand. I've seen stage conjurers do much more mystifying things.'

'But by trickery – not by going right around natural law.'

'What do I know about natural law?' she said reasonably. 'It seems natural to me that if you want to make something plastic behave, you mould something else that's plastic nearby. To make smoke move, you move clay, or something else that's like smoke. Isn't that natural?'

'Not very,' he said wrily. 'It's a law of magic, if that's any comfort to either of us. But it's supposed to be a false law.'

'I've made it work,' she said, shrugging.

He leaned forward. 'I know that. That's why I'm here. If you can do that, there should be other things that you can do, things that can help us. What I want to do is to review with you what Chris thought of your talents, and see whether or not anything occurs to you that we can use.'

She put her hands to her cheeks, and then put them back in her lap again. 'I'll try,' she said.

'Good for you. Chris said he thought witches in the old days were persons with extra-sensory perception and allied gifts. I think he believed also that the magic rituals that were used in witchcraft were just manipulative in intention – symbolic objects needed by the witch to focus her extra-sensory powers. If he was right, the "laws" of magic really were illusions, and what was in operation was something much deeper.'

'I think I follow that,' Doris said. 'Where does it lead?'

'I don't know. But I can at least try you on a catalogue. Have you ever had a prophetic dream, Doris? Or read palms? Or cast horoscopes? Or even had the notion that you could look into the future?'

She shook her head decidedly.

'All right, we'll rule that out. Ever felt that you knew what someone else was thinking?'

'Well, by guesswork ...'

'No, no,' Foote said. 'Have you ever felt certain that you knew ...'

'Never.'

'How about sensing the positions of objects in another room or in another city – no. Well, have you ever been in the vicinity of an unexplained fire? A fire that just seemed to happen because you were there?'

'No, Paul, I've never seen a single fire outside of a fire-place.'

'Ever moved anything larger and harder to handle than a column of smoke?'

Doris frowned. 'Many times,' she said. 'But just little things. There was a soprano with a rusty voice that I had to accompany once. She was overbearing and a terrible stage hog. I tied her shoe-bows together so that she fell when she took her first bow, but it was awfully hard work; I was all in a sweat.'

Foote suppressed an involuntary groan. 'How did you do it?'

'I'm not quite sure. I don't think I could have done it at all if we hadn't wound up the concert with *Das Buch der Haengenden Gaerten.*' She smiled wanly. 'If you don't know Schoenberg's crazy counterpoint that wouldn't mean anything to you.'

'It tells me what I need to know, I'm afraid. There really isn't much left for me to do but ask you whether or not you've ever transformed a woman into a white mouse, or ridden through the air on a broomstick. Doris, doesn't *anything* occur to you? Chris never talked without having something to talk about; when he said that you could help us, he meant it. But he's dead now and we can't ask him for the particulars. It's us to you.'

She burst into tears. Foote got clumsily to his feet, but after that he had no idea what to do.

'Doris . . .'

'I don't know,' she wailed. 'I'm not a witch! I don't want to be a witch! I don't know anything, anything at all, and I'm so tired and so frightened and please go away, please – '

He turned helplessly to go, then started to turn back again. At the same instant, the sound of her weeping was extinguished in the roar of an automatic rifle, somewhere over their heads, exhausting its magazine in a passionate rush.

Foote shot out of the room and back down the stairs. The ground floor still seemed to be deserted under the one light. Aloft there was another end-stopped snarl of gunfire; then Bennington came bouncing down the stairs.

'Watch out tonight,' he panted as soon as he saw Foote. 'He's around. I saw him come out of the woods in wolf form. I emptied the clip, but he's a hard target against those trees. I sprayed another ten rounds around where I saw him go back in, but I'm sure I didn't hit him. The rifle just isn't my weapon.'

'Where were you shooting from?'

'The top of the tower.' His face was very stern. 'Went up for a breath and a last look around, and there he was. I hope he comes back tonight. I want to be the one who kills him.'

'You're not alone.'

'Thank God for that. Well, goodnight. Keep your eyes peeled.'

Foote stood in the dark for a while after Bennington had left. Bennington had given him something to think about. While he waited, Doris picked her way down the stairs and passed him without seeing him. She was carrying a small, bulky object; since he had already put the light out, he could not see what it was. But she went directly to her room.

I want to be the one who kills him.

Even the mild Bennington could say that now; but Foote, who understood the feeling behind it all too well, was startled to find that he could not share it.

How could one hate these afflicted people? Why was it so hard for equal-minded men like Bennington to remember that lycanthropy was a disease like any other, and that it struck its victims only in accordance with its own etiology, without regard for their merits as persons? Bennington had the reputation of being what the Americans called a liberal, all the way to his bones; presumably he could not find it in his heart to hate an alcoholic or an addict. He knew also – he had been the first to point it out – that Jarmoskowski as a human being had been compassionate and kindly, as well as brilliant; and that Caroline, like the poor devil in Andreyev's *The Red Laugh*, had been noble-hearted and gentle and had wished no one evil. Yet he was full of hatred now.

He was afraid, of course, just as Foote was. Foote wondered if it had occurred to him that God might be on the side of the werewolves.

The blasphemy of an exhausted mind; but he had been unable to put the idea from him. Suppose Jarmoskowski should conquer his compulsion and lie out of sight until the seven days were over. Then he could disappear; Scotland was large and sparsely populated. It would not be necessary for him to kill all his victims thereafter – only those he actually needed for food. A nip here, a scratch there...

And then from wherever he hunted, the circle of lycanthropy would grow and widen and engulf...

Perhaps God had decided that proper humans had made a muddle of running the world; had decided to give the *nosferatu*, the undead, a chance at it. Perhaps the human race was on the threshold of that darkness into which he had looked throughout last night.

He ground his teeth and made a noise of exasperation. Shock and exhaustion would drive him as crazy as Newcliffe if he kept this up. He put his hands to his forehead, wiped them on his thighs, and went into the little study.

The grate was cold, and he had no materials for firing it up again. All the same, the room was warmer than his bed would be at this hour. He sat down at the small desk and began to go through Lundgren's book again.

Cases of stigmata. Accounts of Sabbats straight out of Krafft-Ebing. The dancing madness. Theory of familiars. Conjuration and exorcism. The besom as hermaphroditic symbol. Fraser's Laws. Goetha as an international community. Observations of Lucien Levy-Bruehl. The case of Bertrand. Political commentary in *Dracula*. Necromancy *v.* necrophilia. Nordau on magic and modern man. Basic rituals of the Anti-Church. Fetishism and the theory of talismans . . .

Round and round and round, and the mixture as before. Without Chris there was simply no hope of integrating all this material. Nothing would avail them now but the rifles with the silver bullets in them; their reservoir of knowledge of the thing they fought had been destroyed.

Foote looked tiredly at the ship's clock on the mantel over the cold grate. The fruitless expedition through the book had taken him nearly two hours. He would no longer be able to avoid going to bed. He rose stiffly, took up the automatic rifle, put out the light, and went out into the cold hall.

As he passed Doris's room, he saw that the door was now just barely ajar. Inside, two voices murmured.

Foote was an incurable eavesdropper. He stopped and listened.

It was years later before Foote found out exactly what had happened at the beginning. Doris, physically exhausted by her hideous day, emotionally drained by tending the childlike Newcliffe, feeding him from a blunt spoon, parrying his chant about traps and breadknives, and herding him into bed, had fallen asleep almost immediately. It was a sleep dreamless except for a vague, dull undercurrent of despair. When the light tapping against the window-panes finally reached through to her, she had no idea how long she had been lying there.

She struggled to a sitting position and forced her eyelids up. Across the room the moonlight, gleaming in patches against the rotting snow outside, glared through the window. Silhouetted against it was a tall human figure. She could not see its face, but there was no mistaking the red glint of its eyes. She clutched for her rifle and brought it awkwardly into line.

Jarmoskowski did not dodge. He moved his forearms out a little way from his body, palms forward in a gesture that looked almost supplicating, and waited. Indecisively she lowered the gun again. What was he asking for?

As she dropped the muzzle she saw that the fire-control stud was at *automatic*. She shifted it carefully to *repeat*. She was afraid of the recoil Newcliffe had mentioned; she could feel surer of her target if she could throw one shot at a time at it.

Jarmoskowski tapped again and motioned with his finger. Reasoning that he would come in of his own accord if he were able, she took time out to get into her housecoat. Then, holding her finger against the trigger, she went to the window. All its sections were closed tightly, and a crucifix, suspended from a silk thread, hung exactly in the centre of it. She touched it, then opened one of the small panes directly above Jarmoskowski's head.

'Hello, Doris,' he said softly. 'You look a little like a clerk behind that window. May I make a small deposit, miss?'

'Hello.' She was more uncertain than afraid. Was this really happening, or was it just the recurrent nightmare? 'What do you want? I should shoot you. Can you tell me why I shouldn't?'

'Yes, I can. Otherwise I wouldn't have risked exposing myself. That's a nasty-looking weapon.'

'There are ten silver bullets in it.'

'I know that too. I had some fired at me earlier tonight. And I would be a good target for you, so I have no hope of escape – my nostrils are full of rosemary.' He smiled ruefully. 'And Lundgren and Caroline are dead, and I am responsible. I deserve to die; that is why I am here.'

'You'll get your wish, Jan,' she said. 'But you have some other reason, I know. I'll back my wits against yours. I want to ask you questions.'

'Ask.'

'You have your evening clothes on. Paul said they changed with you. How is that possible?'

'But a wolf has clothes,' Jarmoskowski said. 'He is not naked like a man. And surely Chris must have spoken of the effect of the pineal upon the cell radiogens. These little bodies act upon any organic matter, wool, cotton, linen, it hardly matters. When I change, my clothes change with me. I can hardly say how, for it is in the blood – the chromosomes – like musicianship, Doris. Either you can or you can't. If you can – they change.'

'Jan – are there many like you? Chris seemed to think – '

Jarmoskowski's smile became a little mocking. 'Go into a great railroad station some day – Waterloo, or a Metro station, or Grand Central in New York; get up above the crowd on a balcony or stairway and look down at it in a mirror. We do not show in a silvered mirror. Or if you are in America, find one of the street photographers they have there who take "three action pictures of yourself" against your will and try to sell them to you; ask him what percentage of his shots show nothing but background.'

His voice darkened gradually to a sombre diapason. 'Lundgren was right throughout. This werewolfery is now nothing but a disease. It is not pro-survival. Long ago there must have been a number of mutations which brought the pineal gland into use; but none of them survived but the werewolves, and the werewolves are madmen – like me. We are dying out.

'Some day there will be another mutation, the pineal will come into better use, and all men will be able to modify their forms without this terrible cannibalism as a penalty. But for us, the lycanthropes, the failures of evolution, nothing is left.

'It is not good for a man to wander from country to country, knowing that he is a monster to his fellow-men and cursed eternally by his God – if he can claim a God. I went through Europe, playing the piano and giving pleasure, writing music for others to play, meeting people, making friends – and always, sooner or later, there were whisperings and strange looks and dawning horror.

'And whether I was hunted down for the beast I was, or whether there was only a gradually-growing revulsion, they drove me out. Hatred, silver bullets, crucifixes – they are all the same in the end.

'Sometimes, I could spend several months without incident in some one place, and my life would take on a veneer of normality. I could attend to my music, and have people around me that I liked, and be – human. Then the wolfbane bloomed and the pollen freighted the air, and when the moon shone down on that flower my blood surged with the thing I carry within me . . .'

'And then I made apologies to my friends and went north to Sweden, where Lundgren was and where spring came much later.

I loved him, and I think he missed the truth about me until the night before last; I was careful.

'Once or twice I did *not* go north, and then the people who had been my friends would be hammering silver behind my back and waiting for me in dark corners. After years of this few places in Europe would have me. With my reputation as a composer and a pianist spread darker rumours, none of them near the truth, but near enough.

'Towns I had never visited closed their gates to me without a word. Concert halls were booked up too many months in advance for me to use them, inns and hotels were filled indefinitely, people were too busy to talk to me, to listen to my playing, to write me any letters.

'I have been in love. That – I will not describe.

'Eventually I went to America. There no one believes in werewolf. I sought scientific help – which I had never sought from Lundgren, because I was afraid I would do him some harm. But overseas I thought someone would know enough to deal with what I had become. I would say, "I was bitten during a hunt on Graf Hrutkai's estate, and the next fall I had my first seizure ..."

'But it was not so. No matter where I go, the primitive hatred of my kind lies at the heart of the human as it lies at the heart of the dog. There was no help for me.

'I am here to ask for an end to it.'

Slow tears rolled over Doris's cheeks. The voice faded away indefinitely. It did not seem to end at all, but rather to retreat into some limbo where men could not hear it. Jarmoskowski stood silently in the moonlight, his eyes burning bloodily, a sombre sullen scarlet.

Doris said, 'Jan – Jan, I am sorry, I am so sorry. What can I do?'

'Shoot.'

'I – can't!'

'Please, Doris.'

The girl was crying uncontrollably. 'Jan, don't. I can't. You know I can't. Go away, *please* go away.'

Jarmoskowski said, 'Then come with me, Doris. Open the window and come with me.'

'Where?'

'Does it matter? You have denied me the death I ask. Would you deny me this last desperate hope for love, would you deny your own love, your own last and deepest desire? That would be a vile cruelty. It is too late now, too late for you to pretend revulsion. Come with me.'

He held out his hands.

'Say goodbye,' he said. 'Goodbye to these self-righteous humans. I will give you of my blood and we will range the world, wild and uncontrollable, the last of our race. They will remember us, I promise you.'

'Jan ...'

'I am here. Come now.'

Like a somnambulist, she swung the panes out. Jarmoskowski did not move, but looked first at her, then at the crucifix. She lifted one end of the thread and let the little thing tinkle to the floor.

'After us, there shall be no darkness comparable to our darkness,' Jarmoskowski said. 'Let them rest — let the world rest.'

He sprang into the room with so sudden, so feral a motion that he seemed hardly to have moved at all. From the doorway an automatic rifle yammered with demoniac ferocity. The impact of the silver slugs hurled Jarmoskowski back against the side of the window. Foote lowered the smoking muzzle and took one step into the room.

'Too late, Jan,' he said stonily.

Doris wailed like a little girl awakened from a dream. Jarmoskowski's lips moved, but there was not enough left of his lungs. The effort to speak brought a bloody froth to his mouth. He stood for an instant, stretched out a hand toward the girl. Then the long fingers clenched convulsively and the long body folded.

He smiled, put aside that last of all his purposes, and died.

'Why did he come in?' Foote whispered. 'I could never have gotten a clear shot at him if he'd stayed outside.'

He swung on the sobbing girl. 'Doris, you must tell me, if you know. With his hearing, he should have heard me breathing. But he stayed — and he came in, right into my line of fire. *Why?*'

The girl did not answer; but stiffly, as if she had all at once become old, she went to her bedside light and turned it on. Standing beneath it was a grotesque figurine which Foote had difficulty in recognizing as Caroline's telephone doll. All the frills had been stripped off it, and a heavy black line had been pencilled across its innocuous forehead in imitation of Jarmoskowski's eyebrows. Fastened to one of its wrists with a rubber band was one of the fragments of skin Newcliffe had scraped out of his trap; and completely around the doll, on the surface of the table, a pentagram had been drawn in lipstick.

The nascent witch had turned from white magic to black. Doris had rediscovered the malign art of poppetry, and had destroyed her demon lover.

Compassionately, Foote turned to her; and very slowly, as if responding to the gravitational tug of a still-distant planet, the muzzle of his rifle swung too. Together, the man and the machine, they waited for her.

Both would have to be patient.